TURNING
TIDE

Center Point
Large Print

Also by Melody Carlson and available from
Center Point Large Print:

As Time Goes By
We'll Meet Again
Harbor Secrets
Riptide Rumors
Surf Smugglers

THE LEGACY OF SUNSET COVE

TURNING
TIDE

BOOK FOUR

MELODY
CARLSON

CENTER POINT LARGE PRINT
THORNDIKE, MAINE

This Center Point Large Print edition
is published in the year 2021 by arrangement with
WhiteFire Publishing.

The text of this Large Print edition is unabridged.
In other aspects, this book may vary
from the original edition.
Printed in the United States of America
on permanent paper.
Set in 16-point Times New Roman type.

ISBN: 978-1-64358-771-4

The Library of Congress has cataloged this record
under Library of Congress Control Number: 2020946473

CHAPTER 1

Late October 1917

Although Anna McDowell had always enjoyed scooping the latest news, she now cringed whenever anything came in over the wire at the newspaper office. Grim reports from the Great War seemed to dominate all else these days. Even Oregon's exciting prohibition tales of lawless bootleggers and illegal rum-running had been overshadowed by the grisly battles waging around the globe. And the numbers of dead and wounded were unfathomable and growing daily.

And knowing how her good friend and son-in-law Jim Stafford as well as many other young men from Sunset Cove—not to mention the entire country—daily risked life and limb by serving with the Allied Forces overseas . . . well, it put a serious damper on Anna's usual heightened interest in the latest information.

Frank Anderson poked his head into her office. "Did you hear about *this?*" Her lead reporter waved the paper in the air, his fair brows arched with obvious interest.

"What's that?" She looked up from the copy

she was checking, wishing he were about to announce the war had ended but knowing it was unlikely.

"Just in from England. About Ypres."

"Still fighting in Ypres." Her tone sounded jaded even to herself. "How many battles have pummeled that region by now?"

"Several." He came fully into her office. "But this story is different, Anna. Definitely front-page newsworthy, if you ask me."

She nodded, setting down her pencil. She was glad that she and Frank had finally arrived at a first-name basis . . . and that he'd finally come to respect her role as editor in chief of this news-paper. "How is this story different?" She felt a trace of hope. "Is the Kaiser surrendering? Is the war about to end?"

"No." He frowned at the paper strip in his hand. "Says here that thousands of troops from Australia and New Zealand were wiped out this week."

"Oh, my." She sadly shook her head. "Well, that's not very encouraging, Frank. I was hoping it was something more positive."

"You and me both."

"But why did you say this story was different?"

"It's *how* these troops perished that makes this newsworthy."

"Oh, please tell me it's not from a communicable illness." Anxiety surged through her.

"Daniel—I mean Dr. Hollister. He recently wrote to me how diseases were spreading like wildfire overseas. He's grateful to be over there since medical help is so critical right now."

"No, these men didn't die from anything disease-related." Frank pursed his lips.

"What then? Didn't you say they were killed in battle? Tragic, yes, but what makes it news?" Anna wasn't eager to plaster another horrible defeat story across the front page of their small-town paper.

"Because this story is completely related to the weather."

She felt confused. "The *weather?*"

"Yes. It says that due to extra heavy rains over there, our Allied soldiers drowned. Right there on the Ypres battlefield."

"On the battlefield? How is that even possible?"

"It seems that the rain-soaked ground turned into a quagmire of slippery mud. I'm imagining it was similar to quicksand. The men became trapped in the muddy muck, and then they began to sink down into shell craters. Probably left behind from previous battles. And then they drowned."

"In the mud?" She shuddered.

He nodded grimly.

"Oh, Frank, that's so horribly gruesome." She cringed to think of Jim and Lawrence and AJ . . . all the other young men fighting over there. She prayed their friends weren't in Ypres, and yet she knew they were in places equally perilous. And what about relatives and loved ones who'd lost their men . . . drowned in the mud like that? How would they be feeling right now?

"Stupid war." She slammed a fist onto her desktop. "What a waste. A nasty, terrible waste. How many more brave young men must die before the madness ends? Kaiser Wilhelm is the devil himself."

"I agree." Frank leaned forward with an intense expression. "And it makes me want to do something. . . . Anna, I think it's time I joined up too. I'm sure they need more help over there and I'm—"

"But you're exempt, Frank. You've got a wife and children and you're over—"

"That doesn't mean I can't enlist and go over and do my part." He stood up straight as a soldier, narrowing his eyes with determination. "They need me, Anna."

"That may be true, but you're needed here too. Besides your family, this newspaper needs you. We're already shorthanded with Jim and Lawrence—"

"I know, I know." He sighed, his shoulders slumping. "It's just that it makes me feel so . . . useless. Sitting over here while others are—"

"Frank." She locked eyes with him. "Think about your wife and three young sons—what if you'd been over there, and what if you'd been drowned in the mud like those other men? What would Ginger do without you? Imagine how your sweet wife would struggle to raise those rambunctious boys on her own. And please forgive me, but I don't see how the presence of one newspaperman in his late thirties would make much of a difference anyway."

He sighed deeply. "Yes, I suppose you're right. It's just so hard to stand by and watch . . . even from this distance."

"But consider this—we still have some young unmarried men in our town, men who've claimed exemptions but who appear fit and able. I've mentioned it to Chief Rollins, and he said he might look into taking legal action."

"I've heard those rumors too. It's ironic when you consider that a couple of those so-called *exempt* fellows might actually be running rum along the coastline." He scowled. "Not brave enough to fight for their country, but stupid enough to risk their lives to break the law for a few bucks."

"I've had similar thoughts." Anna rolled a fresh sheet of paper into her typewriter. "We need to run some pieces that illuminate this problem. Without naming names, of course. But we could pressure them to do the right thing."

"You really think they'd take notice?" Frank looked doubtful.

"Their friends and relatives might take notice. Maybe they'd put their feet to the fire." She pointed her pencil in the air like a beacon. "In fact, I'm going to attack this head-on in my next editorial. I'll challenge those heel-draggers to step up. I'll remind them that their friends and brothers are over there struggling—and that more soldiers, coming from all corners of this country, could help turn this thing around."

"That's a good plan. And I'll angle my war article in that same direction." Frank's eyes lit with renewed enthusiasm. "Maybe the pen is mightier than the sword after all."

Anna wished that were true as Frank exited her office, but she knew that the pen alone wasn't going to bring this awful war to an end. If only it could. Oh, she knew that good journalism helped. It informed people and brought just causes to the forefront. And being a responsible newspaper-woman had always been important to her—even now as she hammered away at her typewriter.

Everyone needed to do their part. All needed to make sacrifices, to contribute according to their abilities. If they wanted this war to end, they'd all have to pitch in.

She was just finishing her piece when the telephone jangled.

"Your daughter just called," Virginia told her. "She sounded a bit excited. She wants you to call her back at the hospital."

"At the hospital? Why is she at the—"

"Katy didn't say. Just asked you to call her as soon as you were free."

"Yes, of course." Anna quickly hung up and then dialed the hospital's number. But the woman on the other end didn't seem to know anything about anything. Anna considered asking to speak to Sarah Rose, since she was the bookkeeper there, but instead, she snatched up her hat and gloves. It would probably be simpler and quicker to just go over there—and only ten minutes if she walked fast. Plus the fresh sea air would do her good. As Anna walked, she prayed that nothing bad had happened to her daughter.

Katy could be a bit reckless at times. She was known to zip around in Mac's Runabout like she thought she was participating in a motor race. She'd boast about how she picked up a special delivery at the railroad station then dropped off a customer order—making it back to the dress shop in record time. But what if she'd been involved in a crash? Anna took in a calming breath, reminding herself that Katy was an excellent driver. Much better than Anna. Also . . . Katy was expecting. That alone should make her more cautious when driving. Anna hoped so.

Katy's baby wasn't due for about six months, but could she be experiencing a problem with her pregnancy? That happened sometimes. Anna sincerely hoped not. Despite Katy's initial reluctance to have a child so soon after marrying Jim, she'd come full circle on it. She now eagerly looked forward to becoming a mother. She'd even gotten serious about knitting—and not only army socks. Most recently, she'd been working on a lovely robin's egg blue baby cardigan.

As Anna entered the new hospital, she tried not to feel overly anxious—or agitated at the receptionist. She glanced around the vacant waiting area as if searching for clues and hurried up to the front desk. "I just called about my daughter Katy Stafford, and I was told she wasn't—"

"I'm so sorry about that," the woman told her. "You spoke to me, and I wasn't aware at the time that Katy was here at the hospital, but I just learned that she's upstairs in the maternity—"

"Maternity?" Anna gasped and, without waiting to hear more, rushed for the stairway, which she knew would be swifter than the pokey elevator. But by the time she reached the maternity section, she was breathless and shaky. "I—I'm looking for Katy Stafford," she explained to a recently hired nurse. "Is she—"

"Room 204." The nurse pointed down the hallway and, before she could say another word, Anna took off. Ducking into Room 204, she nearly knocked down her own daughter. "Oh, Katy!" she exclaimed. "Are you all right?"

Katy smiled. "Yes, of course, Mother. I'm perfectly fine."

"I tried to call back, but I couldn't get you, so I came. What's wrong?"

"Nothing is wrong. Not really. It's Ellen." Katy guided Anna out of the room and down the hallway. "She's going to have her baby."

"Oh, that's right. Ellen's baby is due, isn't it?"

"Yes, and she'd hoped to have her baby at home to save money," Katy quietly explained. "But she was having some troubles and her mother insisted she come here. Fortunately, I was in the dress shop and had the Runabout. Otherwise Clara was going to call for that new ambulance to fetch her. You know that Doc Hollister has been bragging it up."

"So I've heard. Mac was complaining about the expense, but JD insisted it was needed to reach the outlying places that the hospital wants to serve. Apparently it's very similar to what they're using on the battlefront. Daniel has written about how those Red Cross vehicles are saving lots of lives."

"Well, Ellen actually thought an ambulance ride would be exciting, but Clara thought we should come by car. And so we did."

"Good for you." Anna glanced around. "Is Clara here now?"

"Yes, she's with Ellen. I only called you to let you know what was happening." Katy linked her arm into Anna's. "I thought you'd like to know.

13

But I didn't expect you to leave work just to come here."

"Well, I was due for a break. Besides, this is newsworthy." Anna smiled in relief. "Much happier news than writing about the gruesome old war."

Katy stopped walking and turned to her mother with fearful eyes. "Is there more bad news—about the war? What is it now?"

Anna regretted her words. "Well, it's a war, Katy . . . of course, there's always going to be some bad news. But we can't obsess over it. We must maintain hope."

"Yes, I suppose you're right." Katy sighed deeply.

"How about a cup of tea?" Anna suggested. "We've been like ships in the night ever since you moved in with Ellen. I'd love to catch up with you."

"And I'd love some tea."

Before long they were seated at a small table in the tiny cafeteria located in the hospital basement, and Katy was explaining how Ellen had begun having labor pains early this morning.

"We thought it was indigestion at first. We had spaghetti for dinner last night." Katy giggled. "I doubt Dr. Hollister senior would approve, but it's what Ellen was craving, and I made it for her."

Anna smiled. "Well, maybe you shouldn't

admit this to old Doc Hollister. He's such a stickler about diet."

"He's a stickler about everything." Katy shook her head. "I sure wish Dr. Daniel would come home."

"I do too, honey." Anna patted Katy's hand. "But I'm glad he's helping those young men over there. And maybe the war will end by the time your baby comes into the world."

"I hope so." Katy stirred her tea. "Not just so Dr. Daniel can come home, but I so want Jim to come home . . . to be with me . . . here to welcome his child."

"Well, April is still a ways off," Anna reminded her. "Anything could happen by then."

"I know." Katy still looked uncertain.

"So what's the latest you've heard from Jim?" Anna asked.

"I received a letter sent from England just yesterday." Katy brightened. "He sounded good. He was happy that his unit was preparing to move. I know he's been longing for *active* service." Katy bit her lower lip. "He'd complained before about the endless training and waiting in England. But yesterday's letter was two weeks old, so I suppose he could actually be on the European front by now. Naturally, he can't give out specific details."

"Naturally." Anna wondered if Jim's unit was in Belgium since it was a hot spot for the European front. And she tried not to dwell on today's news . . . or that Jim might possibly be in Ypres. She was aware of the numerous battlefields on the European front. And just because all those poor soldiers had perished in Ypres didn't mean that Jim would be among them. Hadn't Frank said it was Australian and New Zealand troops involved in that muddy mess? Anna sure hoped so. She didn't want to think about Jim leading his troops into something like that . . . or dying on any battlefield.

And the idea of Katy becoming a widowed mother at such a tender age was deeply disturbing. It would be like history repeating itself. Anna lost her husband when Katy was a baby— and she felt certain she couldn't go through that much sadness again. Especially where her daughter was concerned.

CHAPTER 2

After her mother left the hospital to return to the newspaper office, Katy wasn't sure what to do. She knew she was probably needed back at the dress shop since both Clara and Ellen were still here, but she also felt a need to stay nearby. Especially since she'd promised Ellen she would stick by her side throughout this ordeal. But that was because Ellen had declared she didn't need her mother around to help her. Of course, that had changed when Ellen's labor pains had gotten severe. Katy had been so relieved to call Clara . . . and even more relieved when Clara recommended they proceed to the hospital. Maybe this would help them to repair their fractured relationship.

"May I use the telephone?" Katy asked the front receptionist.

"Yes, of course." She pointed to the end of the counter. "That one is for public use."

Katy called the dress shop, relieved to hear her grandmother's voice. "I've been dying of curiosity," Lucille said eagerly. "Is the baby here?"

"Not yet." Katy looked at the big clock above the reception desk, realizing they'd been at the hospital for nearly four hours now. "But I think you should just close the shop, Grandmother."

"Good idea. I'll put out a sign saying we're out for the birth of the baby." She chuckled. "That'll give our customers something to chatter about. And then, how about if I come over there to wait with you?"

"Oh, would you?"

"Of course! It'll be exciting to see the new baby."

Katy promised to meet her in the waiting area and, as she hung up, felt greatly relieved to know that she wouldn't be waiting alone. Most people thought of Katy as a very confident, impetuous, and brave person, but when Katy heard Ellen howling in pain this morning, she'd gotten a startling wakeup call. This would be her in six months or so. And, like Ellen, her husband would be thousands of miles away. It was unsettling.

To distract herself, Katy reached for her handbag. As always, she kept a small sketch pad in it. This was for whenever a new idea for a fashion design came upon her. Sometimes at the most unlikely places. Unfortunately, the wartime fashions were not as inspiring as they'd been a few years ago. Katy missed the lace and ribbons and frills. Nowadays, women's styles had grown more severe. Even somewhat military looking. Katy had done a number of designs like this and, although the younger women liked them, it was taking awhile for them to catch on in their small, conservative community.

Now, with her thoughts on babies, Katy decided to draw something suitable for a newborn infant. Perhaps they would introduce a line of baby clothes at the dress shop. She was just finishing up a pretty christening gown, similar to the one she'd made for Ellen's baby, when Grandmother bustled into the waiting area.

As always, Lucille looked festive and colorful. Katy's grandmother had her own sense of style and, despite the military inspired fashion trends, the older woman still enjoyed her frills and furs. Today she had on a lilac gown with a long gray fur stole slung over her shoulders, and she smelled of lavender.

"Has the baby arrived?" Lucille asked with wide eyes.

"Not that I know of. I asked them to send someone down with the news." Katy put her sketch pad back into her bag.

"What do you think it will be?" Lucille sat down beside her.

"For some reason I think it will be a girl."

"That's probably because you're hoping to have a boy." Lucille winked.

"Maybe so." Katy twisted the handle of her

purse. "Do you remember what it was like to have a baby, Grandmother?"

Lucille chuckled. "That's something a woman never forgets. Oh, we might forget some parts of it, but we generally remember."

"Was it terribly painful?" Katy peered curiously at her.

"Well, darling, that's one of the things a woman tries to forget."

"Oh." Katy nodded.

"Of course childbirth is painful, Katy. But that pain is swallowed up with the joy of holding your baby in your arms."

"So you felt like that? You were joyful when my mother was born?" Katy studied her grandmother closely.

"Yes, as a matter of fact I did feel joyful." Lucille slowly removed a soft leather glove. "I'm well aware that I gained a reputation for not being maternal, but I did feel motherly. At the start anyway. And then, well, things changed."

"Your mother-in-law made it difficult for you." Katy had heard the story about how Mac's mother had dominated the young bride and her child and how she'd eventually made it very easy for Lucille to leave Sunset Cove.

"Unfortunately I wasn't a very strong person back then. I was unable to stand up to Mac's mother. In all honesty, I was probably too young to be a mother."

"Do you think I'm too young?"

"No, darling, I do not. You are so much wiser than I was at your age. Like your mother says sometimes, you are old for your age, Katy. I have no worries about you, dear. You'll be a wonderful mother. And Jim will be a wonderful father."

"I hope so."

Lucille squeezed Katy's hand. "I'm sure it was difficult to see Ellen in pain. Especially since you know your time is coming."

"I'll admit that it was disturbing to hear her this morning." Katy sighed. "But Ellen has a tendency to be a bit, well, melodramatic."

Lucille smiled. "Yes, I'm sure you're right about that."

Katy checked her watch pendant. "But she has been in labor for quite a long time now. Does it usually take this long to have a baby?"

"Often. Though I think it's different for everyone." Lucille frowned slightly. "How has it been living with Ellen?"

"Oh . . . I suppose it's all right."

"I know Ellen really appreciates you being there. Of course, Clara does too. Especially considering how those two haven't gotten along so well of late. But I have been concerned for you, dear. It's nice that you want to help Ellen, but I worry that she might take advantage of you. I don't like to say it, but that girl has a bit of a lazy streak."

Katy smiled. "Yes, well, that's not news."

"I also know that your grandfather misses you."

"He does?" Katy frowned, remembering her chess games with Mac, having tea in his sitting room overlooking the ocean. "I should visit him more—and I want to. But between the dress shop and helping with Ellen and leading our Red Cross chapter . . . well, there's only so much time in the day."

"I know it's not my business, dear, but I hope you'll remember to take care of yourself too. I'm concerned that Ellen—and her new baby—will be very needy. They might run you ragged."

Katy smiled. "Oh, Grandmother, don't worry. I won't let that happen." She looked up to see a nurse coming their way.

"Mrs. Bouchard has given birth," she told them.

"What is it?" Katy asked eagerly.

"A boy." The nurse smiled. "Seven pounds three ounces."

"And how is Mrs. Bouchard?" Lucille asked.

"The mother is doing well. She'll be ready for visitors within the hour. You can view the baby at the nursery if you like."

Katy grabbed Lucille's hand. "Let's go see little Larry now."

"Larry?" Lucille stood.

"Yes. That's what Ellen said the name would be if it was a boy. Larry for Lawrence."

As they rode the elevator up, Katy tried to

suppress the idea that since Ellen had a boy that Katy would automatically have a girl. Even though Ellen had claimed such a thing, Katy knew it was silly. And she really did want a boy. She was already imagining calling him Little Jimmy.

Since there was only one baby in the nursery window, they knew it must be young Larry. But as Katy peered down at the red wrinkled face, she was unimpressed. "He's not very good looking, is he?" she quietly said to Lucille.

"They're never very pretty at the beginning. Even your beautiful mother was rather homely at first."

Katy laughed. "I'll have to keep that in mind."

After a while, they went in to see Ellen. "How are you feeling?" Katy asked gently. "Was it very hard on you?"

Ellen leaned back into her pillow with a loud sigh. "Oh, my . . . don't ask."

"But she's better now," Clara told Katy. "Did you see our beautiful baby boy?"

"Yes, we just saw him." Katy exchanged glances with Lucille. "He's lovely."

"We closed the dress shop in his honor," Lucille told them. "I put a big sign on the front door, saying we were out for a baby's birth."

"How long will you be in the hospital?" Katy asked Ellen.

"Doc Hollister said a week." Ellen lowered

23

her voice. "But I'm worried about the expense."

"I told you I'd help," Clara assured her.

"So will I," Katy offered.

"And I will too," Lucille said.

Ellen's eyes filled with tears. "Thank you all so much. I don't know what I'd do without you."

They took turns hugging her, reassuring her that all would be well until the nurse came in, announcing that visiting time was over. "It's time to bring baby in here. Only one guest can remain." She pointed to Clara. "And I recommend the grandmother."

Relieved by this, Katy leaned down to kiss Ellen's cheek. "I'll come back to visit you tomorrow. In the meantime, I hope you get lots of good rest."

As Katy drove Lucille home, she made a decision. "I think I'll go home to Grandfather's house while Ellen's in the hospital," she declared as she waited for Lucille to get out.

"Oh, good!" Lucille grinned. "He'll be so glad to hear that. Your mother will be too. And Mickey and Bernice."

"And it'll feel like a holiday to me," Katy admitted as her grandmother got out.

Lucille laughed. "I'm sure it will."

As Katy drove two houses down to her grandfather's house, she felt a huge sense of relief. The idea of a week here was really a welcome thought. No more cooking and cleaning and catering to Ellen during her "off" hours. It really would be like taking a vacation!

She parked in the carriage house then went through the back door to the kitchen. "Hello," she called to Bernice as she stirred something on the stove.

"Oh?" Bernice turned then smiled. "My darling girl is back." She hugged Katy. "Are you staying for dinner? We have plenty."

"I'm hoping I can stay for the whole week." As she unpinned her hat, she explained about Ellen and the baby.

"As far as I'm concerned you can stay here till the cows come home." Bernice nodded to a tray she was just setting up for tea. "Want to add another teacup and take that to your grandfather?"

"Certainly." Katy set her hat and gloves on a kitchen chair. "How's he doing anyway?"

"All things considered, not too bad. Well, unless that old Doc Hollister comes sniffing round Lucille. That gets Mac grumbling."

Katy laughed as she picked up the tray. "I know how he feels." She walked slowly through the old house, remembering the pleasure she felt the first time she saw the McDowell house. Having grown up in a tiny city apartment, the old stone estate had felt like a mansion to her. And the view of the sea had thrilled her artist's heart. She didn't realize how much she'd missed it these past couple of months.

"Good afternoon," she said brightly as she went into Mac's private sitting room.

"Katy girl!" Mac's blue eyes twinkled. "To what do I owe this pleasure?"

She set down the tray and then explained about Ellen's baby and her plans to spend a week here. "If you don't mind."

"If I don't mind?" He chuckled as she handed him a teacup. "I was just feeling sorry for myself."

"Why are you feeling sorry for yourself?"

"Oh, just feeling lonely. The house is so quiet these days. Not like it was before. Remember the fun times we had before our boys all went off to war? And then you moved out to help with Ellen. And Anna is always so busy with the newspaper. It's just not the same as it was before."

"I know what you mean." She sat down with her teacup, gazing out over the foggy ocean. "But it won't always be like this."

"No, of course, not. The war will end, the boys will come home and . . ." He brightened. "We'll soon hear the pitter-patter of little feet."

She told him a bit more about baby Larry. "I didn't want to say anything to Ellen, but he wasn't very good looking. He reminded me of a wrinkled old man."

"You mean like me?"

"No, you're a handsome old man."

Mac smiled. "Flattery will get you nowhere."

26

"It's true."

His smile faded. "I wish your grandmother agreed with you there."

"But she does, Grandfather," Katy insisted. "I know she does."

He rubbed his chin with a doubtful expression. "I'm not so sure. She's been spending a whole lot of time with Doc Hollister of late. Or should I say JD as she calls him. *JD*—what kind of name is that for an old codger like him?"

"Well, if she's been spending more time with the old doctor, you have only yourself to blame." She shook her teacup at him.

"What's that supposed to mean?"

"You haven't been inviting her to do things with you."

"The last two times I asked her over for dinner, she already had plans."

"Then you need to book her well in advance, Grandfather. Beat old Doc Hollister to the punch."

"Is that so?" He picked up a ginger cookie.

"I know what we'll do," she said suddenly. "We'll host a dinner party while I'm here. We'll have it on Saturday, and I'll be sure that Grandmother can come. And I'll make sure that Doc Hollister is *not* on the guest list."

His blue eyes sparkled. "That's just the ticket, Katy."

"I'll handle everything."

He chuckled. "I have no doubt about that."

"We'll have Mayor Wally and Thelma. And Chief Rollins and his wife." She counted on her fingers. "And Clara and Randall. You and Grandmother and Mother and me. That's ten. A good-sized dinner party."

Mac grinned at her. "You've always been good medicine for me, Katy girl. I'm so glad you're back. Even if it's only for a week."

Katy wished that it could be for good, but she knew that Ellen expected her to continue sharing the apartment in town. If she hadn't given her word, she would gladly bow out now. Still, she knew that Ellen needed her. Probably more than ever just now.

CHAPTER 3

Anna knew that stepping on toes was just part of the newspaper business, but she tried to avoid it when possible. Unfortunately, it wasn't always possible. So when her editorial piece came out—the one chiding healthy young men who cowered behind feeble excuses to avoid military service—she braced herself for opposition. She didn't have to wait for long, but she couldn't help but feel surprised when it was Daniel's previous employee Norma Barrows who confronted her right in front of Kathleen's Dress Shop.

"I read that editorial you wrote in yesterday's paper," Norma said sharply. "I guess that's what they call a poison pen piece."

"What do you mean?" Anna remained calm.

"Who do you think you are to go round calling out innocent young men? Publicly shaming them in your *yellow* paper?" Norma glared at her.

"I don't think innocent young men would be troubled by what I wrote." Anna studied Norma closely, wondering why she was so upset about this. Did she still resent Anna? Perhaps she'd heard that Anna was engaged to Daniel? Was that what this was about?

"It's bad enough that some of our boys feel embarrassed for being exempted from the draft in the first place, but for you to make them feel even more guilty—well, it's just plain mean. That's what it is. Mean! And I plan to write a letter to the newspaper to defend them." She shook her fist. "Not that you will print it."

"If your letter is honest and printable, I'd be glad to run it. The newspaper is a good forum for open discussion."

"Says you." Norma narrowed her eyes. "If you ask me, the paper was much better off before you came here. In fact, the whole town was better off before you—and your kind—showed up."

Anna felt a rise of indignant outrage. "My kind?"

Norma nodded toward the dress shop. "Well, your uppity daughter for starts. She's barely more than a child and yet she thinks she can dictate her fashion opinions onto the whole town."

"Katy doesn't do—"

"And then you bring your colored friends here to steal employment from perfectly good—"

"Sarah Rose has every right to her job." Anna stood straighter. "She had the training and skills and common sense necessary to manage an

30

office. And both our doctors agreed that she's an essential employee in the records department at the hospital, so perhaps you should take up your grievance with one of them."

"Never mind about that. What really irks me is that stupid article you wrote. It was just plain wrong."

"Well, you're entitled to your opinion." Anna glanced in the dress shop window to see Clara peeking out. They were supposed to be meeting for lunch just now. "But I am curious as to why you're so angry about my opinion piece, Norma. Is this really about the newspaper? Or is this personal?"

"It happens to be personal. At least to me. You see, my boy Edward is one of the unfortunate fellows who is exempt from the draft. And your piece in the newspaper will not help him. Not one bit!"

Anna blinked in surprise. "I didn't realize you had a son. And if he feels badly for being exempt from the military, I am genuinely sorry. My piece wasn't targeted at anyone who can't serve for a *legitimate* reason. It was meant for the young men in town who appear to be . . . well, hiding out from the law."

"Well, you obviously don't know *my* boy." Norma still sounded angry. "And I still plan to write that letter to the newspaper."

"I really hope you'll do that." Anna forced

a small smile. "I'd be glad to run it as soon as possible. It's important for readers to hear both sides of an issue."

Norma made a harrumphing noise then turned on her heel and stormed off. Anna took in a deep breath and slowly shook her head. She had never imagined that Norma Barrows had any children. She just hadn't seemed the motherly type. Anna knew that Norma was about the same age as her, and that she'd been married and divorced, but she was surprised to hear of a grown son.

"What was that all about?" Clara emerged from the dress shop, tugging on her gloves. "I watched it all from inside. Looked like Daniel's old nurse wanted to take your head off. Is she angry that you and Daniel are engaged?"

"I actually wondered the same thing myself." As they walked toward the hotel, Anna explained about Norma's son. "She was very offended by the piece I ran in yesterday's paper."

Clara chuckled. "Have you ever met Norma's boy?"

"No. I didn't even know she had children."

"Just the one boy. Eddie Barrows. He was a friend of AJ's when they were in school. I think he's a year older. Eddie used to work on our fishing boats in the summertime, but several years ago he went to live with his father—somewhere inland. He's only been back in town a few months. And if you ask me, he's healthy as a horse. I've wondered myself why he'd be exempt from service."

"Interesting."

"I've also wondered why he came back to Sunset Cove. He doesn't appear to have employment anywhere. Not from what I've seen."

"Could be one of those ne'er-do-wells . . . trouble brewing . . ."

"I wouldn't be surprised. I used to worry that he was a bad egg. Believe it or not, I didn't like his influence on AJ. That seems rather silly now, considering all the trouble AJ got into last year."

"But that had to do with Albert. A father probably has more influence than a friend, don't you think?"

"Yes, I'm sure you're right." Clara sighed. "Sometimes it's easier to just forget all that happened. I'm so glad it's behind us now."

"And you can be proud of AJ for going over there to serve his country. His complete turn-around has certainly given me hope."

Clara smiled. "I am proud of my boy. And I'm grateful to you and Randall for the way you helped him find his way, Anna. I'll always appreciate the way you both believed in my son when no one else did."

Anna considered this. AJ had taken a bad path . . . but only because his father had led him down

33

it. Now she felt curious about Eddie Barrows. If Clara considered him a bad influence, it might be worth keeping an eye on him. But as they went into the hotel, she knew it was time to change the subject. And so she inquired about Ellen and the baby.

"I stopped off there this morning before I went to work. They both seem well," Clara said. "And that was a beautiful bouquet of autumn roses that you left for Ellen. Very kind of you."

"Well, I wanted to celebrate her motherhood. And today, we will celebrate your grandmotherhood."

Clara smiled. "Between you and me, I don't feel old enough to be a grandmother."

"Well, we both had our children early in life," Anna reminded her. "Besides that we're still in our thirties—that's not so terribly old."

After they were seated, Clara pointed to the shining diamond on Anna's ring finger. "And you're like a young girl yourself, Anna. Engaged to be married . . . Well, when this war ends."

"For all we know you might be engaged too . . . in time."

"I'm not so sure." Clara waved a dismissive hand. "For all I know, Randall might be a confirmed bachelor."

"I don't think so." Anna smiled. "I've seen him look at you, Clara. I think he's simply been waiting for the right timing."

"Speaking of Randall, we're both looking forward to the dinner party at your father's house this weekend. It's been awhile since we've attended a social gathering."

"Well, as you know, that's Katy's doing." Anna explained Katy's strategy to get Lucille into Mac's company without the older doctor's intrusive presence.

"That Katy. She's always up to something good. And I'm glad she's taken some time to be home with you and your father . . . you know, while Ellen's in the hospital." Clara frowned slightly. "Do you think Katy will really want to go back to living with Ellen next week? I mean, with the baby there and all? That's a lot to take on. And I hate to admit it, but Ellen can be a handful sometimes."

Anna shrugged. "I guess it's something the girls will have to work out." She didn't want to say more on the subject because she'd already offended one mother today. But she did feel that Ellen was a handful. The young woman still had some growing up to do. And Anna hoped her daughter wouldn't get pulled in too tightly into helping Ellen. Maybe Ellen would reach out to her mother more now that the baby was here. Maybe she'd appreciate Clara more. If all went well, perhaps they could bury the hatchet and even live together. Anna wanted to suggest as much, but she knew it wasn't her place.

. . .

Katy had concealed her personal disappointment over Saturday night's dinner party. After investing so much time and energy, she'd hoped for a truly enjoyable evening. But for the most part it had felt rather flat and close to boring. Probably because the guests were mostly older and because the younger, more interesting fellows were off at war. But at least her grandparents had seemed to enjoy themselves. And Grandfather had seemed sweetly appreciative when she'd told him goodbye this morning.

As Katy drove the Runabout to the hospital, she had mixed feelings. On one hand, it might be interesting to be around someone closer to her age again. On the other hand, it was Ellen. Sometimes she could be lighthearted and fun. Other times, she could be such a letdown. If Katy's share of the rent wasn't paid up until the end of November, she might even consider not going back to the apartment at all. And then, instead of helping with Ellen's finances, Katy could invest that money in Liberty Bonds. She was always trying to get others to buy them because she knew that every dollar spent on a bond helped US soldiers overseas. Her goal was to purchase as many as she could afford . . . until the war ended and Jim came home.

But Ellen still claimed that she needed Katy's help. She'd needed her during her pregnancy and now it seemed she needed her to help with the baby at home. In a weak moment, Katy had agreed. As she parked the car under the porte cochere in front, Katy figured that—if nothing else—continuing to live with Ellen might be good preparation for when Katy became a mother herself. It was like on-the-job training.

Katy found Ellen in the downstairs waiting area, seated in a high-backed wheelchair with her baby in her lap. But instead of looking like a happy mother about to go home with her new bundle of joy, Ellen's brow was creased. She looked seriously disgruntled.

"What on earth is wrong?" Katy quietly asked.

"Oh, just everything." Ellen scowled at a hospital orderly standing nearby. "The head nurse was mean to me this morning. The baby was very fussy. And then on top of all else, you are late."

"I'm sorry. It's only a few minutes past eight." She looked at the wheelchair. "Are you unable to walk?"

"Of course I can walk. But the hospital policy is that I must be wheeled out to the car."

"Right." Katy picked up Ellen's overnight bag then followed as an orderly wheeled Ellen outside. "Are you excited to go home?"

"I guess so."

Katy opened the car door, holding the baby as Ellen slowly climbed in. "Here's your little darling." She handed Baby Larry over. "And don't worry, I'll drive very carefully." Katy laughed to remember the way she'd torn through town to get Ellen to the hospital just a week ago. She'd been so worried Ellen might have the baby in the car, and then it had taken hours and hours for him to come at all.

Neither of them spoke as Katy slowly drove through town. Perhaps Ellen was tired. By the time Katy was parking, the baby was starting to cry. Katy hurried around to help Ellen out of the car, once again holding the baby. "Will you be able to go up the stairs?" Katy asked with concern. "Are you strong enough?"

"I think so. You carry the baby and then come back to get my overnight bag later."

Katy didn't argue. Instead, with the howling baby in her arms, she led the way up and unlocked the door to the apartment. "Home sweet home." She smiled as they went inside. A few months ago, she'd helped Ellen give this place a full makeover, but it still looked a bit shabby around the edges. Especially after having just been at Grandfather's lovely home.

"It stinks in here." Ellen sniffed the air.

"You're right. It does." Katy glanced toward the kitchen. "I guess we left dirty dishes in the sink that last night. We were in such a hurry to get—"

"You mean you didn't even clean it up yet?"

Ellen took the baby from Katy with a scowl. "That doesn't seem like you."

"I, uh, actually I haven't really been here since we took you to the hospital that day. I mean besides just grabbing some of my things and leaving."

"Where have you been all this time?" Ellen demanded.

Katy explained about going home and then excused herself to fetch Ellen's bag from the car. This was not starting out well. Maybe it was a mistake. Perhaps Katy would simply clean up the kitchen, do some general straightening, get Ellen settled, and then announce that she'd decided to go back home to live. Wasn't that the sensible thing?

But by the time she got back upstairs, Ellen was sitting on the sofa—sobbing. And the baby was howling too. "What on earth is wrong?" Katy dropped the overnight bag to the floor. "What happened?"

"I'm just so miserable," Ellen choked out. "I'll never be a good mother. I don't know how to do this. And Lawrence is so far away. What will I do? *What will I do?*"

"I, uh, I don't know." Katy sat next to her. "I guess you'll just take it one step at a time." She reached for the baby, doing her best to comfort the squalling infant.

"I can't do this, Katy. I really can't do this."

"Do you want me to call your mother? She might know what—"

"No!" Ellen shook her head. "Mother already thinks I'm a failure. I won't let her see me like this."

Katy stood, still holding the baby—jiggling him up and down like she'd seen someone do once, trying as best she could to soothe the child. And then after a minute or so, he quieted down a bit, but he was still fussing. "Could he be hungry?" Katy asked as Ellen loudly blew her nose.

"I don't know. What time is it?" She looked at the wall clock. "Yes, I suppose that could be it."

Katy handed the baby back to her. "Why don't you feed him, and I'll attack that kitchen." Not waiting for Ellen to object, she hurried off to wash the crusty dishes. While the water was heating, she wondered how she could graciously escape this place. Why had she ever agreed to be roommates in the first place?

Finally, the kitchen was clean and the baby was quiet. As Katy dried her hands, she organized her words. "So . . . Ellen," she began carefully. "I've been thinking. It will be rather tight with you and the baby. I'm sure you'll want to keep him in your room with you. And, well, there's only one bedroom. So I'm thinking it would be better if I just went back home to—"

"No—no!" Ellen cried. "You can't abandon me, Katy. Everyone else has abandoned me already.

40

My husband and my brother are both overseas. My father is dead. And—"

"There's your mother, Ellen. She would be happy to help—"

"She would just tell me that I'm doing everything wrong. She'd make me miserable. You know she would."

Katy wasn't so sure but knew it was pointless to argue. And perhaps it was unkind and selfish to leave Ellen on her first day home. "Well, I just thought maybe you'd have more room if I were gone," she said quietly.

"This is a sofa bed," Ellen pointed out. "You could sleep out here if the baby's noise disturbs you."

"Yes . . . I'd thought of that." Katy glanced at the clock. "I guess we can talk about this later. Right now, it's time to go to work. I have a customer coming in for a fitting at ten."

"What if I need help?" Ellen said meekly. "What will I do?"

"Just call down to the shop." Katy reached for her handbag. "Someone can come up."

"And we need some groceries," Ellen told her. "I'm sure of it."

"Why don't you call the mercantile and have some things sent over?"

"Oh, yes . . . I guess I could do that."

"Get some rest." Katy paused by the door. "And try to think happy thoughts, Ellen. It does you no good to worry and fret. And I doubt it helps the baby much either."

"I don't think he could possibly know the difference."

Katy shrugged. "Maybe not . . . but just the same." She forced a smile. "Try to have a good day. It's your first day home with your baby—it should be exciting and fun, don't you think?"

Ellen's expression suggested nothing of the sort. But instead of pursuing the subject of infant feelings further, Katy simply ducked out the door and, grateful to escape to the dress shop, hurried downstairs. This was not going to be easy.

Somehow Katy would get through it . . . or get out.

CHAPTER 4

Although she'd specifically asked Virginia to be on the lookout, Anna wasn't too surprised that Norma Barrows' letter didn't show up at the newspaper. A couple weeks later, Anna assigned a follow-up article to Frank.

"I want a piece about the fellows who are exempt from the draft," she told him at their editorial meeting. "Perhaps remind our readers as to why some men are exempt. And you might even interview a few of them. Spotlight how they contribute to the war effort in other ways."

"Maybe I should just interview myself," Frank said wryly.

"Or me," Reginald said. "Although most folks can see I'm too old to be of any use over there. But I know of a few fellows who claim exempt status but look fit enough to serve. At least to me."

Anna studied Reginald. Among other things, he handled the society column and human-interest stories. Some folks called him the town gossip, which might've been fitting since he did have a talent for scooping local tittle-tattle. Some that was print-worthy and some that was not. "Well, that's just the point of this article," she pointed out. "It's unfair to judge young men by appearances. We need to be supportive of the ones who are truly exempt."

"Want me to interview Eddie Barrows too?" Frank made some notes.

"Why not? Might make his mother proud."

"What if Frank digs up something that *doesn't* make her proud?" Reginald asked with a sly expression.

She lifted her brows. "Is there something you specifically know about Eddie Barrows?"

"I know that he's a lazy good-for-nothing."

"How do you know that?" she asked.

"My mother is good friends with Eddie's mother. Shortly after he moved back to town, my mom hired him to paint her house. Sort of as a favor to Norma. He insisted on being paid in advance, which wasn't easy for Mom. She's a widow. And I had to help her out with it. So Eddie got the paint and started in. And he was actually doing a decent job . . . at first. But then he kept making excuses and not showing up. Maybe got one-fourth done, if that. Now that winter's setting in, Eddie assured her he'll finish it in the spring." He scowled. "Bet I'll have to do it myself. Especially if I get my hands on Eddie first. I'd like to break both his legs."

44

"Well, we won't write about *that* in the paper." She turned back to Frank. "Maybe you shouldn't interview Eddie after all."

They finished up their meeting, and Anna stopped by Virginia's desk to pick up her mail. "A letter from England." Virginia waved an envelope.

"Daniel." Anna eagerly grabbed the letter. "I haven't heard from him for a couple of weeks."

"I expect he's busy over there."

"I'm sure you're right about that." Anna picked up the letter opener from Virginia's desk, carefully slitting the envelope. As she walked back to her office, she slid out the single sheet of stationary. The letter had been written nearly three weeks ago. In her office, she closed the door and hungrily read.

16 October 1917

Dear Anna,

Thank you for your wonderful letters. You have no idea how much I appreciate your faithfulness to write me. I wish I had more time to write back, but the demands at the base hospital are great. I haven't written much about the work I'm doing. I worry it's too dreadful to describe in detail. I'm sure many people assume that doctors primarily treat actual battle injuries like gunshot and shrapnel

45

wounds, but I feel I've spent more time treating diseases like dysentery, tetanus, diphtheria, and pneumonia. Because this war is being fought in filthy, muddy trenches, infection runs rampant amongst our troops. The conditions on the battlefield are so grueling that soldiers are regularly rotated in and out of service simply to preserve life. The stories we hear at the hospital are gruesome.

The need for good hygiene care on the battlefront is desperate, but I fear the message is not getting through. Even here at the hospital I am constantly reminding medical personnel to wash their hands before treating patients. Florence Nightingale wrote a book on this, but unfortunately, busy people get careless and disease is spread.

I have requested a transfer to the continent. I want to be closer to the battlefront. I feel I could be of more use over there, and I could learn so much about medicine. We have some impressively experienced physicians working there, and I would be privileged to serve under them.

I am telling you this because it means my letters will be fewer in upcoming months, and I don't want you to worry. Just pray for me, my darling, and for all the brave young men out there in the trenches. Pray that this war ends soon.

Yours Truly,

Captain Daniel Hollister, MD

• • •

By mid-November, Katy was worn to a frazzle. But she didn't want to concede this to anyone. It would be like admitting defeat. Especially since her mother and grandmother and even Clara had warned her that she'd taken on too much by living with Ellen. Somehow she had to get through it. And she'd convinced herself that as soon as Ellen became more comfortable with motherhood, Katy's responsibilities in their home would lighten. The problem was that Ellen did not seem to be adjusting. In fact, her resentments toward being a mother, her baby's fussiness, and even Katy seemed to be growing.

But when she came home to discover a strange young man sitting in their apartment, right next to Ellen on the sofa, Katy was mad. "What's going on here?" she asked in a sharp tone.

"Katy, I'd like you to meet Eddie Barrows," Ellen said lightly. "He's an old friend of my family."

"Oh?" Katy felt a bit guilty for having misjudged the situation, and yet she felt suspicious too. Ellen should know better than to entertain a gentleman in their apartment.

The dark-haired man stood up, making an overly dramatic bow. "Pleased to make your acquaintance, Miss Katy."

"It's *missus,*" she corrected. "Mrs. Stafford."

"Oh, yes. Pleased to meet you *Mrs.* Stafford." His amber colored eyes sparked with interest. "Ellen has told me a bit about her roommate, but not that she was so pretty."

"Oh, Eddie." Ellen stood. "You're such a flatterer." She turned to Katy. "Eddie brought me the grocery order from the mercantile. I was so surprised to see him that I had to invite him in to catch up. He and AJ were school chums."

"I see." Katy unpinned her hat, hanging it on the hook by the door.

"Eddie moved away from Sunset Cove when he was fifteen," Ellen continued. "He's only been back a couple of months."

With her back to them, Katy unbuttoned her coat. Hopefully Mr. Barrows would take the hint, excuse himself, and be on his way. But Ellen kept talking, almost as if she wanted him to stay.

"I hear your baby," Katy told Ellen. "Sounds like he's getting hungry."

"Oh, he's okay. He ate a couple of hours ago."

"Well, it sounds like he needs something," Katy said with more emphasis.

"You can check on him if you want. Doc Hollister said that it's good for babies to cry. It helps to develop their lungs."

"Well, it hurts my ears," Katy said with irritation. Then turning her back on Ellen and Eddie, she went to check on Baby Larry. She gently scooped him up from his bassinette, speaking soothingly and gently rocking him. "Did you miss me, little guy?" Feeling some dampness seeping through his gown, Katy carried him over to the bureau they'd been using to change and dress him. Of course, he was wet. He was always wet. Sometimes Katy wondered if Ellen ever changed his diapers. But questioning this only led to fights.

After he was changed and seemingly content, Katy carried him out to the living room. Eddie was still there. "Here." Katy handed him to Ellen. "His diaper needed changing."

"I was just asking Eddie to stay for dinner," Ellen told Katy.

"You did?" Katy stared at her.

"Eddie doesn't really have many friends in town. And I thought we might appreciate some manly conversation for a change."

"Does that mean you're cooking dinner tonight?" Katy asked.

"Well, I *do* know how to cook," Ellen said defensively.

"Great." Katy picked up a fashion magazine and sat down on the sofa. "I'm glad to hear that." Ordinarily a comment like that could lead to an argument, but maybe with Eddie here to witness . . . perhaps Ellen would hold back.

"Well, if I'm going to cook, you should take care of the baby." Ellen held little Larry in front of Katy.

"Fine." Ellen dropped the magazine and took the baby from her. Then, taking in a deep breath, she mentally counted to ten. And controlling herself from declaring to Ellen that this was it and she was going back home to live, Katy focused her attention on the baby. Oh, she wasn't going to let this whole thing slide. She planned to give Ellen a piece of her mind. A good-sized piece. But it could wait until after dinner . . . after this unwelcome dinner guest went home.

Oddly enough, Ellen seemed to be in surprisingly good spirits as she fixed them dinner. She even hummed to herself. And Eddie actually helped her by setting the table. Sure, it wasn't much of a dinner, but it was remarkable that Ellen was able to do it. It was progress.

Still, when they were finished, Katy felt aggravated. "Well, Eddie," she said as she began to clear the table. "Unless you're inclined to wash dishes, I think we ladies will have to call it a night." Without offering to help, Eddie thanked them both, put on his hat and coat, and made his departure.

"That was rude," Ellen told Katy.

"What was rude?" Katy set her plate in the sink.

"Getting rid of Eddie like that."

Katy turned to face Ellen. "I do not approve of entertaining young men here, Ellen. I don't care if he's an old family friend. You're a married woman. So am I. And it's not proper having someone like Eddie here."

"Someone like Eddie?" Ellen glared at her. "What's that supposed to mean?"

"It means that he is obviously not a gentleman."

"How can you possibly say that?"

"A gentleman would not have come into this apartment with you while you were home alone."

"I wasn't alone. Baby Larry was here." She smirked.

"You *know* what I mean."

"Are you suggesting that I am not a lady?" Ellen narrowed her eyes.

"I don't know." Katy held up her hands, well aware she'd just stepped over the line and not sure she even cared. But the fight was begun. Voices were raised and before long the baby was howling too. Ellen played the victim—she was too young to be stuck home alone with a baby day after day . . . unable to fit into any of her stylish clothes . . . missing her husband who was off at war . . . pinching pennies just to get by . . . and so on.

"You can feel sorry for yourself, if you want." Katy spoke loudly to be heard over Baby Larry's cries. "But you made your own choices and it's time you took responsibility for them. You're a mother and a wife. If you don't like it, you've only yourself to blame. Everyone's got problems, Ellen. That's just life. But it's time you grew up. And just so you know, I'm done carrying the load for you. And I'm sick of living like this."

"And I'm sick of you!" Ellen stormed off to the bedroom.

After Ellen slammed the bedroom door, Katy grabbed a few of her things and quietly slipped out of the detestable apartment. She was going home! Her mother and grandmother were right. Clara was right. Katy could not keep rescuing Ellen.

As Katy went into the quiet house, she began to feel a little guilty. Not over Ellen. But over Baby Larry. He deserved better. But what more could she do? Seeing no one in the darkened house, she tiptoed up the stairs. But as she reached the second-floor landing, tears began to flow.

"Katy?" Anna poked her head out of her bedroom. "Goodness, you scared me. I thought you were a burglar. What are you doing—" She stopped, seeing the tears streaming down. "Oh, Katy—what's wrong?"

"I'm a failure." Katy collapsed into her mother's arms, sobbing.

"No, you are not." Anna led Katy into her bedroom, easing her into the overstuffed chair.

"Now, tell me, darling, whatever is the matter?"

Katy poured out the story, not sparing any details, clear up to the unwelcome dinner guest this evening. "I just can't take it anymore."

"You don't have to, Katy. You have a home here with us. We've all missed you." Anna gave her a handkerchief. "And you need to take care of yourself, darling. You've got a child of your own to think about. And the dress shop . . . and your Red Cross chapter. Let Clara tend to Ellen."

"But Ellen fights with her mother."

"Sounds like Ellen fights with you too."

Katy chuckled a bit. "That's true."

"And this young man that came to dinner?" Anna grimly shook her head. "That's not good. Who was he, anyway?"

"A friend of AJ's. Eddie something. I can't recall his last name."

"Eddie Barrows?"

"Yes. That's right. Do you know him?"

"Remember Nurse Barrows? That's her son."

"Oh. Well, I don't like him. And I don't think it's right for Ellen to entertain him in our apartment. I mean *her* apartment, because I'm not going back."

"Good for you. And I agree with you, it's not right for Ellen to have gentlemen callers either. Even if it's innocent, it will get people to talking."

Katy sniffed. "I don't feel guilty for leaving Ellen. But I do feel bad for leaving Baby Larry.

And a little guilty for not telling Ellen I was going. I didn't even leave a note. And Ellen was pretty upset."

Anna pursed her lips. "How about if I give Clara a telephone call? Maybe she could go check on Ellen."

"Yes, I'd appreciate that." Katy sighed. "I'm so tired, Mother."

"You are going straight to bed, Katy. Doctor's orders." Anna reached for her hand. "I might not be a doctor, but I'm engaged to one. And I'm certain that he would agree with me on this. You need some good rest. Let someone take care of you for a change."

"That sounds nice." Katy sighed. "It's good to be home."

Later on, after she was snuggled into her warm comfortable bed, Katy knew she'd made the right decision. Not only for herself, but for her baby too. If she hadn't been so strong-willed and stubborn, she probably would've left Ellen long before this. At least she was home now.

Her thoughts shifted to Jim . . . where was he sleeping tonight? Hopefully not in some muddy trench like she'd been reading about in the newspapers. Although so far, it didn't sound like American troops were seeing much if any action just yet. Maybe they wouldn't. But as usual, before going to sleep, she prayed for Jim's well-being, health, and safety. And she felt certain Jim would be happy to hear that she was back with her family again. His last letter had expressed concern about her living situation with Ellen. And someday, God willing, she would be in her very own home with her husband and baby.

CHAPTER 5

Katy managed to avoid any direct interactions with Ellen during the next week. She knew that Clara had reached out to her daughter, even inviting Ellen and the baby to move into her two-bedroom apartment above the dress shop. But Ellen had refused.

"I don't know how she'll be able to pay her rent," Clara confided to Ellen as they opened up the dress shop together.

"Well, the rent's covered until December first," Katy told her. "But after that, well, I don't see how she can stay there either."

"I told her what you said about returning to work, that she could bring the baby here and sew in the back room. But she wouldn't hear of it."

Katy could just imagine Ellen on her high horse . . . too good to rub elbows with the other two women who sewed for the dress shop. "Maybe she just needs time to figure things out." Katy adjusted the mannequin to show off the dark green velveteen jacket better. It was one of her own creations, somewhat military looking with its double-breasted brass buttons, but cut in a way to flatter a feminine figure. She would've liked to wear it herself except that her expanding waistline probably couldn't squeeze into it.

"I'm a bit worried, Katy." Lowering her voice, Clara glanced over her shoulder to be sure the door to the workroom was shut. "Ellen has been seen in the company of Eddie Barrows."

Katy bristled. "Oh?" She tried to sound unconcerned. "When was that?"

"Your grandmother saw them together two days ago. Ellen had little Larry out in the baby buggy and Eddie was strolling alongside her—right down Main Street. At first Lucille thought it was simply a chance encounter. But then she observed Eddie going to the apartment with Ellen." Clara frowned. "Lucille claimed he was helping her carry the baby buggy up the stairs, but it concerns me just the same."

"I can understand your concerns, but maybe he was just helping her. It's a challenge to get the baby and the clunky buggy up those narrow stairs. I know because I've done it before myself. It always takes two trips."

"Yes, I'm sure you're right. I'm probably making a mountain out of a molehill."

Katy felt torn. Should she express her own concerns to Clara, or would that simply make a touchy situation worse? After all, it could've been just an innocent encounter. And Ellen probably appreciated help with the awkward buggy. Just the same, Katy planned to warn Ellen about guarding her reputation . . . if she ever got the chance. She straightened the feather on a felt hat then turned to Clara. "Well, it's time for me to go open up for the Red Cross meeting. Bernice made ginger cookies, and I want to get them set out before the ladies arrive."

"You're such a good girl, Katy." Clara's smile looked slightly sad. "I suppose I'd hoped you would help Ellen to find her way."

"I think she'll find her way. But it might take her awhile. And, quite honestly, if I thought it would've really helped Ellen, I would have continued living with her, but—"

"Oh, don't get me wrong. I believe you did the right thing in moving back home. Hopefully Ellen will realize that and take me up on my offer."

"I'm sure she will." Katy pulled on her gloves. "Just give her time." But as Katy went out to her car, she didn't feel as confident as she'd tried to sound. Ellen could be very willful—and she was easily offended. Any opposition from Katy or Clara might drive her straight into an untoward friendship with Eddie Barrows. It wouldn't matter nearly so much, except that Katy knew Baby Larry could pay the price for his mother's lack of good judgment.

• • •

Anna braced herself as Frank waved a page from the telegraph machine through her opened office door.

"Don't give me that look—this is *good* news."

"Let's hear it then!"

"It happened on Tuesday," he began. "The Brits rolled out a record number of tanks and infantry, launching an artillery attack on the German trenches near Cambrai, France. They gained five miles and wreaked havoc on two German divisions. Britain is touting it as a *spectacular success* and—get this, Anna—for the first time since 1914, church bells rang in England."

"Oh, that is fabulous news." Anna clapped her hands. "Maybe this *is* the beginning of the end."

"And US troops have yet to officially set foot on the Western Front."

"Maybe they won't have to at all. Wouldn't that be wonderful?"

"Well, I wouldn't count on that. I think US troops will be absolutely necessary. Already the Brits have lost so many soldiers. But hopefully the tide is turning—or about to turn."

"I pray that it is." She smiled. "And what a great story to run right before Thanksgiving too. It should lift everyone's spirits."

"Speaking of Thanksgiving, I wanted to ask for next Friday off. Ginger wants us to go to her parents for a long weekend."

"Yes, of course. I meant to say something at this morning's meeting. We'll put out the Thanksgiving edition and nothing else until the following week. I just got Mac's approval."

"That's a great plan." He nodded. "I'll get to work on this story. The headline will be 'Brit Bells Ring Out.' Something we can all be thankful for."

Of course, thinking about Thanksgiving reminded her of another piece of tricky business she had yet to manage. She'd promised Daniel to include his father in holiday celebrations—to make him feel part of the family. But Mac and JD were not exactly on friendly terms these days, and at the mere mention of inviting JD for Thanksgiving, Mac had grown moody and terse. Still, she couldn't let Daniel down—not while he was over there helping all those servicemen. Besides that, JD would one day be her father-in-law, so Mac would have to get beyond this jealous rivalry over Lucille's attentions.

Thoughts of Lucille gave Anna an idea. She would ask her mother to host Thanksgiving dinner. And if Mac wanted to stay home and pout, he could. But Anna didn't think he would. He wouldn't like the idea of Lucille and JD spending time together without his presence. To this end, she walked down to the dress shop at noon. The weather, unlike yesterday's rainstorm, was clear and unseasonably warm. A great day for a walk. Except that it made her miss Daniel. She wondered what he was doing now. Because of the time difference, she hoped he was done with his work day, but she wouldn't be surprised if he was still caring for the wounded. She just prayed he was taking care of himself too.

She was nearly to the dress shop when she spotted Ellen pushing her baby carriage on the other side of the street. Next to her was a tall young man. For a brief moment, Anna thought it was Lawrence, but then she realized that was impossible. According to Clara, Lawrence's unit had recently shipped overseas. Anna waved to Ellen, trying not to stare too curiously at the young man. Perhaps he was a relative, in town for the upcoming holiday.

She went into the dress shop to find Clara straightening the glove shelves. After greeting her friend, she mentioned just seeing Ellen on the street. "And she was accompanied by a young man that I don't recognize. Do you have family visiting?"

"What did he look like?" Clara's brow creased.

"Look like?" Anna considered. "He was tall and thin. Dark hair. Not bad looking, although I observed him from across the street."

"Eddie Barrows," Clara said quietly.

"Norma Barrows' son?"

Clara glanced around the shop. "He's been keeping company with my daughter."

"Oh?" Anna didn't know what else to say.

"I told her it was a bad idea." Clara sighed. "It seems she didn't listen."

"Well, you did mention he'd been friends with AJ," Anna said.

"That's true. But it was years ago. I'm afraid this is something entirely different."

Anna didn't have any advice, but she knew she'd be deeply disturbed if it was her daughter parading around in public with another man. This younger generation might take on life differently than their elders, but young married women befriending young men would not sit well with anyone of any age. Especially in a town as small as Sunset Cove. "I'm looking for my mother," she told Clara.

"She's in back with Katy. I think she goes home early today."

"Oh, good." She grasped Clara's hand. "Don't fret over Ellen. I'm sure she'll come to her senses about this."

"I hope you're right."

Anna found Lucille just pulling on her coat. "Do you have time to go to lunch with your favorite daughter?" she asked.

"I'd love to." Lucille smiled.

"What about *your* favorite daughter?" Katy grinned. "Am I invited too?"

"Of course." Anna hugged Katy. "I was just thinking pleasant thoughts about you." Katy didn't plan to disclose that it was in light of seeing Ellen just now.

"Then let's go." Katy pinned on her hat.

As they went outside, Ellen and Eddie were just stopping outside the building that Ellen lived in. Ellen was picking up the baby and Eddie was handling the baby buggy.

"Ellen," Katy said loudly. "How are you?"

Ellen looked up with a surprised expression. "I'm fine, thank you," she answered crisply.

"And how is Baby Larry?" Katy persisted, peeking at the bundled-up infant.

"He's doing just fine—thank you."

Katy looked at Eddie now. "I'd like you to meet my mother and grandmother, Eddie." She properly introduced everyone.

"It's good to see you, Ellen. Your baby looks well." Anna touched Larry's rounded cheek. "And how is your husband doing? Have you heard from Lawrence lately?"

"Not since his unit went overseas," Ellen said quietly. "We've sort of lost touch."

"But you must continue to write him regularly," Lucille told her. "Soldiers expect their wives to remain faithfully in touch. Even if husbands are unable to answer, they need encouragement from their wives. And I'm sure Lawrence will want to hear how his young son is faring."

Anna eyed Eddie. "You're not in uniform. Does that mean you're exempt?"

"That's right," he answered crisply.

"We recently wrote about that in our newspaper," she continued. "It was so refreshing to hear how young men are contributing to the war effort in their own unique ways."

"And Eddie has been helping me. He carries the baby carriage up the stairs for me, and he's helped with lots of other things." Ellen narrowed her eyes at Katy. "Chores that someone else *used* to help me with, before they got too busy to give me the time of day. You see, it's not easy being a new mother . . . on my own. It's nice when someone steps in to help. Maybe you'll see that for yourself someday." Ellen looked at Anna. "Although your family will probably come to your rescue."

"I hope my mother will be by my side when my time comes." Katy looped her arm through Anna's.

"Your mother tells me that she's invited you more than once to go live with her," Anna told Ellen. "I should think she would be marvelous help."

"I prefer to live independently." Ellen stuck out her chin. "Now if you'll excuse us, it's time for Larry's nap." Without another word, she disappeared into the stairwell, with Eddie and the baby carriage clomping up after her.

"Well, well." Lucille just shook her head. "Poor Clara."

"Poor Baby Larry," Katy said.

"Poor Lawrence." Anna sighed to remember how Ellen's husband had made such a fine turn-around last summer. And now this? Hopefully Lawrence wouldn't hear of it. And hopefully, things weren't as bad as they appeared.

CHAPTER 6

Anna was relieved that Lucille was eager and willing to host Thanksgiving. Of course, Mac threw a small fit when he heard that JD Hollister was on the guest list.

"Why did Lucille go and invite that old blowhard?" Mac demanded at breakfast.

"As a matter of fact, I invited him," Anna confessed. "JD is Daniel's father. He has no family in town and, like it or not, he will someday be my father-in-law." She set down her coffee cup with a clink. "At least I hope so."

"You hope so?" Mac's brow furrowed. "What does that mean? Are you planning to break your engagement?"

"No, of course not. But Daniel's job is perilous."

"Why's that?" Katy asked. "I thought he was working in a military hospital in England."

"Not anymore. He asked to be transferred to the Western Front." Anna sighed to think of what Daniel's life must be like these days.

"Even so, aren't doctors safe over there? I

assume the medical units are located well away from active battles."

"Some mobile units are quite close to the battlefront. And, although they should be exempt from enemy fire, that's not always the case. I've heard of a few medical units that suffered attacks by unscrupulous Huns."

Mac grimly shook his head. "What's this world coming to?"

"Even Red Cross nurses get injured . . . and sometimes killed," Anna continued. "Although infectious diseases pose a greater risk. Medical personnel get exposed to everything."

Katy frowned. "I didn't know that about Red Cross nurses. I think I'll tell my chapter about this. It might motivate them to work even harder for the cause. Speaking of my chapter, we're meeting this morning." She laid her napkin next to her plate and stood. Then going over to Mac, she kissed his cheek. "Don't worry too much about old Doc Hollister," she told him. "I'm pretty sure Grandmother likes you better."

Mac didn't look confident, but he thanked Katy just the same. After she left, he turned to Anna. "I still don't see why you invited JD to our Thanksgiving celebration," he complained.

"Because I promised Daniel I'd help his father to feel at home with us while Daniel's serving overseas. So try to put your biased opinions aside, Mac. Because if you don't, I'll warn you, you could end up being very lonely."

"What's that supposed to mean?"

"It means that in all likelihood JD is going to be my father-in-law and that means he will be part of my family. Please don't make me choose between you and him."

"Are you saying you'd choose him over me?"

"That would be your choice, Mac. If you can't abide JD's company, you will be cutting yourself out of our family gatherings." Anna slowly stood. "And if you treat JD badly around Lucille, you will simply arouse her sympathy toward the old doctor. I would think you'd know that by now."

He frowned but didn't say anything.

"So hopefully you'll want to join us for Thanksgiving. And now I need to go to work. Have a good day, Mac." As she left the dining room, she heard him grumbling to himself. But hopefully, he'd gotten the message.

On her way to work, Anna prayed for Daniel's safety . . . and that God would use him mightily to help the wounded servicemen. Not for the first time, she wondered why everyone couldn't just get along. Whether it was the power-hungry Kaiser in Europe or her own territorial father here at home, it was a shame that some people seemed to thrive upon conflict. Would they ever learn?

Katy wished she felt more enthusiasm about Thanksgiving this year. But like all their other recent get-togethers, it just seemed a bit flat. "I wonder if the US soldiers celebrate Thanksgiving over there," she said as she helped serve dessert.

"Oh, I'm sure they do," Lucille told her. "It would be un-American not to."

"With turkey and dressing and pumpkin pie?" Katy asked her.

"Well, that would be hard to say." Lucille turned to Anna. "You're a newswoman, what do you think?"

"I doubt that they're eating turkey over there." Anna frowned as if she knew more than she wanted to say.

"What do they eat?" Katy demanded.

"Well, I just read an article about the rations they eat in the trenches." Anna set down her fork. "It's not very appealing and perhaps not the best dinner conversation."

"But I want to know," Katy insisted.

"Mostly they eat canned corned beef," Anna said quickly. "And they used to have biscuits, but flour has been in short supply, so they have some sort of beet biscuits now."

"Beet biscuits?" Mac scowled. "That sounds downright unappealing."

"Well, unless you're starving," Sarah Rose said quietly.

Katy set a piece of pumpkin pie down at her own place setting. "Suddenly I don't feel very hungry."

"Depriving yourself of dessert is not going to help your soldier husband," Dr. Hollister declared. "In fact, I'm sure Jim would be dismayed to think you were not taking advantage of the good food available to you and your baby today."

"If Katy doesn't feel like eating, she doesn't have to," Mac said sharply.

"It's ridiculous to waste a perfectly good piece of pie—especially when it's been made with rationed items." Dr. Hollister scowled at Mac. "Giving in to silly feminine emotionalism helps no one."

"Katy isn't giving in to silly feminine emotionalism," Mac shot back at him. "She is simply a precious girl with sympathetic feelings."

And now the two old men were arguing and Katy couldn't take anymore. Without even excusing herself, she rushed to the kitchen and out the back door. Once she was outside, she took in a deep breath. "Oh, Jim," she whispered into the brisk sea breeze, "please, come home as soon as possible, darling. I need you." Then, bowing her head, she asked God to take care of Jim . . . to bring him home safely.

"There you are." Lucille came out the back door, quickly wrapping a woolen shawl around Katy's shoulders. "We don't need you catching a chill."

"Thank you." Katy smiled stiffly. "Are the old codgers still going at it?"

"Unfortunately, yes." Lucille chuckled. "Sometimes I think they enjoy sparring."

"For your sake, they probably do."

"That's why I thought it best to remove myself. Anna is in there trying to play the mediator, but I think it's pointless."

"I told Grandfather that I think you must love him best." Katy studied her grandmother, trying to read her expression.

"You did, did you?"

"Well, don't you? I mean you were married to him. Surely, you loved him then."

"Yes, I suppose I did. But it was a very young, immature sort of love, Katy. That's probably why it turned out badly."

"That and your mother-in-law."

"That's true."

"But you do like Grandfather, don't you?" Katy felt worried.

"Yes, of course, I do. There is much I admire about Mac."

"If he proposed marriage to you . . . would you say yes?"

"I honestly don't know the answer to that, Katy. But mostly I hope that he won't ask. Not yet anyway. I don't feel ready to be married to anyone at the moment. I've rather enjoyed my independence."

"Independence?" Katy sighed, pulling the shawl more tightly around her neck. "I used to imagine that I would be such an independent woman. And now look at me."

Lucille looked at her. "You seem quite independent to me, Katy. You're part owner of your own business. You design lovely clothes. You'll be a mother in the springtime. You head up the local Red Cross. And you seem to be holding together quite nicely while your husband serves overseas." She patted both Katy's cheeks. "I am rather proud of you, darling."

"Thank you." Katy smiled. "That actually means a lot to me."

"I know you've been missing Jim," she said softly. "But that's only natural. And I'm sure it won't be too long until he comes home. Just be patient."

Katy nodded. "I'm trying."

"I know you'd never be as foolish as your friend Ellen." Lucille shook her head. "That girl seems to be on the path to destruction."

"I felt sort of guilty for not inviting her to join us today, but I doubt she would've come anyway."

"Clara said she refused to join her and Randall at his mother's."

"Oh, dear, do you think she's home alone with the baby?"

Lucille shrugged, but her eyes suggested uncertainty.

"Maybe I should take her some leftovers," Katy

said suddenly. "Maybe it could be like a peace offering."

"I can ask Sally to put something together."

"If you think it's a good idea . . . I don't know if Ellen will appreciate it."

"If she's hungry she will. And I'm sure she misses you, Katy. Maybe you can talk some sense into that foolish girl."

"I just hope I don't find Eddie Barrows there."

"I'll bet he's spending Thanksgiving with his mother." Lucille reached for Katy's hand. "Let's get inside where it's warm."

It didn't take long to put together a basket of Thanksgiving food, and soon Katy was knocking on the apartment door, cringing to think of what she would say or do if Eddie was there. But the door opened and Ellen, still wearing her house-coat, did not appear to be expecting visitors.

"Oh, it's you." Ellen peered curiously at Katy. "What do you want?"

Katy held out the basket. "To be your friend. And to share some Thanksgiving dinner with you."

"Oh?" Ellen opened the door wider, allowing Katy into a very messy looking apartment. "Okay, come in."

Katy cleared a spot on the kitchen table to set the basket and then, hearing the baby's crying, offered to go check on him. The bedroom was as messy as the rest of the house and Baby Larry, not surprisingly, needed changing. By the time Katy took a clean and dry baby back out, Ellen was already eating.

Jostling the baby, Katy got him to quiet down then sat across from Ellen. "I think Baby Larry is getting bigger," she said in a tone more cheerful than she felt.

"He should be bigger, he eats every two hours."

"I'm sure that must be hard on you." Katy studied the dark circles under Ellen's eyes. "I bet you don't get much rest."

"That's for sure." Ellen forked into the dressing.

"I know you don't want to hear this, Ellen, but I don't see why you don't live with your mother. She really wants—"

"She wants to tell me how to live my life."

"I don't think that's true."

"Oh, yeah?" Ellen glared at her. "She was up here yesterday—lecturing me about spending time with Eddie. You should have heard her harping at me."

"Well, that's because she loves—"

"That's because she wants to control me, Katy. And to make matters worse, she holds you up as my example. Nothing would make her happier than if I could be more like you." Ellen wrinkled her nose. "And, trust me, it gets under my skin."

"I'm sorry about that."

"Well, I'm sorry my mother feels the need to control my every move."

"Well, it's not as if she's been able to." Katy reminded Ellen of how she'd run off to marry Lawrence against her mother's will. "And I honestly don't think she wants to control you, Ellen. I think she simply wants to help you. And she wants to be a grandmother. I suspect she's a bit lonely."

"She is *not* lonely. She has Randall. They're always together. In fact, that's where she is right now. With Randall and his mother. And here I am all alone."

Katy wanted to point out her own presence just now, but didn't. "My grandmother said you were invited to join Randall's family today."

"My mother didn't really want me there. She just put on a pretense for Randall's sake. How would it look if she didn't invite me? I could tell she was relieved that I said no. Less embarrassing for her since, according to my mother, I have a tarnished reputation now. But I didn't do anything wrong!"

Katy didn't know what to say. "Well, I just wanted to make sure you were okay." She stood, still jostling the baby. "And I wanted to hold this sweet baby again." She smiled. "I've missed you both."

"Really?" Ellen brightened slightly. "Would you consider moving back with me?"

Katy sighed. "I just can't do that, Ellen. Even old Doc Hollister told me I've been doing too much." She handed the baby back to Ellen. "I have to take it easier . . . for my own baby's sake."

Ellen's lower lip protruded. "Yes, I suppose that's true."

"How will you get by . . . I mean with your budget. Will you really be able to stay here on what little you get from the war department?"

"It won't be easy." Ellen nuzzled her baby. "But we'll get by somehow."

"I know you don't want to work at the shop, but maybe you'd like to do some piece work sewing here at home."

Ellen's eyes lit up. "Would you let me do that?"

"Of course. You probably heard I had to let both the fulltime seamstresses go . . . because of the war rationing and all. But we still have work that needs doing. And I'm considering starting a line of specialty children's clothing."

"Oh, I'd love to work on that. And it would give me something to keep me busy in the evenings. It can get awfully lonely up here."

"Yes . . . I'm sure." Katy smiled sadly. She couldn't imagine living up here by herself with a baby. "I would be lonely too. And I don't want to lecture you, Ellen, but you should heed your mother's advice when it comes to socializing with Eddie."

Ellen frowned.

"But I believe you, and I'll try to help people

understand that nothing wrong happened. But you need to be more careful." Katy pointed to Baby Larry. "For his sake as much as for yours." She hugged them both. "And when I bring up the sewing, I'll make sure to stay and visit a bit."

"Would you really? That would be so nice."

Katy assured her that she would, but as she left the dismal apartment, she felt uneasy. The truth was she would rather avoid interacting with Ellen. Especially if Ellen ignored their warnings and persisted in seeing Eddie Barrows. If that happened, Katy would cut herself off from Ellen. But hopefully this would be the end of that nonsense. Katy prayed that Ellen would come to her senses.

CHAPTER 7

Early December 1917

Anna could hardly believe the news she'd just heard. "Give that to me one more time, Frank. Did I hear you right?"

He nodded glumly. "The Norwegian supply ship, *SS Imo*, collided with the French cargo ship, *SS Mont Blanc*. Two thousand died and nine thousand were injured. It occurred up in Nova Scotia yesterday."

"And this was an accident—not an act of war?"

"That's what it says—*accidental collision*. That French cargo ship was loaded with explosives meant for the Western Front. The whole place must've blown sky high."

"That's so horrible." Anna shuddered.

"Horrible for the victims and bad for the allied forces waiting for the explosives." He frowned. "Front page, eh?"

"Yes." As he left, Anna wished they could find a bit of good news to print in the paper too, but it had been dark days lately. Not just in Europe, but all over. And hopes of the US helping to bring this war to a swift end were waning. Christmas on the home front would probably be bleak this year. But it would be much bleaker . . . and deadlier . . . in the trenches.

"Letter just came for you." Virginia stuck her head into Anna's office. "Thought you might want it."

"From my Daniel?" Anna leaped from her desk, eagerly grabbing it. "Thank you!" She snatched up her letter opener, quickly slitting the envelope open then carefully unfolding the single page with trembling fingers. Hopefully all was well with him.

17 November 1917

Dear Anna,

I'm sorry it has taken me so long to write back to you, but I thank you for your letters. They are like beacons of light from a faraway utopia. Those sweet memories of Sunset Cove, and warm thoughts of you, are what keep me going.

As you must know, the front lines are intense. I often work sixteen hours a day and sometimes longer. My only spare time is for sleep, and I am so weary that even the bombs and artillery do not keep me awake.

I spend most of my day in surgery, going from one severely wounded patient to the next. Although I am learning new medical techniques, I regret the lives that cannot be saved and I ache for the lives that will never be the same again. War is hell. There is no other way to describe the atrocities here.

On a more positive note, I'm happy to report that modern technology is changing the outcome for patients. Motorized ambulances are now being utilized to transport the wounded to receive more immediate care. I cannot describe the importance of this expedience. It is the difference between life and death for many of our soldiers. I am grateful for it . . . and grateful that I am of use here.

Please, continue to pray for all of our troops. Pray that this horrific war ends soon and that we can return to our former lives and abide peaceably together for the rest of our days.

Yours Truly,
Captain Daniel Hollister MD

After reading the letter twice, Anna proceeded to write Daniel a long, detailed response, telling him everything she could think of to bolster his spirits. Was she painting too cheery of a home-front picture? She didn't think so. Daniel needed encouragement to help him to continue doing the important work over there. As much as she missed him and as concerned as she felt for his safety, she was proud to think of him saving lives. She knew he'd done the right thing by going. She just prayed he would make it home.

She addressed the letter then took it out to Virginia. "Please send this out as soon as possible."

"That was quick." Virginia pressed the stamp more tightly to the envelope. "How is our good doctor faring these days?"

"I'm afraid he's worn out," Anna admitted. "But he's doing a good job. And he needs our prayers more than ever."

"I pray for all our boys over there." Virginia pulled on her coat. "If I take this to the post office right now, it'll make the afternoon train."

Anna thanked her and was just heading back to her office when Frank waved to her from the telegraph machine. "More news?" she asked.

"From Washington DC," he told her. "We've just declared war on Austria-Hungary."

"I suppose it's about time we stood up to Germany's allies." She read the short report. "Do you think it'll bring this madness to an end sooner?"

"I'm sure that's what everyone is hoping for."

"Wouldn't it be wonderful if it could end before Christmas?" She tried to imagine how she'd feel if Daniel could come home by then but immediately knew that was unrealistic.

"It would be a real miracle if that happened," Frank told her. "But I won't be holding my breath."

"No, of course not." She took the report from him. "I'll handle this one since you're doing the explosion story." As she returned to her office, she began constructing the piece in her head. She would give the article a positive spin in order to lift everyone's spirits. And it wasn't as if she were making this up, because the US declaration of war against German allies really should help propel this war to a quicker end. It just made sense.

Katy tried to suppress feelings of discouragement as she drove her grandmother home from the dress shop. Her biggest disappointment today came from not receiving a letter from Jim. It had been six weeks now since she'd heard anything from him. And that had only been a postcard sent from Belgium in late October, announcing that he and his unit had safely made it to the continent. And that meant they were probably headed for battle—perhaps immersed in it right now.

"Well, don't take it to heart," Lucille said as Katy stopped in front of her house. "After all, no news is good news. If anything bad had happened to Jim, you would've heard." She patted Katy's hand. "And don't forget, it's better to pray than to worry, dear."

"Yes, I know that's true. But for some reason I felt certain I'd hear something from him today." Katy sighed. She really had felt something inside of her this morning. And it wasn't just the fluttery movements of the baby she was carrying. It had been different. And she'd imagined it was related to her husband. Hopefully it didn't mean that Jim had been hurt . . . or worse. She couldn't bear to even say those words aloud.

"I do hope you'll get some rest, Katy. I agree with JD that you push yourself too hard. For Jim's sake, as much as for your own and your baby's, I must insist that you stay home from the shop all day tomorrow."

"But it's Saturday and—"

"Never mind about that. You know that Clara and I can handle everything just fine on our own. Besides that, it's been so quiet there lately . . . I've wondered if we should consider only opening a few days a week. Perhaps Thursday through Saturday. Those have always been our busiest days."

"But what about holiday shoppers? Christmas is only two and a half weeks away."

"What with war deprivations and people's struggles to make ends meet . . ." Lucille grimly shook her head. "Folks are pinching their pennies. Clara and I discussed it at lunchtime today. We both feel that going to three days a week makes good sense."

Katy considered this. Only one lady had stepped into the shop today, and she only bought a pair of stockings. "You could be right, Grandmother."

"Then you agree?" Lucille looked surprised.

Katy sighed then nodded. "Yes. For now I do agree."

Lucille patted her hand. "When this war ends, business will pick up. In the meantime, we can be thankful to keep our little shop from going completely under. Many enterprises—all over the country—are suffering."

"Unless they're manufacturing guns, boots, or bayonets." Katy forced a smile as Lucille climbed out of the car. But as she went home, she felt that heavy blanket of gloom return. Perhaps it was best that she wasn't going to work tomorrow. Maybe she'd spend the entire day in bed.

The house was quiet as she went inside. Although she could see dinner preparations and something on the stove, Bernice was nowhere to be seen. Katy tiptoed through the living room and then, instead of going in to chat with her grandfather like she often did after work, she went straight upstairs to her room. As she unbuttoned her dark green woolen coat—one of the severe, almost military-like styles she'd designed in the fall—she suddenly felt weary and dowdy . . . and very thick through her midsection.

Of course, she knew that pregnancy meant the

loss of one's figure. But as a girl who'd enjoyed fitted lacy gowns and femininity, she hadn't really been prepared for this. And as she studied her image in her bureau mirror, she felt seriously disturbed. Who was that tired, frumpy woman? What had happened to young, vibrant Katy McDowell?

"You should be thankful Jim isn't here to see you like this," she told her reflection. "You look nothing like the bride he wed last summer." She sat down in her easy chair and, after struggling to unbutton her shoes, leaned back, closed her eyes, and promptly fell asleep.

Katy woke disoriented, jarring at the sound of Bernice's dinner bell. Still tired, she considered ignoring it and going directly to bed, but realizing she was hungry, she put on her house-slippers and padded downstairs. Her mother and grandfather were in their places, discussing—as usual—the newspaper business as well as the latest news. They paused to greet her and ask a blessing and then continued talking about the most recent events.

"Just when I felt like we had a bit of good news to lift everyone's spirits, and then we hear about *Jacob Jones*." Anna shook her head.

"Who is Jacob Jones?" Katy asked with only a fragment of curiosity.

"Not who, but what," Mac said. "The *Jacob Jones* was a US ship that was sunk yesterday."

"Oh . . ." Katy wasn't sure she wanted to hear the details.

"It was a destroyer ship," Anna explained. "Not far from England, it was torpedoed by a German U-boat. It sank within eight minutes. Can you imagine that? Eight minutes."

"Did they say how many lives were lost?" Mac asked.

"No. I assume we'll hear more later. The news came too late for tomorrow's paper. I'll run the *Jacob Jones* story on the front page of our next paper."

"Well, I doubt there were many survivors," Mac said glumly. "That German sub probably made sure of it. Those blood-thirsty Huns are out to destroy all—"

"Stop—stop!" Katy held up her hands. "All you two ever talk about is war-war-war. I get so sick of hearing war stories. Stop!" She stood up with clenched fists.

"Oh, Katy girl." Mac set down his fork. "I am so sorry."

"I just can't take anymore. I haven't heard from Jim for so long and I just—I just—I just can't take more bad war news." As Katy broke into tears, Anna leapt from her chair, embracing her, gently stroking her hair.

"Oh, sweetheart. I didn't realize it affected you so. You're always so strong and capable. But how insensitive of us." She turned to Mac. "We will practice some restraint in our conversations. Especially at mealtimes."

"I'm sorry to fall apart like this. And I know you didn't mean to upset me. Really, I'll be fine." Katy used her linen napkin to blot her tears. "It's just that I felt so worn and weary tonight. Maybe I should excuse myself to—"

"Please, don't do that. Just sit down again," Anna urged. "I promise we will only speak of pleasant things now. You can eat your dinner in peace."

"Yes, we should all eat our meals in peace," Mac reiterated. "It's a consequence of covering the current events. We newspaper folks can become callous and grim."

"I won't always be so overly sensitive," Katy said quietly. "I don't know what's wrong with me today. Everything just seems to set me off."

"You're with child," Mac reminded her. "And you're concerned for your husband. That alone is plenty."

"Let's talk about something else," Anna suggested. "How was the dress shop today, Katy? Any interesting customers?"

"Not particularly. In fact, it was very slow." Katy explained the new plan to cut back on the days they'd be open. "Grandmother and Clara feel it's wise, and I'm inclined to agree."

"I think that's a good idea," Anna told her. "At least until this war ends. But even if the war gets over before your baby arrives, I still hope that you'll take some time off from the shop. I realize you're a modern, independent woman, but you're only human, dear."

"I think I'm realizing that." Katy sighed. "It's just that I like to be busy. And I think it helps to distract me from worrying about Jim."

"Why don't you work on some paintings?" Mac asked. "I still think you gave up your art too soon. You were just getting good at it."

"Dress designing is a form of art too," Anna pointed out.

He smiled. "I suppose that's true. You're a girl of many talents."

Already Katy was feeling better. As sad as it was to have Jim so far away and out of touch, it was a comfort having family around. Of course, this reminded her of Ellen. And so, although she had planned to keep it to herself, she told them about stopping by Ellen's at lunchtime. "I took her some sewing and, I wasn't going to say anything, but I strongly suspect that Eddie had been there."

"Oh, dear." Anna shook her head. "I thought Ellen was done with that nonsense."

"I thought so too."

"What made you think that young rascal had been there?" Mac asked with a furrowed brow.

Katy held up a finger. "For one thing, her apartment was surprisingly clean." She held up a second finger. "And Ellen was all gussied up and she was in good spirits."

"But maybe that was for you, Katy. Perhaps she was glad that you were coming," Anna said hopefully.

"She didn't know I was coming." Katy held up a third finger. "Last but not least, there was a man's hat hanging on her coat rack. And I feel almost completely certain it belongs to Eddie Barrows."

Both Mac and Anna looked dismayed.

"Perhaps it was Lawrence's," Anna said.

"No. Ellen wanted more room in her room and closet—for the baby's things. So I helped her to pack up all of Lawrence's clothing. And I carried it all upstairs to the storage attic."

"Oh." Anna grimaced.

"And I'm sure I recognized the hat as Eddie's. But when I said this to her, she denied it."

"Did she say who the hat belonged to?" Mac asked.

"She claimed it was AJ's." Katy buttered her roll.

"So how did AJ's hat get there? Maybe he skipped out on the war to pay his sister a little visit." Mac scowled.

"Perhaps Ellen held onto one of her brother's hats to help keep him in her thoughts." Anna's expression suggested she didn't really believe this herself.

"That would be a nice gesture, but I lived in that apartment long enough to know she didn't have any of her brother's hats there. Besides that, she and AJ weren't exactly on speaking terms. You must remember how she treated him after he got in trouble with the law last year."

"Well, this is disappointing. I'd really hoped Ellen was growing up. I wonder what Clara will think. Did you tell her?" Anna asked.

Katy shook her head. "No. I don't see how that will help anything. I only told you two because I needed to talk to someone. And I know you'll keep quiet about it. I suppose there's a slight chance I could be wrong. But I'm pretty sure I saw that hat on Eddie's head before."

"I'm sorry for your sake, Katy. You've been a good friend to that girl. I don't think she deserves it." Mac reached for the butter.

"I don't know . . . but now I don't feel I want Ellen to sew for the dress shop anymore. I thought it was a good idea at the time, but if she's still seeing Eddie . . . Well, maybe I need to just step away. And since we're cutting back on work anyway . . ."

"That's right." Mac nodded firmly. "Leave that wanton woman to her own devices, Katy. You stay out of her messes. Mark my word, no good'll come of it."

"I think your grandfather could be right about avoiding Ellen," Anna agreed. "Although I do feel sorry for the baby. And for Lawrence too. Ultimately I feel sorriest for Ellen—she is risking everything . . . for nothing."

Katy felt sorry for the little Bouchard family too. But perhaps it was like one of her grand-father's favorite adages. *You make your bed . . . you lie in it.* Maybe that's what Ellen had done, or was doing right now. And what more—besides praying—could Katy do for her troubled friend?

CHAPTER 8

Anna wished that the newspaper could contain more good news during the week preceding Christmas, but after Russia had signed an armistice with Germany, the writing had been on the wall—and all over the front pages of every US newspaper including the *Sunset Times*. It was no secret that the German divisions previously occupied with Russians were now on the move. Free to leave the Eastern Front, they had been quickly redeployed to the Western Front. Now they would direct all their military might against the Allied Forces. It would not be a merry Christmas over there—or anywhere, for that matter. This war was like a thick black cloud that had encompassed the entire earth.

According to her last letter from Daniel, he was already overwhelmed with both battle casualties and serious war related illnesses. She had no idea how much this new development would impact his work. To make matters worse, Daniel and other physicians were predicting a serious epidemic that could possibly overshadow the mortality rates caused by the Great War. Of course, as he pointed out, if there were no war, it would be much easier for the medical community to prevent this wildfire spread of disease.

"I'm going out to find some good news," Anna told Frank as she put on her hat.

"Where are you going to look for it?" he asked.

"Kathleen's Dress Shop." She smiled as she pulled on her gloves. "They are hosting a holiday tea and fashion show this afternoon. I'm going there to cover the story—and to enjoy it myself."

"I'm glad someone gets to have fun." His tone was slightly sarcastic. "In the meantime, I'll hold down the fort."

"I'm sure you can. But if you need me, you know where to find me. And I'll be back in time to turn in my fashion show piece. Just save me some room on page four next to Katy's fashion column." They discussed the length and suggestions for images. Then Anna took in a deep breath and stepped outside. Determined to distance herself from the wartime news, and hoping for a happy reprieve, she casually strolled down Main Street.

Anna knew how much Katy and Lucille had been anticipating today's festivities. Bernice had been making cookies the past few days and planned to be on hand to serve refreshments. According to Katy, today's event was not because the shop hoped to make sales, but simply as a way to show appreciation to the faithful customers throughout the past year. And the show was by invitation only.

The shop smelled good and was beautifully decorated for Christmas. With several rows of folding wooden chairs already filled with local ladies, there was barely room to get inside. But Anna took a chair in the back, close to where a friend of Clara's was quietly playing violin. Before long, the high school girls, not much younger than Katy, began to model holiday outfits while Lucille, acting as the master of ceremonies, described the dresses with dramatic flourish. Anna jotted down notes, listing names and details that she knew their readership would appreciate.

All in all, the event was a pure delight and, after the show and teatime wrapped up, Anna could see that all the guests had been thoroughly entertained and appreciative. It even appeared that Lucille had written up some purchases afterward.

"This was perfectly lovely," Anna quietly told Katy. "Well done."

"Thank you." Katy waved goodbye to the last pair of stragglers. "I hope everyone enjoyed it." She picked up a cookie platter.

"I'm sure they did. How about if I help you clean things up?" Anna glanced around the cluttered dress shop.

"That'd be great. Clara and Lucille are helping the models in the back room. But since we plan to be open tomorrow, we need to put this place back together. We borrowed these chairs from City Hall. I'm supposed to set them outside, and Mayor Wally will be by to pick them up in about an hour."

"Let me take care of the chairs," Anna said. As she folded chairs, leaning them by the door, she asked about Ellen. "I didn't see her here today."

"Yes, I felt a little guilty about it, but Clara insisted. She felt Ellen's presence here would be an unnecessary distraction. I suppose she's right. It seems everyone in town is gossiping about her lately."

"I understand." To change the topic, Anna told Katy that she planned to write a piece about the holiday show for tomorrow's paper. "It's partially done, but I still need to go back and drop in some names and details. It'll run alongside your fashion column. By the way, I liked what you wrote. Suggesting ideas for reworking old adult clothing items for children's pieces was excellent." Anna was taking some chairs outside when she noticed the messenger boy coming down the street on his bicycle. She watched for a moment, knowing that telegrams often brought bad news. Not wanting to see where the boy stopped, she went back inside.

She was folding another chair when the

messenger boy, with a telegram in hand, entered the shop. Katy set down the silver tea set with a loud clang. As she walked toward the uniformed boy, her face visibly paled. Anna rushed to her side, supporting Katy's elbow as she mutely held out her hand for the telegram.

"Telegram for Mrs. Clara Krauss," the messenger boy announced formally. "Is this her address?"

"Actually, her apartment is above the dress shop," Anna said nervously.

"But she uses this address," Katy said in a flat voice. "And she is here now. I can give it to her."

Anna reached for change in her jacket pocket, handing the boy a tip and thanking him. Then she turned to Katy. "What is it? Can you tell?"

Katy, still staring at the telegram, just shook her head.

"Shall I get Clara?" Without waiting for an answer, Anna hurried to the back room which was a flurry of clothing and partially dressed young women. "Clara?" Anna called over the noisy voices. "Can you come out into the shop?"

Clara nodded, laughing. "Gladly!"

Anna put an arm around Clara's waist as they headed for the door. "You have a telegram," she said quietly.

"A telegram?"

"Yes. Katy has it for you."

Clara hastened her pace and, hurrying out to Katy, took the manila colored stationary from her. With trembling fingers, she opened it. "Oh, no—oh, no. No, no, no." Anna eased Clara down to one of the remaining wooden chairs, watching as her friend collapsed into uncontrollable sobs and the telegram floated down to the floor.

Katy sat in a chair next to Clara, wrapping her arms around her heaving shoulders without speaking, and Anna picked up the envelope and silently read the typed message.

MRS CLARA KRAUSS
THE SECRETARY OF WAR DESIRES
TO SEND HIS DEEP REGRETS THAT
YOUR SON, PRIVATE ALBERT J
KRAUSS, WAS KILLED IN ACTION
ON FIFTEEN NOVEMBER IN
FRANCE. LETTER TO FOLLOW.
C. RADCLIFF ADJUTANT GENERAL

Anna refolded the telegram and then, scooting a chair next to Clara, sat down with tear-filled eyes. "I'm so very sorry," she said quietly. "So very, very sorry." She put her arm around Clara too.

"AJ?" Katy whispered.

Anna simply nodded.

"Oh, dear, dear Clara." Katy began to cry. "I'm so sorry."

"AJ did such a remarkable job of turning his life around. He did the right thing even though it was difficult and dangerous. AJ turned it around . . . and did the right thing. He made us all so proud of him." Anna knew she was rambling but couldn't seem to stop herself. "And enlisting in the army like that. Such a brave boy. We can all be proud of him, Clara. Such a fine young man and—and . . ." And then she began to sob with Clara and Katy. Words were not enough.

"Ellen," Clara said suddenly. "Someone needs to tell Ellen."

Katy's eyes grew wide.

"I'll go," Anna offered. "I'll tell her."

"Thank you," Clara muttered.

"Yes." Katy nodded with appreciation.

With the telegram still in hand, Anna hurried outside and down the street, practically running up the darkened stairway to Ellen's apartment. *Please, don't let Eddie be there,* Anna prayed silently as she knocked loudly on the door. After a moment, the door opened wide and Ellen, dressed in a pretty blue dress, was smiling brightly. But her smile instantly vanished.

"Oh, it's you." She scowled darkly. "What do you want?"

"I need to—to speak to you," Anna said breathlessly.

"Well, if you're here to lecture me about my private life, I don't have time for—"

"No, it's not that." Anna handed Ellen the telegram, waiting as she read it.

"What?" Ellen looked at Anna with troubled eyes. "Is this for real?"

"Of course, it's for real. Your mother just received it at the dress shop."

"AJ?" Ellen's voice cracked. "Is he—is he really dead? AJ is dead?"

Anna could only nod. "Your mother is still at the shop."

Without bothering for her hat or coat, Ellen pushed past Anna, running toward the stairs. "I need to see her." Anna was about to shut the door and follow Ellen when she remembered about the baby. Unsure of what to do, she decided to remain there with him.

She went inside, closing the door, and looked around. The apartment was clean and tidy, just like Katy had described her last visit with Ellen. But something about it didn't feel right. And the little kitchen table was set with two places with something cooking on the stove. Of course . . . Ellen was expecting company.

Feeling disgusted and weary, Anna turned off the stove and went to the bedroom to check on the baby. Sleeping peacefully in his crib, with a curled fist in his mouth, he was blissfully unaware. No worries over the fact his uncle had perished in the war, or that his father was over there fighting right now . . . or, that his young mother had been exercising very poor judgment.

As Anna adjusted the blanket more snugly around the sleeping infant, she wondered how it would feel to do this for her own grandchild. It was only a few months away now. Her heart went out to Lawrence, who'd never held his child. Was he out there in some muddy trench? Did he have a photo of his baby? Would he make it back to meet him? And what about Jim? Would he make it home? Would he ever get to see his child?

This simply reminded her of AJ again, and now fresh tears were coming. She tiptoed out of the room and, pacing in the tiny apartment, let her tears flow freely. All she'd said about AJ earlier had been true. Sure, he'd made his mistakes, but he'd turned his life around . . . and now he was gone. Anna wiped her tears, praying that God would sort it all out . . . and that this war would soon end.

A knock on the door interrupted her prayer. Thinking it was Ellen, possibly locked out, Anna hurried to open it. But seeing it was Eddie Barrows—and looking as if he owned the place— Anna was tempted to slam the door right in his surprisingly smug face.

"What are *you* doing here?" He glared at her as if she, not him, were the intruder.

"I came here to tell Ellen that her brother has been killed in the war." Anna watched closely for his response, but the interloper didn't even blink.

"Oh, well, that's too bad. But Ellen never cared much for her brother anyway. Maybe you hadn't heard that he was running rum." Eddie's eyes narrowed slightly.

"It's true that AJ lost his way for a while, but he straightened things out before enlisting in the army." Her indignation increased.

"Yeah, maybe so, but it's nothing to me anyway. Guess it would've been better if that news had been about Ellen's husband."

"How dare you say such a thing about Lawrence?"

"I'm sure Ellen feels the same. From what I've heard, her man's a real simp."

"Have you no respect for the brave young men who are serving their country right now?"

"I never said that."

"Your attitude says everything. And I don't like to question a young man who claims he's exempt from military service, but I'd sure like to know why you've been excluded."

"Why? So you can print it in your little newspaper?"

"Just plain curiosity." She looked him up and down. "You appear physically fit to me, Mr. Barrows. Although I've noticed that you don't seem to be gainfully employed anywhere. But perhaps you're not healthy. Although you're obviously well enough to run around town and seem to have no challenges going up and down the steep stairway to Ellen's apartment. Not that you have any business coming up here to spend time with a married woman."

"Which is none of your business."

"Just so you know, Ellen won't see you tonight. She's with her mother right now."

"Well, that won't last long. Ellen hates her mother." His smug smile returned. "I'll just wait here for her."

Anna was so infuriated that she suddenly wished she were a man—and that she could punch this selfish upstart right in his crooked nose. Instead, she went straight to the bedroom, gathered up the sleeping baby, wrapped him in blankets and, without saying another word, marched out of the apartment. But instead of returning to the dress shop, where she hoped Ellen and Clara were reuniting—and she didn't want to distract them—Anna continued on down to the newspaper office. She supposed she might be accused of kidnapping, but at the moment she didn't care.

Virginia's eyes grew wide when Anna walked into the newspaper office with a baby in her arms. "Where on earth did you get *that?*" Virginia touched the baby's cheek. "I know it can't be Katy's."

"Meet Larry Bouchard," Anna said crisply. "Lawrence's son."

"I see." Virginia nodded with a furrowed brow.

"Come with me." Anna tipped her head toward her office and, behind closed doors, quickly explained the situation.

Virginia chuckled. "Well, I think you did the right thing, Anna. And since Lawrence was a newspaper employee, it seems fitting we should offer refuge to his little son. But where is the mother?"

Anna sighed deeply then told Virginia the rest of the story.

Virginia sadly shook her head. "Oh, my. Poor dear Clara. She will be devastated."

"Yes." Anna handed the baby over to Virginia. "If you can mind her grandbaby and perhaps give the dress shop a call to report on the missing child's whereabouts, I will attempt to get some work done before press-time."

"Will do."

"And could you give Chief Rollins a call for me? Tell him I'd like to talk to him if he has time."

"Are you turning yourself in for kidnapping?" she asked wryly.

Anna attempted a weak smile. "Thanks, Virginia." After the older woman left, Anna went straight to her typewriter, quickly finishing the piece she'd started earlier, and then called Frank. "I have that fashion show article ready for you," she said. "But I want you to make room for a small piece on the front page."

When Frank picked up the first piece, she explained about AJ. "I just want to write something for the front page. He's Sunset Cove's first war fatality, and I feel he deserves to be honored for it."

"I'm sorry to hear that." Frank frowned as he stepped out of her office. "I sure hope Jim and Lawrence and the others fare better."

"Right. But you know as well as I do, this war is going to get worse before it gets better." She turned her attention back to her typewriter.

"*If* it gets better." He quietly closed the door.

As Anna pounded the keys of her typewriter, she wondered. . . . Would it ever get better? What if Germany won this gruesome Great War? What would the fate of the world become then? It was too horrible to even imagine. *God help us!*

CHAPTER 9

K aty had been sweetly stunned to witness
Ellen and Clara embracing, weeping
together as they both grieved the loss of AJ.
Apologies and forgiveness flowed freely between
them and, by the time Lucille came into the
shop to announce that Virginia had called from
the newspaper and that Baby Larry was being
cared for there, mother and daughter were
reunited.

"What is going on here?" Lucille asked with a
bewildered expression.

Katy quickly explained about AJ and then
Lucille had tears running down her powdered
cheeks too. She hugged both Clara and Ellen,
expressing her deep regrets. "But why is the baby
at the newspaper office?" Lucille asked them.

"Oh, dear." Ellen covered her mouth with her
hand. "I nearly forgot about Larry. I left Anna
with him. Is he okay?"

"Yes, I'm sure he's fine," Lucille told her.
"Virginia at the newspaper office is caring for
him. Apparently Anna took him there."

"Why would she do that?" Clara looked puzzled.

Ellen looked at her mother with a sheepish expression. "Eddie was coming over tonight. He might've arrived when Anna was there."

Without saying anything, Clara closed her eyes with a pained expression.

Ellen grasped Clara's hands in hers. "I'm so sorry, Mother. I will never see him again. I promise you I won't. And you were right—it was wrong for me to spend time with him. But that's all over with now. And I swear to you nothing serious happened between us. I just needed a friend—that's all. I was so lonely."

Clara opened her eyes, looking directly at Ellen. "We're all the family we have now, Ellen. You and me and the baby. We need to stay together . . . to be strong."

"Do you still want me to live with you?" she asked meekly.

"Of course, I do." Clara nodded eagerly. "Let's not waste time. I'd like you to move in with me tonight."

"All of my stuff?" Ellen looked uncertain. "And the baby's stuff too?"

"We can get those lively high school girls to help," Lucille said suddenly. "They're so full of energy, I'm sure they'll be willing. Especially if I offer them a little tip."

Suddenly everyone was in motion. Ellen

headed for the newspaper office to collect her baby. "I'll bring him straight to your place," she told Clara.

"And I'll drive the high school girls over to your apartment in the Runabout," Katy offered. "I can figure out what you and the baby will need for the next few days. The girls can load it up, and we'll bring it back over to Clara's apartment."

"And send those girls back here afterward," Lucille told Katy. "They can help put the shop back to order. And then I'll give them their tips."

As she drove the boisterous girls, Katy wasn't sure what to expect at Ellen's apartment. What if that crumb Eddie Barrows was up there? When she parked on the street, she observed lights on in the apartment. Seeing a shadow figure pacing back and forth, she felt sure it was Eddie. "You girls wait here until I call down for you." Then without explaining the situation, she hurried on up and simply opened the door.

"Ellen is not coming back here tonight," she told Eddie as soon as she entered the apartment with what she hoped was an air of authority. "And you shouldn't be here either."

"Why not?" He glared at her.

"Because Ellen and the baby are moving in with her mother. She is done with this place for good."

"I don't believe you. Ellen can't stand her mother."

"Think what you like, but Ellen sent us here to get her things. So unless you want the moving crew to come find your unwanted presence here, you might want to beat it." She opened the window and hollered down to the street. "You movers come on up now—we've got work to do!"

Just like that, Eddie disappeared. He probably expected to meet burly men in the stairwell—not the giddy high school girls. Not that Katy cared. She was just glad the creep was gone. Hopefully for good. And hopefully Ellen would keep the promise she'd just made to Clara.

The breakfast table was exceptionally subdued on Saturday morning. Both Anna and Katy were worn out from their emotional evening the night before. And then, before anyone had a chance to tell Mac the bad news about AJ, he'd read the article on the front page of Saturday's morning paper.

"That was a generous piece you wrote about young AJ," Mac quietly told Anna. "Can't say how sad it makes me to hear about his death."

"Yes . . . especially after all he'd been through." Anna picked up a piece of toast. "I had high hopes for him."

"My heart goes out to poor Clara." Mac stirred his coffee. "No parent wants to outlive their child."

"Well, if there was any good to come out of the bad, it's that Clara and Ellen have buried the hatchet." Katy explained about helping to get Ellen settled in last night. "And I had a chance to tell off that creep Eddie Barrows. I was so vexed, but I managed to maintain some dignity."

"Good for you. I'm not sure that I did as well, but I told him off too." Anna smiled sheepishly. "I kept wishing I were a man so I could sock him in the nose."

Mac smiled. "I'd like to have seen that."

"But I do think Ellen was sincere in her promise not to see Eddie again," Katy told them. "She even apologized to me for playing the floozy."

"Playing the floozy?" Anna frowned.

"Those were her words, not mine." Katy forked into her eggs.

"Well, I spoke to Chief Rollins last night," Anna confided. "I asked him to look into Eddie Barrows's claim of exemption. I recently read an article about selfish young men who never registered for the draft. They relocate to other towns then use the pretense that they're exempt for some reason. Often they're not questioned. But it's illegal, and it's up to local law enforcement to investigate."

"Is Harvey looking into it?" Mac asked.

"He promised to do some investigating." Anna felt slightly guilty for pressuring him last night. "But to be honest, I think Harvey is more interested in retirement these days."

"Yes, I'm afraid you're right. Hopefully, he'll find the right man to fill his shoes." Mac sipped his coffee.

"In the meantime, I hope he'll do his job." Katy set down her fork with a clang. "It's plain to see Eddie Barrows is a no-good grifter! And if he's eluding the draft, he deserves to be held accountable. Especially when you consider how AJ just lost his life serving his country. And what about good guys like Jim and Lawrence over there right now? They're risking everything while a creep like Eddie Barrows struts around making trouble here. It just gets me steamed!"

"Well, don't get too steamed." Anna forced a smile to conceal her concern. Katy didn't need to get worked up over this. "For one thing, Eddie Barrows isn't worth it. And besides that, I'm sure Chief Rollins will figure things out." At least she hoped he would. And if he didn't, she would put Frank onto it as an investigative reporter. Hopefully he'd make Eddie uncomfortable. Perhaps Eddie would want to relocate to a different town and that would be the end of it. And if not, and at the very least, it would make an interesting news story. Anna could just see the headline. *Local Man Eludes Draft.* And she would have no compunction about printing it on the front page.

• • •

Anna knew something was up when Clara burst into her office with flushed cheeks and overly bright eyes. For a moment, Anna braced herself. Had Ellen received a telegram regarding Lawrence? But for some reason this felt like good news. "What is going on?" Anna asked eagerly.

"You're not going to believe this." Clara waved what looked like an official letter in the air.

"Please, sit down and tell me." Anna waved to the chair opposite her cluttered desk, waiting.

Clara flopped down and, without removing her gloves, began to read what sounded like a very official letter, stating that AJ had died a hero's death and that he would be honored posthumously with a very impressive award. "The Medal of Honor," Clara said with moist eyes. "Can you believe it?"

"The Medal of Honor is the military's most prestigious award," Anna told her. "Only the President of the United States can award that."

"Yes, and it was signed by the president himself. And there's another letter too. Written by General Abernathy. Randall said that's AJ's commanding officer. I let Randall read the letter because I was so flabbergasted, I couldn't even think straight. Can you believe it arrived special delivery from the White House? Just this morning. It's incredible—they're giving such an honor to my boy."

"I think it's wonderful, Clara. I'd like to write an article for the front page about this. Would you allow us to print the actual letter with it?"

"Yes, of course."

Anna made a note to remind Frank to save space in Saturday's paper. "And it's just in time for AJ's funeral service too."

"Yes, that's what Randall and I were just talking about. I asked him to read both the letters for me at the service."

"Do the letters say why AJ is to receive this award?"

"Yes, the details are in the general's letter. I must admit I didn't understand it all at first, but Randall helped me. I'll try to translate the story to you." She picked up the letter. "General Abernathy heard the testimony of AJ's fellow soldiers. Apparently their foxhole was on the front line and they were surrounded by the enemy and undergoing heavy fire. But they were nearly out of ammunition, and it seemed the units to the rear of them had retreated. It was so dire, the soldiers felt certain none would survive. AJ, who the men said was the best shot, loaded his rifle and took all the ammunition they had left just as it was getting dark. He jumped out of their foxhole and advanced to the next one. He exposed himself to enemy fire but he just kept going, all the while shooting at the Huns. He got close enough to drive them back a ways and then he managed to hold them off for several hours. Long enough for his men to retreat to safety. Even though he killed a good number of the enemy . . . well, it was too much. One against so many. AJ couldn't survive." Clara paused to wipe her tears with a handkerchief.

"Oh, Clara, I always knew that boy had a hero inside of him." Anna was crying too. "I'm so proud of him."

Clara blew her nose. "Well, I always knew he had a devil-may-care attitude and loved taking risks. And, of course, he grew up hunting with his dad. But I never dreamed he'd do something like this."

"You should be very, very proud of your boy. No, not *boy*. AJ was a man."

"Yes. And I am proud."

"Sunset Cove will be very proud of him too, Clara. We will make certain of it."

And they did make certain of it. Not only did the *Sunset Times* run a full front page about AJ's military service and the Medal of Honor, it seemed the entire town turned out for AJ's funeral service shortly after the new year began. The packed church had standing room only for late-comers. Reverend Williamson welcomed everyone, opening the service with Clara's favorite hymn, "It Is Well with My Soul." He continued with a brief message, finally declaring: "Greater love hath no soldier than this, that he lay down his life for his country. That's what AJ Krauss did. He laid down his life." Next he introduced the US senator who had traveled to Sunset Cove from the state's capital for the service.

The senator explained he was there on behalf of President Woodrow Wilson. "Unfortunately, the duties of the presidential office during war-time prohibited him from coming, but he does send his best regards and regrets." Now the good senator described, in more detail, the soldiers' eye-witness accounts of AJ's heroic actions in battle. Finally, he explained the significance of the Medal of Honor and presented it, along with a US flag, to Clara.

After the senator sat down, Randall stood to give AJ's eulogy. As Clara's good friend and the attorney who helped AJ out of his legal troubles, Randall was able to give an accurate and touching account of AJ's short life. He concluded by saying that with Clara's permission, he wanted to read the last letter that AJ ever wrote.

"As you can imagine, AJ wasn't much of a letter writer. In fact, he wasn't much of an academic scholar. And he didn't mind who knew it." Randall smiled as he unfolded the letter. "Clara only got four letters from her son while he served in the US Army. But this letter is significant for several reasons. Written and mailed only five days before AJ lost his life, it has almost a prophetic quality to it. I was greatly touched by it." And now he read.

Dear Mom,

I know I'm not a good letter writer, but thanks much for writing to me anyway. I like hearing the latest news about town and people, and I can't wait to meet my little nephew. Give him a kiss from Uncle AJ.

The reason I wanted to write you tonight is to say some pretty important stuff. First off, I'm just so rip-snorting glad to be a soldier in the US Army. I guess I dragged my heels at first, only cuz I didn't know how great it'd be. The fellas in my unit are the Best. I don't wanna sound mushy, but I love every single one of em. From Big John clear down to Stinky and Peewee. I know those names won't mean a doggone thing to you, Mom, but they're like brothers to me. I'm so proud to fight alongside em. And I'd be proud to die for any single one of em. Especially the guys with wives and kids back home. Pray we all make it out of here okay.

Anyway, I want to tell you that if for some reason I don't make it home—now don't you start bawling about this, Mom, cuz it's just a fact of war—some soldiers die. Probably not me though. Like Sergeant Flannigan says I'm one tough cookie. And that's the doggone truth! But if something happens to me, I need you to know that I really do believe in Jesus Christ now. You always used to beg me to say this before, but it never felt real to me. Now it does! They say there's no atheists in foxholes, and I guess that's the truth all right.

So you need to know if I don't make it home to Sunset Cove, I'm sure-fired certain I'll make it home to Heaven. It's important to me that you and Ellen and even my little nephew know that. If you have any doubts, you can read First Thessalonians 4:13-18. Preacher Stan (that's his nickname) read those scriptures to us—after two soldier brothers got killed last week.

Anyhow, I know I messed up at home and I've already told you I'm sorry about that. I've also told God that I'm sorry— about lots of other things too. But I know I'm forgiven. It feels awful good to be forgiven.

I still hope I can make up for some of my mess ups at home by being a good soldier over here. So that's all I want to say for tonight, Mom. Oh, yeah, and I love you. I love Ellen and her baby too. And I love my other friends back in Sunset Cove. Keep praying for us.

Your Son Always, Love,
Albert John Krauss

As Anna blotted tears with her handkerchief, she could hear others sniffling and even some sobs. Just a year ago, no one would've shed a tear for AJ Krauss—and today she felt fairly sure there wasn't a dry eye in the whole church. Randall cleared his throat and set the letter aside. "I'd like to read the scripture that AJ mentioned in his letter to his mother."

Some of the words seemed to slip right past Anna, but this much she knew: AJ was secure with God now. She reached over to grasp Ellen's hand, giving it a gentle squeeze. How touching that AJ wanted to be certain his mother understood. For their final hymn, they sang "Amazing Grace," and then Reverend Williamson led them in a prayer for the servicemen still fighting the Great War over there, specifically listing the names of the young men from Sunset Cove . . . including Captain Daniel Hollister and Sergeant Jim Stafford. Anna hoped and prayed their prayers were being heeded.

CHAPTER 10

Katy had always loved Christmastime—the fun of decorations and preparations, finding the perfect gifts for loved ones, baking fancy treats. . . . But this year, Christmas felt relatively bleak. Besides the sad news about AJ, there was the aggravation of rationing. Due to the war, sugar and flour and wool and a lot of other things were scarce. And if the men overseas had to live without comforts, it seemed only fair those on the home front should sacrifice too. Katy had been more than willing. A big fancy Christmas would've only made everyone feel worse.

But now it was New Year's Eve, and it still seemed that no one felt much like celebrating. To remedy this, Lucille had planned a small dinner party.

"I don't want to go," Mac complained as they were putting on their coats.

"Oh, Grandpa." Katy helped him with his woolen scarf. "You do too."

"No, I don't," he said stubbornly.

"Come on, Mac," Anna urged. "If you're not there, everyone will wonder why."

"Tell them I'm sick," he growled.

Katy huffed. "But that's a lie."

"I'm sick of JD Hollister."

"Oh, Grandfather," Katy scolded. "What an unkind thing to say."

"It's the truth."

"Look, Mac, if it makes you feel any better, I will do everything I can to distract JD from monopolizing all of Lucille's attentions." Anna stuck his hat on his head.

"How do you plan to do that?" He looked doubtful as Katy helped to button his coat.

"Well, I got a letter from Daniel two days ago. I'll tell him all about that."

Mac brightened slightly.

"And I'll ask him about the new doctor at the hospital," Katy offered. "You know how he can go on and on about that."

"Yes," Anna agreed. "Sarah Rose told me that Dr. Myers isn't measuring up to JD's high expectations."

"Of course he's not. No one is as good a physician as himself," Mac said with sarcasm. "We've all heard him bluster about that. You'd think the man invented medicine."

Katy looped her arm into Mac's as he reached for his cane. "And you shouldn't complain so much, Grandfather. After all, you've only yourself to blame if JD's attentions toward Grandmother aggravate you."

"I'm to blame?" His furry brows arched.

"Yes, like I've told you more than once, you should make your intentions toward Grandmother clear and plain."

Anna nudged him with her elbow. "Katy is right, Mac. If you really want to secure your position with Lucille, you should speak up. For once and for all, you should state your position. That would put an end to this silly rivalry between you and JD."

Mac made a harrumphing sound. "When I need advice on such matters, I will let you two know. And as far as this evening goes, do not expect me to stay there until midnight to see in the New Year."

"That is, unless Doc Hollister lingers," Katy teased. "He might want to sing 'Auld Lang Syne.' "

"I'll remind him that old folks need earlier bedtimes," Mac grumbled. "The old goat's told *me* that more than once."

Katy and Anna laughed as they went outside. But as they walked to Lucille's house, Katy wished that her grandfather would take their advice. It would be so wonderful to see her grandparents reunited. It seemed obvious that they still loved each other. And for them to be able to grow older together . . . well, it just made sense. But for some reason, Grandfather continually dragged his heels when it came to talk of marriage.

And even though Lucille claimed she enjoyed her independence, Katy suspected her grandmother was lonely, that she longed for something more. Sometimes she could almost see it in her eyes. But Grandfather could be so stubborn. And even more so when JD was around.

They were barely in the house and removing their wraps when the sound of JD's voice came wafting toward them. He was telling Lucille about the time he saved the life of a young woman who'd been in a motorcar accident. "I performed the first successful blood transfusion at our hospital, and it's been recorded in the medical—"

"Oh, there you are," Lucille called out, hurrying over to greet them. "I'm so glad to see you all. Happy New Year!" As they hugged, Lucille whispered in Katy's ear. "Just in time. JD's gory hospital stories have nearly destroyed my appetite."

Katy laughed. "Reinforcements have arrived," she whispered back. Then she turned to her grandfather. "Why don't you show Grandmother what I gave you for Christmas?"

As Mac showed the tie that Lucille had helped Katy pick out, Katy went over and sat next to Doc Hollister on the couch. "Happy New Year," she told him. "1918—doesn't that have a nice ring to it?"

He shrugged. "I don't see why it sounds any different than 1917."

Katy turned to where Sarah Rose was sitting quietly in a chair by the window, perusing one of Lucille's magazines. "Happy New Year to you too, Sarah Rose."

Sarah Rose thanked her. "And I must agree with you, Katy, I like the sound of 1918. Maybe this is the year the war will end."

"I don't think so," JD said grimly. "According to what I've been reading, this war could drag on for at least two more years."

"Oh, goodness, I hope not." Katy forced a smile for the old doctor. "So, tell me, how are you doing? How's your health these days?"

"As well as possible . . . all things considered." He glanced over to where Mac and Lucille were pleasantly visiting on the far side of the room.

"Is it your heart?" Katy asked, knowing full well this would invite a long medical explanation about angina. But then she changed topics to ask about the hospital, and he told her about the new doctor who wasn't pulling his weight.

"He called me to assist him in an appendectomy operation last week, but I quickly discovered that he is not an experienced surgeon." As he continued to go into gruesome detail about the surgery, Katy glanced helplessly at her mother.

"JD," Anna said suddenly. "I don't think I told

you about the last letter I got from Daniel just two days ago."

JD brightened. "You heard from Daniel?"

"Yes." Anna sat on the other side of JD. "Yes, it was very interesting." As Anna began sharing the latest on his son, Katy jumped at the sound of the doorbell.

"I'll get that," she called out to her grandmother. Not surprisingly, it was Clara, Ellen, and the baby. And Randall and his mother Marjorie right behind them. Katy greeted everyone and, holding Baby Larry, waited for them to remove their coats. "Here's my favorite young man," she cooed to the baby. "Want me to help you off with your bunny suit?" She carried the baby to Lucille's spare bedroom, unbuttoning the warm knit suit. "Look at you," she said. "Growing up so nicely."

Ellen sat by her on the bed, adjusting the baby's little booties. "He seems to get bigger every day."

"I bet he'll be walking soon." Katy held him on her lap, peering straight at his chubby face and sparkling blue eyes.

"Oh, no, he won't be walking for ages, Katy. Babies don't usually walk before their first birthday. I've been reading up on it. Randall's mother gave me a book about it for Christmas, and I'm becoming quite the expert. I know when babies start to roll over and crawl and get teeth and all sorts of things."

"Good for you, Ellen. Maybe I should borrow your book when you're done." She put her face close to Larry's. "Your daddy will be so proud of you."

"I sent Lawrence a photograph with the baby and me. Mother paid to have it taken . . . after we heard about AJ. I wish I'd done it sooner, so he could've had it by Christmas. I just wasn't thinking right."

"Well, at least he'll have it soon. And I'm sure he will treasure it."

"I sent a picture to Lawrence's family in San Francisco too," Ellen said. "Along with a letter. Lucille encouraged me to reach out to them."

"That's wonderful. I'm sure they will be glad to hear from you."

Ellen frowned. "I'm not so sure. They didn't know that Lawrence enlisted. His mother had insisted that he would be exempt because of his feet. I hope they're not upset that he went in anyway. And, after all, his feet were just fine."

"Hopefully, they'll be proud to discover they have a son serving over there. And a beautiful grandson right here." Katy handed the baby back to Ellen. "Not to mention a daughter-in-law who is doing a great job being a mommy."

"Thanks." Ellen looked sad. "But I don't really deserve that. I wasn't doing such a good job . . . not until we lost AJ."

"Well, I think AJ would be proud of you now,

Ellen. And of his nephew. And maybe he's sort of like a godfather to Larry now. You know, up there in heaven looking down on him, watching over."

Ellen brightened. "I never thought of it like that. But I like it."

Katy stood. "I should probably go back out there. I promised Mac to keep JD occupied."

"Is Mac feeling jealous again?" Ellen chuckled.

Katy nodded. "Mother and I will be taking turns with him."

"I can help too. I'll ask him some baby questions. He loves to tell me that everything I'm doing is wrong."

Katy laughed. She'd experienced the same thing with pregnancy advice. Doc Hollister seemed to get pleasure with finding fault with anyone about anything when it came to the topic of medicine.

After a couple of hours of distracting JD for Mac's sake, Anna was weary. And although it wasn't yet midnight, she wanted to go home and write a letter to Daniel. She remembered Mac's insistence that he wouldn't remain to see the New Year in, but right now, he was sitting down to a game of cards with Lucille and JD and Marjorie. The four of them were quite boisterous too, acting as if they were the young ones tonight. Meanwhile, Ellen and Katy both looked sleepy,

125

and Randall and Clara were having a quiet, intimate conversation over by the window.

Anna went to the kitchen to find Sarah Rose at the sink. "Can I be of any help?" Anna offered.

"I'm almost done washing up," Sarah Rose told her.

"And I've got the dessert tray almost ready," Sally said.

Just the same, Anna picked up a tea towel and began to dry the crystal goblets lined up on the counter. "I think perhaps I'll call it a night before midnight," she quietly told Sarah Rose. "I can't keep up with those old people."

Sarah Rose chuckled. "You and me both. How about if we make our excuses and go home together?"

"Perfect." Anna smiled. "I'm so glad you decided to move back into Mac's house. Although I'm sorry it's a longer walk to the hospital for you."

"I don't mind the walk at all. Gives me a chance to clear my head—both coming and going. And the view of the ocean along the way is well worth it." She handed Anna a goblet. "Although Doc Hollister is not so glad. He keeps suggesting his house is closer."

"That's because he wants you to keep house for him," Anna reminded her.

"Believe me, I know." Sarah Rose shook her head.

"You couldn't pay me enough money to keep house for that old blowhard," Sally said as she moved the hot teakettle to the back of the stove.

Anna and Sarah Rose both giggled.

"And if he asks Miss Lucille to marry him and gets a notion to move in here, I will be packing my bags—just as fast as you can say Jack Robinson."

"Oh, I don't think you need to worry about that," Anna reassured her.

Sally's eyes grew wide. "You don't know the half of it."

"What do you mean?"

"I mean I heard them earlier. If that old doctor wasn't hinting at matrimony, my name's not Sally Pruitt."

"Are you sure?" Anna felt worried now.

"And, if I'm not mistaken, that bulge in the chest pocket of his vest is about the size of a small jewelry box. Probably with a fancy ring inside."

Anna exchanged worried glances with Sarah Rose.

"So if Miss Lucille should say yes, I'll say no thank you very much—and *goodbye*." She set the silver teapot on the tray with a loud clang.

"Well, that's very, uh, interesting." Anna glanced toward the door. "I think I'll go take a peek to see how things are developing out there."

"You can tell them tea and dessert is about

ready to be served in the dining room," Sally said.

As Anna returned to the living room, she tried to concoct a way to call Mac aside—to give him a warning about Sally's suspicions. But the foursome seemed to be genuinely enjoying themselves at the card table, and she hated to interrupt. So she decided to simply let fate take its course.

"How's the game going?" She lingered by the card table long enough to see there was a slight bulge in JD's vest pocket. Perhaps Sally was right.

"JD and I are winning," Lucille told Anna.

"Good." Anna winked at Mac. "It's nice to know my parents are so talented."

"You know what they say," Marjorie quipped. "Lucky in cards . . ."

They all laughed.

"Well, Sally said to tell you that tea and dessert is about to be served in the dining room."

"Wonderful." Lucille smiled. "We'll take a short break after this hand, then come back to finish the game."

"And Sarah Rose and I would like to say goodnight," Anna told her. "We're both too tired to see in the New Year. But we thank you for a lovely evening."

"Are you going home now?" Katy asked with a disappointed expression.

"Yes. Do you want to come with us?" Anna quietly asked her.

Katy looked slightly torn. "No, no, that's all right. I think I'll stick around for tea and dessert. Apple cobbler and whipped cream sounds pretty tempting." She patted her round midsection. "And it's not as if I'm watching my figure these days."

Anna smiled. "You and Mac can walk home together."

"And I'll have her here to keep me company," Ellen told Anna.

Feeling that there was little—if nothing—Anna could do to change the course of this evening, she told everyone goodbye, and she and Sarah Rose walked home.

"Do you really think Miss Lucille would consent to marry Dr. Hollister?" Sarah Rose asked as they went into Mac's house.

"I don't think she loves him." Anna removed her coat.

"You're probably right. But I do recall how proud she was when she heard you were marrying Dr. Daniel. I remember her saying how impressive it was for you to become a doctor's wife."

"She said that?"

"I heard her say that to your father. Not long after you got engaged."

Anna just shook her head. "Well, I'm sure it

won't be long until we hear about it. I mean, if JD really does propose to Lucille. And I suppose it might seem a romantic gesture to do so on New Year's Eve."

"Oh, my." Sarah Rose pursed her lips. "Do you think we'll hear your father yelling from clear over there tonight? Right around midnight?"

Anna giggled then grew sober. "Goodness, I hope not." But as she went to her room, she wondered. What sort of fit would Mac throw if JD really did propose—and if Lucille actually accepted? This was just the sort of thing to make the society column news in the paper next week. And if Reginald got wind of it, he would probably have a real heyday with the story.

CHAPTER 11

"A m I the only one having breakfast today?" Anna asked Bernice as she filled her coffee cup. "I'm not surprised Katy wanted to sleep in after her late night, but where's Mac? He's always an early riser."

"He had Mickey bring his breakfast on a tray to his sitting room." Bernice set a basket of muffins on the table with a troubled frown. "Do you suppose he's not feeling well?"

"I don't know." Anna reached for the jam.

"Seems odd to me. But Mickey's not talking." Bernice studied Anna. "Did you have a falling out with your father?"

"No." Anna sighed to recall Sarah Rose's suspicions about JD and Lucille. "But I have a feeling I know what's up." She picked up her plate and coffee. "I think I'll go join him."

"Well, don't keep me in the dark," Bernice declared. "I've been working for that man for longer than you've been alive, Anna, and I have every right to know what's going on."

"Yes, I'll definitely let you know." Anna forced a

smile as she left. Hopefully, she was wrong about this. Mac was probably just tired from staying up so late. Seeing the door cracked slightly open, Anna let herself in, quietly greeting her father.

"Harrumph." He glowered at her. "I told Mickey I was eating alone."

"Well, I was eating alone too." She sat across from him, setting her breakfast on the end table. "And I preferred to eat with company."

"I'm not good company, Anna." He frowned down at his barely touched breakfast. "Not in the least."

"That's all right." She picked up her coffee and casually sipped. "I have a feeling I know why too."

His brow creased. "Humph. Am I the only one who got the rug ripped out from under him last night? Did everyone else know about this—this idiotic debacle old Doc Blowhard has brought upon us?"

Anna was disappointed but not surprised. "Katy tried to warn you, Mac. She suspected that JD had intentions for Lucille."

His response was a low growl.

"But I find it hard to believe that Lucille accepted his proposal." She set her cup down. "Are you saying she did?"

"Not exactly." His pale blue eyes looked seriously troubled. "But she didn't turn him down either."

"Oh?"

"Confound it. She told him she would think about it. *Think about it!*"

Anna couldn't help but chuckle. "So how did the old doctor take that?"

"He was none too pleased, but he said he'd wait for her answer."

"And what do you think her answer will be?"

"Durned if I know." He hit the table with his good fist. "But I knew from the get-go that old usurper would be trouble."

"Then you should've beaten him to the punch, Grandfather." Katy stepped into the sitting room. "I told you so more than once."

"Good morning," Anna said brightly to her. "How are you feeling after your late night?"

"Tired." Katy sat down. "Bernice said she'd bring my breakfast in here." She grinned. "I guess we're having a little breakfast party."

"Party?" Mac growled. "More like a funeral."

"Oh, Grandfather, don't be so dramatic," Katy said lightly. "This is all your own making."

"My own making?"

"Grandmother has sent you signs . . . signs that you continually ignore."

"What sort of signs?" he demanded.

"You've heard her say how she gets lonely rattling around in her big old house by herself. Just her and Sally most of the time. And Sally doesn't offer much companionship. The only

133

reason Grandmother keeps coming to work in the dress shop is to have us girls to chat with— because there's just not that much work to do there right now. She's just lonely."

"I did hear her asking you to move in with her before Christmas," Mac pointed out to Katy. "I suppose that was because she was lonely."

"But she knew I wanted to stay here," Katy told him. "I think she said it for your benefit. But you're not very good at taking a hint."

"Well, I also remember her saying she was an independent woman," he defended himself. "Lucille made it clear from the start that she had her own means to live, and she bought that house, and the only signals I got from her were to keep my distance."

"That was at first," Anna told him. "She wanted time to herself, to figure things out. She wasn't even sure that she would remain in Sunset Cove."

"But then she realized how much she loves her family," Katy told him.

"Meaning you and your mother." His frown lines deepened.

"Well, I noticed something interesting last night." Katy's eyes twinkled.

"What's that?" He studied her.

"I never heard old Doc Hollister mention the word love."

Mac rubbed his chin. "Yes, I think you're right about that."

"And I know that love is important to Grandmother."

"I'll bet the only person that old codger doctor loves is himself," Mac said curtly.

"And I've never heard Lucille use the word *love* when referring to JD," Anna said quietly. "To be honest, I can't even imagine it." She felt guilty for saying this—after all, JD was Daniel's father. But as hard as she tried, Anna had difficulty feeling the slightest bit of affection for the man who would one day be her father-in-law.

"So what are you two saying?" Mac demanded.

"I'm saying that I believe Grandmother is the type of woman who wants a man to declare his undying love for her." Katy sighed. "She is a romantic."

"I must agree with Katy." Anna nodded.

"Then why did she tell JD she would *think* about it?"

"Because she was uncomfortable," Katy explained. "The way JD proposed was so awkward, Grandfather. In front of all of us like that? What on earth was she supposed to say?"

"No!" Mac shouted. "She was supposed to say no."

"Maybe she will do that today," Anna suggested.

"Or maybe she'll be feeling lonely this morning," Katy taunted. "Maybe she'll decide that even old Doc Hollister is better than being

135

alone. At least he knows how to carry on a conversation—"

"With himself!" Mac reached for his cane. "Katy, dear, will you go tell Mickey I need him to help me dress?"

"No need for that," Bernice said from the doorway where she'd just appeared with a breakfast tray. "I'll go get him."

"And I'll take my breakfast in the dining room," Katy told her.

As Anna and Katy made their exit, they both had trouble containing their giggles. "Mac is going on the warpath," Anna whispered to her daughter. "Unless I'm wrong, I think he plans to give JD some serious competition."

"It's about time."

"Hopefully, it's not too late."

Within a few days, the big news was circulating town. And by Saturday Reginald had the story ready for the society column. Lucille and Mac were officially engaged. They planned to repeat their wedding vows in February. Everyone in town seemed happy for them. Everyone except JD Hollister. According to Sarah Rose, who frequently checked in on the old man, JD had remained holed up in his house for more than a week now.

"He sleeps in all morning," she confided to Anna. "And when he does get up, he sits around in his dressing gown. And he won't eat much of anything. And he hasn't been to the hospital. Not once since he got the bad news on New Year's Day." Sarah Rose frowned. "Even when I told him that Dr. Myers made a mistake in the surgery the other day, he didn't seem to care. I'm feeling very worried for him."

"I'll check on him during my lunch hour tomorrow," Anna had promised yesterday. But now it was tomorrow, and Anna had no idea what she would say or do to make this situation better. But for Daniel's sake—and because of her promise to look after his father—she knew she had to do this. But when she discovered the old doctor slumped on the living room couch in a worn dressing gown, she knew that Sarah Rose was right to be concerned.

She cheerfully greeted him and, acting as if nothing whatsoever was wrong, sat down and began to chatter at him about the latest news. "I suppose you've heard about President Wilson's Fourteen Points by now," she said.

"What? Points?" He peered at her as if he'd just realized she was there.

"Fourteen principles for peace," she explained. "That's what they're calling it—Fourteen Points. We printed it in the newspaper yesterday. Maybe you didn't see it."

"No . . . I didn't." He rubbed his gristly gray whiskers. It looked as if he hadn't shaved in days.

And Anna suddenly felt a pang of compassion for the old man. Still, what was she to do? And so she continued to ramble, explaining how Wilson outlined fourteen steps he felt were necessary to obtain world peace. "Of course, it's a somewhat idealistic plan, but if it were possible, if all parties could agree . . . well, it's possible that the war could end and the world could return to living in peace."

"Peace?" He scowled. "When has the world ever had real and lasting peace?"

"Well, I suppose there has always been some sort of war going on somewhere," she conceded. "But not like it is now. I don't think the world has ever seen anything like the Great War."

"That's only because of mobility," he declared. "Modernizations of travel. Ships and trains and planes. That and the development of improved and superior armaments designed to easily kill the enemy. Making it possible for all nations to take up arms and fight. You add those things to greedy leaders puffed up with national pride— and what do you get?"

"The Great War." She nodded. "I never looked at it quite like that, Dr. Hollister. Modernizations *have* made it easier for countries to go to war. I think you are absolutely right. In fact, if you don't mind, I'd like to write an editorial piece on this very thing."

He looked slightly surprised. "You would?"

"Yes, I would. It sounds as if you've given this subject quite a bit of thought."

He slowly nodded. "I suppose I have."

"Perhaps I can make some notes of your thoughts." She reached for her ever-handy note-book. "If you don't mind."

"I, uh, I suppose I don't mind."

"But I'm hungry," she told him. "It's my lunch hour. Do you mind if I go find something in the kitchen?" She stood. "Perhaps you'd like something too?"

"No, thank you. But Sarah Rose has left food in the ice chest. Help yourself."

"I'll be right back." As Anna went to the kitchen, she concocted a plan. She would fix them both a plate of food and then, besides coaxing him to eat, she would attempt to feed his wounded ego by engaging him in more discussion of Wilson's Fourteen Points.

"Here you go." She handed him a plate and sat down. "I don't like to eat alone." And now she began to explain Wilson's first point. "He's trying to encourage open conversations between countries," she explained while he nibbled on his lunch. "No more private agreements or secret disclosures between countries. All should be frankly and openly discussed in full public view. What do you think of that?"

He shrugged. "I suppose if you can get countries to agree, it makes sense."

She went on to explain Wilson's points about equality in trade and freedom of maritime navigation and reduction of armaments . . . and the many other things pertaining to the actual countries involved in the war. And all the while, JD would nod and comment . . . and eat.

"Sounds like our president has some good sense," he finally said, setting his empty plate aside. "I hope the other countries will listen."

"I do too. I would be so happy to see this war ended and our men coming home." She sighed. "I miss Daniel."

He nodded. "I do too."

"But I know how much he's needed over there. And I can tell by his letters that he is learning so much about medicine."

"Yes." JD brightened a bit. "In his last letter, Daniel wrote how privileged he'd been to work under some very renowned and internationally respected physicians—names we've only read about in the journals. He's learning the sort of medicine he could never experience in this country." He almost smiled. "I suppose I envy him."

"But I'm sure whatever he learns over there, he will gladly share with you."

"Yes . . . I look forward to that."

"Dr. Hollister," she began carefully, "I know you feel badly about how, you know, how everything went with my mother . . . and my father."

He cleared his throat, looking down as he adjusted the crooked lapels of his dressing gown. "Well, it was rather unexpected . . . a disappointment, I suppose."

"And I suspect it was a blow to your pride."

He looked up with steely eyes but said nothing.

"I just want to assure you that no one in this town dwells on such things for long. And I suspect that no one outside of our small circle even heard about New Year's Eve. And I expect that's pretty much forgotten by now. So I really wouldn't let it trouble you."

He cleared his throat again. "Yes . . . you could be right."

"And perhaps it's none of my business, but as much as you favored Lucille, I was never under the impression you were in love with her. But I could be wrong."

"In love?" His frown looked confused. "I am a man of science. Not of the sentimental type."

"Yes. But my mother is sentimental. Perhaps you didn't realize it before. It seems that she still loves my father and, as it turns out, he still loves her. So you probably can see that it's for the best."

He nodded. "I suppose you're right. I had never really thought about love."

"I wondered about that."

"What about you and Daniel? Do you love each other like that? After all, Daniel is a man of science too."

"That's true. But it seems you have raised a good man with a warm heart. He does love me as much as I love him."

Dr. Hollister nodded. "That's good to know. And to be completely honest, I suppose I was simply looking for a companion. Someone to grow old with me. Lucille seemed as good a choice as any."

"Then be encouraged. There are numerous older women in this town who would welcome your intelligent conversation and companionship." She even began to list a few names. "Perhaps they're not as colorful as Lucille, but good women all the same."

"I hope you're right. I've been told that I can be rather off-putting."

Anna smiled. "You might have more luck if you practiced a bit of reserve."

"So I've been told." He sighed.

"I must admit that I'm usually intimidated by you," she confessed. "But not today. I've enjoyed our conversation."

He blinked. "You have?"

"Yes. And I look forward to more like this. I'd like to hear more of your thoughts on world events and medicine and whatnot. But not in the form of a lecture."

"I suppose I do that . . . sometimes."

"It's so much nicer to share a two-way conversation."

"I'll try to remember that." His pale lips curled up ever so slightly. "I think your mother tried to tell me the very same thing . . . more than once."

Anna checked her watch. "Well, thank you for the lunch and conversation." She stood, picking up their plates. "And if you don't mind, I'd like to make this a regular thing. Perhaps we can schedule lunches like this, once or twice a week."

"I'd like that." He actually smiled.

"So would I." As she took the dishes to the kitchen, she realized that she sincerely did want to spend some more time with JD. And not just for Daniel's sake either. She could see that JD was simply a lonely old man . . . probably in need of some gentle feminine training and persuasion. Perhaps some old dogs could learn new tricks.

CHAPTER 12

During the next few weeks, Anna went out of her way to spend time with JD. At first it was for lunch . . . and then as the old doctor got back to his old routines and running the hospital, it changed into morning coffee or afternoon tea. At first, Anna felt they were making real progress in their friendship—but more recently it felt like a lost cause. The more JD returned to his old self, the more he returned to complaining. Mostly about their backward small town and the incompetence of his entire staff. It seemed no one measured up to JD's high expectations.

"I suspect God himself would be a disappointment to JD," Anna told Sarah Rose as they walked home together after Anna had met JD for tea at the hospital.

"I'm afraid you're right about that." Sarah glumly shook her head. "I know Dr. Hollister is never pleased with anything I do."

"That shouldn't surprise you."

"Yes, but I've been thinking it might be time for me to move on."

"Move on?" Anna turned to Sarah. "From Sunset Cove?"

"I don't know." Sarah frowned. "To be honest, I'm not eager to return to Portland. There's not much for me there."

"If you like living here, you should stay. And if you aren't comfortable at the hospital, there's always the dress shop."

"And, as Dr. Hollister likes to remind me, I could be a fulltime housekeeper for him."

"Would you really want to do that?"

Sarah's brow creased. "As odd as it must sound, I do care about that cantankerous old man."

Anna laughed. "Yes, that does sound odd."

"I'm sure it's partly due to the respect I have for his son."

"Yes . . . and Daniel had respect for you too, Sarah."

"And I'm so proud of the way young Dr. Hollister is serving overseas. I want to do what I can to help his father while he's gone."

"I know exactly what you mean." Anna sighed. "That's why I've gone out of my way to reach out to JD. But today, when the old curmudgeon started to snipe at my newspaper—well, I had difficulty biting my tongue."

"That's understandable."

"So you wouldn't mind keeping house fulltime for JD? Would you be a live-in?"

"It would probably be easier that way." Sarah

shook her head. "But I'd miss the view from my room at your father's house. Still, I'd have the whole second floor to myself there. Dr. Hollister never goes upstairs."

"I can see how that might be nice for you. If you can put up with JD's disgruntled opinions over everything."

"Like I said, I'm used to it. And it's not only him that's making me uncomfortable at the hospital . . . there are other factors too."

Anna wasn't surprised. "I wondered about that."

"It wouldn't be too bad if I had Dr. Hollister's support."

"He's not like Daniel."

"No, not at all. So, tell me the truth, Miss Anna. What do you think? Should I quit the hospital and keep house for the old curmudgeon, as you call him?"

Anna chuckled. "If that's what you want. And perhaps it will be only temporary. Maybe when Daniel comes home and takes charge of the hospital again . . . maybe you'd want to return to work there."

"Maybe. In the meantime, I think Dr. Hollister needs me."

Anna patted Sarah's back. "You're a good woman, Sarah Rose. I'm ashamed to admit that you're far more gracious to JD than I am. And someday that old curmudgeon will be my father-in-law."

"Yes. That's part of the reason I want to help him, Miss Anna. You and Miss Katy have been so good to me. I feel I owe it to you."

Anna looked into Sarah's dark eyes. "You do not owe me a thing, Sarah Rose. When I think of how much you helped me with Katy when she was little—whatever would I have done without you?" She grabbed her hand, squeezing it. "You are like family to me. You owe me nothing."

"Thank you. But I still want to help Dr. Hollister. I've prayed about it for the past several weeks, and I feel that's what God wants me to do, and I believe God will give me the strength and grace to do it."

"Well, to put up with that man day in and day out, I'm sure you'll achieve sainthood and have even more jewels in your heavenly crown for your kind generosity."

Sarah Rose threw back her head and laughed. "And if that's so, I will simply cast that crown down at the feet of my Savior."

Katy insisted on helping with Lucille and Mac's wedding. Partly as a way to thank her grandmother for the way she'd helped with Katy's wedding, and partly because Katy just enjoyed the whole process so much. Plus it provided a good distraction from her own "delicate" condition and rapidly expanding waistline—and her growing concerns for her husband's welfare. It had gotten so that she didn't even want to read the newspapers anymore.

"I don't know why you're going to so much trouble," Mac told her as she supervised the fitting of his new pinstriped suit.

"How many grandchildren get to help their grandparents get married?" she teased.

"You have a point there." Mac held out his good arm as Clara adjusted the cuff of his sleeve. "But I would've been happy to marry your grandmother in the courthouse."

"Lucille wanted a big wedding," Clara mumbled with pins between her lips.

"That's right," Katy agreed. "Grandmother never got to have one before. And I think she deserves it."

"Yes. The bride should have her big day." Clara stood up to examine the waistcoat.

"What about you?" Mac said. "When is Randall going to step up and make you his bride?"

Clara blushed then busied herself with the fitting.

"Oh, Grandfather," Katy scolded. "You know that's none of your business."

"Someone needs to light a fire under that man," Mac continued. "Does he want to be a bachelor forever?"

"I'm sure Mr. Douglas knows what he's doing," Katy said primly. "Anyway, this is about *your* wedding day, Grandfather. And it's only a week away."

"That's another thing. Why does it have to be on Valentine's Day?" Mac frowned. "Seems a bit frivolous to me."

"Frivolous?" Katy adjusted his black satin tie. "I was the one who suggested it, and I happen to think it's very romantic. Mother and Grandmother agreed."

"As did I." Clara measured the other sleeve. "And Ellen too."

He chuckled. "You ladies far outnumber me. What chance do I have?"

"None." Katy grinned. "And now I need to get back to the dress shop to check on Grandmother's gown."

"Oh, wait until you see that," Clara told Mac. "It's gorgeous."

"Yes. It's very elegant." Katy pinned on her hat. "But I still have a lot of finish work to do yet. I expect it'll take several more days to get it all done."

"You're not overdoing it, are you?" He narrowed his eyes at Katy. "In my day, women in the family way didn't go running about as much as you do." He turned to Clara. "Don't you agree with me?"

"These younger women have their own ideas." Clara re-pinned the cuff on his bad arm.

"That's right." Katy smiled. "And besides, Dr.

Daniel assured me I could continue my normal activities for as long as I felt like it. And I feel like it."

"What does *old* Doc Hollister say about that?"

Katy laughed. "Really, Grandfather? Don't tell me you've begun to respect the 'old codger's' opinions?"

"Now that he's not interfering with my personal life anymore, I have no problems with the old doctor. After all, the best man won." He winked at Clara.

"So this was about competition?" Katy tugged on her gloves. "I'm sure my grandmother would not like the sound of that."

"No, no, of course not." He chuckled. "Your grandmother knows full and well that I love her. She never would've agreed to marriage if I hadn't said that."

"Just don't you forget it," Katy warned as she headed for the door. But as she left, she couldn't help but giggle. Her grandparents might be old in some ways, but they still acted like they were her age at times. And despite her grandfather's protests, she suspected he looked as eagerly forward to the wedding as she did. Anyway, she hoped so. She was going to a lot of trouble to make this day special. And, despite her less than lovely figure, she planned to enjoy it. She only wished that Jim could be there to enjoy it with her.

Anna was working on an editorial about President Wilson's most recent speech to congress. This time he'd spoke about "Four Principles," and in Anna's opinion, this speech was much more concise and understandable than the previous longwinded fourteen points. Most importantly, the first principle was solely dedicated to bringing "a peace that was permanent." Wouldn't that be something? Anna hoped and prayed that the rest of the world would agree. If such a devastating war resulted in world peace, it would almost be worth it. But, like JD was quick to point out, world peace was not likely. Still, it seemed a good goal. And she'd tried to put an optimistic tone into her editorial. Readers deserved something positive.

"Is your editorial ready for press yet?" Frank asked her.

"Yes." She rolled it out of the typewriter. "Just finished."

"Mac's big day is almost here." Frank took the piece, glancing over it.

"Yes. He's eager to get it behind him."

"Like most grooms." Frank chuckled. "Speaking of the soon to be newlyweds, where will they be living?"

"Mac insists on remaining in his house. And Lucille seems happy about it."

"Will she sell her house?"

"She hasn't mentioned anything. Why, are you interested?"

"Ginger is. She always complains that our boys are going to outgrow our little house. But I'm afraid Lucille's house would be too much of a stretch on the meager salary of a lowly newspaper editor." He grinned. "That is, unless there's a raise in my future."

"No one will be getting any raises until this war is over, Frank. You know that."

"Well, you can't blame a man for trying." He started to leave then stopped. "Hey, I almost forgot—did you hear about Eddie Barrows?"

"No. Hopefully he's not up to more mischief. I haven't seen him around town lately."

"That's because he headed east. But I heard through the grapevine that he's been arrested for draft evasion."

"So someone caught up with him." She shook her head. "Well, good. Maybe a little jail time will give him the opportunity to think."

"I'm guessing he'll get shipped off to boot camp. I hear they can make it pretty hard on ablebodied men who don't register with the Selective Service."

"Hopefully they'll knock some sense into him while they're at it." She covered her typewriter. "I think I'll call it a day if you've got everything under control here. I promised Katy I'd come home early to help with some of the wedding preparations. Although I tend to agree with Mac, a simpler service might've been nice. I'm pretty sure that when Daniel and I get married, we won't go to so much trouble."

"Speaking of Daniel, how's the good doctor doing these days? Any news?"

"He doesn't write as often as I do, but that's understandable. He puts in long, hard days with little time off for anything more than eating and sleeping. But he tries to keep his letters uplifting, and he's very appreciative of the great doctors he's serving under. But he does seem growingly concerned with the possibility of disease. He mentioned some new type of influenza that's been spreading through the troops. He and other prominent physicians are concerned it could become epidemic in time. Perhaps worldwide."

"How's that?"

"With so many people traveling abroad . . . displaced immigrants . . . servicemen coming and going. If they carry germs with them, it could spread uncontrollably. At least that's his theory. Hopefully he's wrong."

"Hopefully."

Anna smiled as she buttoned her winter coat. "Well, at least we can distract ourselves for a bit with wedding festivities this week. I assume you and Ginger will be attending. Katy said everyone at the paper was invited."

"Wouldn't miss it for the world. Sounds like most of the town will be there too."

"It'll give everyone a much-needed break from the focus on war. I know I'm looking forward to it."

As Anna walked over to the dress shop where she'd agreed to help with the wedding preparations, she thought about Daniel . . . and with each step, she prayed for his safety and welfare. Just a few days ago, she'd read a United Press news story about a French medical unit that had been accidentally obliterated by a careless German bomb. And she could be wrong, but Anna still wondered if it had truly been an accident. It was chilling to think that German troops would target field hospitals, but with all their other atrocities, anything seemed possible.

Thinking of Daniel made Anna wonder. . . . Would they ever really have a wedding? Even just a simple civil service with a couple of witnesses? Not because she didn't think he'd make it home safely—she refused to let her mind go there. But so many times she'd gotten her hopes up with Daniel . . . and one thing had led to another . . . and then she'd been disappointed. What if he changed his mind during their time apart? Perhaps the advances in modern medicine would become so important to him that, like his father, he'd decide that Sunset Cove was too remote for a doctor to learn and grow. Or what if some pretty Red Cross nurse stole his heart while saving a soldier's life? She could imagine that. Oh, she knew it was silly to fret over such things, but anything could happen.

But for now, she remained determined to stay focused on her parents' nuptials. She would celebrate their big day with enthusiasm. And despite having her beloved so far away, she would be happy for the sake of her family. And maybe someday her day would come too.

CHAPTER 13

Although the dress shop was closed for the day of the wedding, Katy had dropped by to pick up a few of the decorations they'd stored there. As she was loading them into the Runabout she heard someone calling her name—her married name.

"Mrs. James Stafford?"

She looked over her shoulder to see a uniformed delivery boy walking his bicycle down the sidewalk toward her. "Yes?" she answered with a trembling voice.

"Telegram for you," he said solemnly.

"Thank you." She dug out some change from her purse for a tip then waited as he wheeled his bike away, but her hands were shaking too hard to open the telegram. She could see it was from the Department of War. With wobbly knees, she went inside of the dress shop, closing and locking the door behind her. Once in the back room, she picked up a pair of dressmakers sheers and slit the envelope open.

Her heart was pounding so hard that she could

hear it in her ears, and her hands were shaking so badly that the typewritten words blurred before her. Sitting down, she took a deep breath and, bracing herself for the worse, slowly read.

MRS JAMES STAFFORD:
THE SECRETARY OF WAR SENDS
HIS REGRETS THAT YOUR
HUSBAND, LIEUTENANT JAMES
STAFFORD HAS BEEN INJURED IN
BATTLE ON NINE FEBRUARY IN
FRANCE. LETTER TO FOLLOW.
TC ATKINSON GENERAL

"He's not dead," she said aloud. "Not dead." Even so, the tears were trickling down her cheeks. "But he's hurt. Injured. How badly?" She stood up, pacing back and forth as she ran all the grim possibilities through her head. Was he severely injured? Were they life threatening wounds? Where was he being treated? And how could she possibly get any answers to these questions?

She sat back down and let the tears flow. "Oh, Jim, Jim," she sobbed. "Please, be okay." And then she bowed her head and prayed . . . and prayed. "Please, God, let him be okay. Bring him home to me . . . and to his baby." She touched her swollen middle, realizing that it might be only her and the baby, without Jim, forever. It could happen. Maybe it already had happened.

The ringing phone snapped her out of her grim thoughts and, trying to compose herself, she answered.

"Oh, good, you're still there," Clara said on the other end. "Lucille just called me to say she left her shoes at the shop. Remember she had them for trying on her gown the last time? Can you drop them by her house before you go to the church to decorate?"

"Yes," she said curtly. "I'm just on my way now." As she hung up the phone, she knew that she would have to keep her bad news to herself until the wedding festivities were completely over. She had no intentions of putting a serious damper on what was meant to be a very happy occasion. There would be time for that later.

As she drove over to her grandmother's, Katy practiced smiling. She rehearsed some light lines of conversation. Finally, she told herself that she would simply stay very busy throughout the day, or else remain in the background. Somehow she had to get through the next several hours.

She handed off the shoes to Clara, who was helping Lucille to get ready. "I'll see you at the church." Katy forced a shaky smile. "I've got a lot to do before three." Thankfully, Clara seemed oblivious to Katy's pain, giving her the confidence that perhaps she could pull this off. But as she gathered up the cherry blossoms that she'd arranged to have for the wedding, she realized her hands were still shaking. Telling herself to calm down, she loaded the bucket of blooms into the rumble seat and took another deep breath—once again praying that God would watch over Jim and bring him safely home.

At the church, she busied herself with the flower arrangements. Because it was only mid-February, the selection was limited. And because Grandmother loved pink roses, Katy had made some very realistic looking ones from crepe paper. She mixed these with the cherry blossoms and greenery and red satin hearts for Valentine's Day, and the final effect of these bouquets along the center aisle was surprisingly attractive. Hopefully her grandparents would like it too.

Katy had also gleaned a couple dozen pink and red tulips that she used for arrangements beside the altar. Mixing the tulips with more cherry blossoms and ivy made the bouquets appear more festive than they really were, but Katy was pleased.

She kept herself busy with preparations, taking time to make everything as perfect as possible until she could hear people arriving. She went to greet her grandmother and mother and Clara, and then excused herself to go home to change. "I think everything is in order here," she assured them, kissing her grandmother's soft powdery cheek. "I hope you like it."

"I love it," Lucille gushed. "It's far better than I

imagined. But then I should've known my artistic granddaughter would make it look grand. Thank you, darling." Lucille paused, looking intently into her eyes. "Is everything all right, dear?"

"Yes," she smiled brightly. "Everything's fine. I just need to get changed, and perhaps I'll put my feet up a bit."

"Yes, yes. No need to be here until shortly before three." Lucille patted her shoulder. "I'd appreciate it if you took it easy until then, Katy."

Katy nodded. "Thanks. I will." And before anyone else could question her, and grateful that her mother was distracted with Clara and Ellen, Katy hurried out.

Anna hid her amusement that her mother had insisted on wearing a wedding veil for her wedding ceremony. She knew that if she and Daniel ever did marry, no veil would be involved. Just the same, she took her time, helping Lucille arrange the lacy trimmed veil just right. "You look very beautiful," Anna said quietly.

"For an older woman," Lucille added.

"For any aged woman." Anna smiled.

"Thank you, dear." Lucille lowered her voice. "Do you think Katy is all right?"

"What do you mean?" Anna felt a wave of concern. "Was something wrong?"

"I don't know. I just felt that she wasn't feeling well . . . or something."

Anna considered this. "Well, she was probably just tired. I keep telling her not to overdo it, reminding her that she's with child. But I'm not sure she ever listens."

"Maybe it's catching up with her." Lucille smoothed the skirt of her dress.

"I know she's not happy that she can't fit into any of her pretty dresses." Anna adjusted the edge of the veil.

"And perhaps she was thinking of her own wedding day last summer," Lucille said sadly. "And missing her groom. They had so little time together."

"Yes, that's probably it. But don't worry. Knowing Katy, she will cheer up when the festivities begin. She loves these celebrations."

"I'm sure you're right."

As Anna continued helping Lucille, she wasn't so sure. Katy had been so excited about the wedding today, it was hard to imagine her not being happy about it now. In fact, she had just told Anna this morning that she wanted to be around to be sure Lucille's wedding outfit was perfect. And now she wasn't even here.

As three o'clock drew near, Anna felt more worried. Katy was still not back. What if something was wrong? Could it be with the baby? Should she call home? Or send someone to check on her? Then, just as Muriel began to play the organ, Anna spotted her daughter ducking into the back of the church. Wearing her loose pink silk gown, Katy looked pretty as usual and, from what Anna could see, all was well. She'd probably just needed a little rest.

Anna went to greet her, and then it was time for the wedding to begin. Anna had felt surprised and honored when Lucille had asked her to stand up with her. Next to Mac was his best friend, and the town's mayor, Wally Morris. As Anna walked down the aisle ahead of her mother, she wondered again if it would ever really be her getting married again. Would Daniel ever be standing where Mac was standing, gazing lovingly at her?

Then instead of dwelling on that, she reminded herself this was her parents' wedding. She was here to celebrate their big day. And smiling widely, she took her place up front and watched as her mother, looking much younger than her years, made her way down the aisle.

The church was packed, and after the wedding vows were repeated and Mac and Lucille were pronounced man and wife, the whole church erupted in applause and cheers. A little unconventional perhaps, but sweet. This reuniting had been a long time coming, and it seemed everyone was rejoicing with the bride and groom.

After the wedding, the reception was held at the Grange Hall. Like the church, it had been decorated with cherry blossoms and paper roses.

Katy had spent yesterday afternoon getting it just perfect. Hearts and flowers everywhere, pink and red and white—very festive. But when Anna spotted Katy on the sidelines, behind the refreshment table, she could tell that all was not well with her normally energetic young daughter. And so, after greeting the guests and playing the part of the devoted daughter, Anna made her way over to Katy. "Are you feeling well?" she quietly asked.

"Oh, yes." Katy nodded vigorously. "I'm fine."

"You don't look fine." Anna studied her daughter's red-rimmed eyes. "I can tell, honey, something is definitely wrong."

"Not now, Mother," Katy hissed.

"But I—"

"Not now!" Katy turned abruptly and marched off toward the kitchen.

Anna wondered if she'd done something to offend her, but taking Katy's hint—that she didn't want to talk now—Anna went off in search of someone else to visit with. Still, she felt troubled. Something was definitely wrong with Katy.

Katy felt trapped in the kitchen but, making herself appear useful and busy, decided to make it work for her. At least until Mother backed off from her incessant questioning. In an hour or so, her grandparents would have to depart for the westbound train—since Mac's plan was to

163

take Lucille to the state capital for a week-long honeymoon. Randall Douglas had offered to take them to the station in his big fancy car. After that, Katy would be free to go home. And then, if her mother insisted, Katy would explain about the telegram. But not until then.

Finally, she could tell by the clock and the cheering going on out there, the bride and groom were probably preparing to leave. Katy hurried out, grabbing a handful of rice to toss upon them as they made their flamboyant exit. She blew kisses to both of them, keeping a happy smile pasted on her face until Randall's car was out of sight.

"That was very nice." Anna slipped an arm around Katy. "And now we need to talk, my dear."

"I want to go home," Katy said quietly. "I've got the Runabout if you want to ride with me. Bernice promised to oversee the clean-up."

"Let me say goodbye to Clara and a few others first," Anna told her.

"I'll wait in the car." Katy grabbed her purse and the wrap she'd left by the door and hurried outside. She didn't want to face anyone right now. Not even her own mother. She just wanted to go home and cry herself to sleep. But finally her mother came, and she was barely inside the Runabout when Katy blurted out her news.

"He's been hurt, Mother. Jim has been wounded in action."

"Oh, no." Anna's eyes grew big. "Is it bad?"

"I don't know." Katy dug in her purse to retrieve the wrinkled telegram. "Here."

Anna quickly read the brief message then turned to Katy with tear-filled eyes. "Oh, honey, I'm so sorry. When did you get this?"

"Around noon." Katy was crying again too.

"And you were keeping it all to yourself throughout the whole wedding and reception?"

Katy barely nodded, then Anna embraced her, holding her tightly. "You poor thing. I'm so sorry. But how brave you were not to burden your grandparents with the news. I'm just so sorry, Katy."

"I—I don't know what to think or do, Mother. My mind has been spinning in circles. What if he's in terrible pain? The telegram doesn't say much, but I'm not sure if that's good or bad. For all I know Jim could be dead by now." She choked back a sob.

"Let's not go there." Anna pointed to the steering wheel. "And I will drive us home."

After trading places, Katy allowed her tears to fall freely again. And, grateful that her mother didn't try to hush her, Katy leaned back and sobbed like a small child as Anna silently drove them home.

Anna guided Katy into the quiet house and,

settling her in Mac's private sitting room, went to make them some tea. By the time she returned, Katy had regained some composure, but her tears were still trickling down. "I know I should be stronger than this," she mumbled as she took the teacup from her mother.

"Why should you be stronger?" Anna demanded as she sat down. "You've had some very shocking news. Of course you're upset. I'm upset too. Not only is Jim your dear husband, he's my good friend. I'm so very sorry to hear he's been hurt. It's all very upsetting."

Katy just nodded, sipping her tea. It was worse than upsetting. It felt as if her whole world had crumbled with that telegram. Her hopes for her happy little family reuniting after the war . . . Jim working at the newspaper while she cared for the baby and created beautiful designs for the dress shop . . . someday they would travel together . . . perhaps to Paris like Jim had promised her. Poor Jim, if he did survive, he'd never want to return to the country where he'd been injured.

"I know I'll probably sound trite," Anna said carefully. "But after our tears are shed, I think all we can really do is to pray for him . . . and to wait to hear more news."

"Is that really all?" Katy looked up in desperation. "Because I'm not sure I can stand the waiting part. Not for very long."

"I have an idea," Anna said suddenly. "Perhaps

we can contact Daniel, and he can get some news to us. After all, Jim must be in one of the US Army hospitals. Daniel must have a way to communicate between the hospitals."

"Yes!" Katy said eagerly. "Please, please ask Dr. Daniel to find Jim. Maybe he can help treat him too. He's such a good doctor."

"I'll send Daniel a telegram right now." Anna set down her teacup and stood. "I'll call it in to the telegraph station. I'm not sure how long it takes a telegram to reach France, or on to his medical unit on the Western Front, but we will certainly give it our best try."

As Anna hurried to the phone, Katy tried not to remember the gruesome stories she'd overheard during the many times her mother and grandfather discussed the war—the inhumanity of the German troops, or the battlefield injuries that soldiers suffered at their hands. Like mustard gas or shrapnel wounds that became horribly infected. She'd tried to block such tales from her mind, but somehow they'd remained dormant and hidden—ready to assault her in the middle of the night. As she waited for her mother to return, Katy did as Anna had said—she earnestly prayed for Jim . . . prayed that it wasn't already too late.

CHAPTER 14

By the time Mac and Lucille returned from their honeymoon trip, Anna still hadn't heard back from Daniel. As a result, Katy was not doing well. Anna had even discussed it with JD, explaining that she wasn't eating right or sleeping much. "I'm very worried," she confessed. "And I don't know what to do for her. We all try to help her, but she's so distraught and worn out."

"Is she still working at the dress shop?"

"I've tried to keep her from it, but she's a stubborn girl. She's gone in a few times." Anna sighed. "But I'm concerned for her and the baby. She just looks so tired and even has dark circles under her eyes."

"Well, we could put her in the hospital," he suggested. "That way she'd have round-the-clock care."

"Do you think that's really necessary?"

"It's necessary that she gets good nutrition and adequate rest." He frowned. "She needs peace and quiet."

"Mac's house isn't exactly quiet, with all of us

coming and going." She didn't want to mention that it had become even busier with Lucille living there now.

"Katy would be better off somewhere restful . . . with someone to care for her. Perhaps the hospital is the best place."

Anna wasn't sure. "Bernice has been trying to look out for Katy, but it's not easy when she refuses help."

"I know what we can do." He held a finger in the air. "Move her to my house and have Sarah Rose care for her. I know those two are close, and Sarah Rose would make a very good nurse for Katy."

"Really, you think so?" Anna was surprised to hear him praise Sarah Rose.

"Sarah Rose doesn't have proper training, but she's proven herself a responsible caregiver."

"And I think Katy would listen to Sarah Rose. But I'm not sure I can get her to agree to move there."

"Tell her it's there or the hospital," he said firmly. "Doctor's orders. If necessary, I'll come tell her that myself. She has a responsibility to her baby."

"Yes, I'm sure you're right." Anna smiled. "Thank you, JD. I'm glad I spoke to you about this."

"I wish Daniel would get back to us." He frowned. "I sent him a telegram too."

"I'm sure he's terribly busy. And communications to the Western Front, with the war raging like it is, are probably challenging."

"Seems to me it would be better not to send word of the wounded at all, if they don't share the patient's condition. Just gives family more to fret over."

"I couldn't agree more." Anna didn't want to admit that not hearing back from Daniel had even added to her concerns. Although she was certain he was busy, she also knew he was serving in a dangerous area.

Katy was actually relieved to move into Dr. Hollister's house. She didn't want to admit it, but she'd felt guilty for putting a damper on her grandparents' newly married state. As a result, she'd skipped some meals and tried to maintain a low profile. Then when her mother had mentioned being hospitalized, Katy had eagerly agreed to move to Dr. Hollister's house. The idea of being cared for by Sarah Rose was surprisingly comforting.

"I hope you don't mind being upstairs," Sarah told her as she helped Katy settle into the room she'd prepared. "But there's only one bedroom downstairs, and Dr. Hollister is using that."

"I don't mind a bit." Katy sat in the easy chair by the window.

"But I don't want you going up and down the

stairs," Sarah warned as she began to unpack Katy's bags. "You've got the bathroom right down the hall, and I'll bring your meals up."

"You mean I'm to be stuck up here?"

"That's right. Dr. Hollister gave me strict orders." Sarah shook out a white flannel nightgown.

"What about going to the dress shop? Or my Red Cross meetings?"

"Dr. Hollister said you are in confinement now. For the welfare of yourself and your baby, you are to remain up here. You will rest and eat and regain your strength. You can read or draw." She pointed to Katy's knitting basket where a nearly finished pale blue baby sweater was waiting. "Or knit. But that's all."

Katy frowned but said nothing.

"Darling girl." Sarah Rose knelt beside her, taking her hand. "You are plum worn out. It's not good for you or your baby. And if you don't agree to these conditions, Dr. Hollister says he will put you in the hospital. Wouldn't you rather be here with me?"

"Yes, yes . . . of course."

"And remember, you're not just doing this for yourself. Think of your man. He won't want to come home to a sickly wife and baby."

"You mean . . . *if* he comes home."

"Oh, Katy darling, don't stop believing that he'll come home."

"My one consolation is that I haven't received a War Department telegram informing me he's passed." Katy took in a ragged sigh. "But I brace myself for that every single day."

"Instead of bracing yourself for bad news, you should be praying." Sarah stood, putting her hands on her hips.

"I do that too. But I'm not sure God is listening."

"Of course he's listening. But sometimes his answer is to *wait*."

"Wait—wait—wait," Katy exclaimed. "I get so doggone sick of waiting."

"You've never been a very patient girl." Sarah's smile looked sad. "But you have no choice this time. You've got about six weeks to wait for that baby . . . and who knows how long you'll be waiting for your man. Just be thankful you still have both of them to wait for."

Katy nodded, remembering that Sarah Rose had lost both her baby and her man. She knew what she was talking about. "I'll try to be more patient," Katy promised.

"And now we're going to get you into bed."

"Bed?" Katy frowned. "It's the middle of the day."

"Doctor's orders." Sarah Rose was already unbuttoning the back of Katy's dress. And before long, wearing her warm flannel nightgown, Katy was tucked into bed.

"I feel like a child."

"Good. Pretend you're a little girl and that Sarah Rose is putting you down for your nap. And if you take a good long one, I'll bring you up some tea and cookies this afternoon."

Katy leaned back into the pillow, closing her eyes. It seemed pointless to protest . . . and she didn't want to be hospitalized . . . so she gave in . . . drifting to sleep.

After several days of Sarah Rose's gentle care in the quiet house, Katy felt a little better. She'd even finished the baby sweater and was now working on some soft yellow booties. But she still worried about Jim. It had been more than two weeks since she'd gotten that telegram—shouldn't she have heard something more by now? That wasn't the only thing troubling her though. Katy questioned this need for "confinement."

"I told you what the doctor said," Sarah Rose reminded her as she picked up the lunch tray. "It's this or the hospital."

"Fine," Katy growled.

"And I have some good news for you."

"About Jim?" Katy sat up.

"No. About your grandmother. She plans to visit you this afternoon."

"Oh . . . that's nice. Have you heard from my mother?"

"Yes. She called this morning to see if she

could pop in to see you tomorrow. You know this is her busy day at the newspaper."

"Yes . . . I know." Katy didn't want to admit that she missed her mother.

"And I told your grandmother not to come until three. After you've had your afternoon nap."

Katy patted her bulging mid-section. "Hopefully the baby won't keep kicking me in the ribs."

"Looks to be a big baby." Sarah Rose put her cool hand on Katy's forehead and then checked her pulse like she often did throughout the day. "My guess is that it's a boy."

"I hope so. Baby Jimmy . . . or Baby Jamie. I haven't made up my mind."

"Well, there's time for that." Sarah drew the drapes, turned off the light, and quietly slipped out of the room.

Although Katy closed her eyes, she felt certain she wouldn't sleep. She didn't even want to sleep. Not after the nightmare she'd had last night— finding Jim bloody and lifeless, face down in the mud. She still couldn't shake that image from her memory. And now she felt more certain than ever that she'd lost him. She couldn't even pray.

A knocking on the door made her sit up in bed, but before she could answer, the door burst open and her mother stepped in. "I'm sorry to disturb your nap," Anna said quickly, turning on the bedside light. "But this telegram came from Daniel, and I knew you'd want to—"

"What does it say?" Katy demanded.

"Daniel has seen Jim," Anna told her. "He is alive. But he's been seriously wounded."

"Yes?" Katy leaned forward.

"He's lost his arm, Katy." Anna's expression was hard to read.

"His arm?" Katy slowly nodded. "Is that all?"

Anna blinked. "Isn't that enough?"

"Yes, that's plenty." Katy couldn't help but smile. "But at least he's alive, Mother. That's the main thing. And so other than missing his arm, is he really okay?"

"Daniel only mentioned the amputated arm and that Jim was being treated in an army hospital in England, and that he would be sent home when he's strong enough. Think about it, Katy, Jim might make it here before your baby comes."

"Did the telegram say that?" she asked eagerly.

"No. But that's more than a month off. It seems possible."

"Did Dr. Daniel say which arm Jim lost?" Katy asked quietly . . . the reality of Jim's injury sinking in.

"No, he didn't."

"Hopefully it's the left arm. Then he can write me a letter."

"Well, even if it's his right arm, he can learn to use his left."

"Like Grandfather, after his stroke?"

"Yes. Mac has gotten quite adept at using his left hand to write."

"Maybe Grandfather will be an encouragement to Jim." And now, despite her earlier relief, Katy felt tears coming. "Oh, poor, poor Jim."

"But at least he's alive, Katy. Remember that."

"I know, but I was just thinking of how much he likes hunting and fishing . . . and typing out stories for the newspaper."

"Mac has learned to manage the typewriter fairly well. It slows him down some, but he can do it. Jim will be able to as well." Anna sat down on Katy's bed, giving her a comforting hug. "Let's just be thankful he's alive. And that he'll soon be home to see his wife and child. I hate to say it, but I was very worried that it was going to be much worse. I'm really relieved. You should be too."

"I know." She sobbed. "But it's just hard to think of Jim like that . . . with only one arm. He must be so very sad."

"Well, we'll just have to do whatever we can to cheer him up. The address of the hospital is there—so you can write to him." Anna handed Katy the wrinkled telegram as well as a hand-kerchief. "Try not to worry too much, Katy. Just rejoice that he's alive."

Katy nodded, blotting her tears with the hand-kerchief.

"I'd stay longer, honey, but I've got a news-paper to get to the press."

"I know. Thank you for coming, Mother." Katy nodded. "And you're right, it is very good news. I'm so happy Jim's alive. Really, I am."

But after Anna left, Katy began to cry again. She told herself that they were tears of relief . . . but they were mixed with tears of grief. Losing an arm would be hard on an active man like Jim. She knew it. But she would do all she could to help him recover from it. And one arm was enough to hold her . . . and their baby.

Knowing she would be unable to sleep now, Katy reached for her stationary and began to pen a letter to her beloved, assuring him that she would love him just as much with only one arm as she did with two. Perhaps even more! She was just finishing it up when her grandmother arrived.

"I brought you magazines." Lucille kissed Katy's cheek as she set recent issues of *Cosmopolitan*, *Vogue*, and *Ladies' Home Journal* on the bed. Katy thanked her and then asked if she'd heard the latest news.

"News?" Lucille sat down in the easy chair, unpinning her hat.

"Jim is alive." Katy set her pen and paper aside and told her grandmother about Daniel's tele-gram.

"That's wonderful news." Lucille's smile faded. "Well, except for the part about losing his arm. I'm sorry about that. But as you know, your grandfather has little use of his right arm, but he makes do. I think his bum-leg troubles him more than the lame arm. At least Jim has both legs."

Katy agreed and then, to change the subject, they began to peruse *Vogue* together, commenting on the changing fashions, shorter dress lengths, hat styles, and daintier looking shoes. "I think shortages of leather are the reason," Lucille said as they admired a pair of delicate pumps that were partly cloth and partly leather with a grosgrain bow on top. "But aren't those pretty with that springy dress?"

"Yes. I am looking forward to being able to wear clothes like that again." She pointed to her swollen belly. "Do you think I'll ever get my waistline back?"

"Of course, you will. But you'll be so caught up with your sweet baby and husband, you probably won't even notice. Do you know when Jim will come home?" She flipped a page.

"No. But Mother feels it could be soon. Perhaps even before the baby comes."

"Wouldn't that be wonderful to have him here to greet his child?"

"Yes. But I wonder where we will live. I never really gave it any thought before . . . probably because I didn't expect him to be home this soon. I suppose Dr. Hollister would probably let us stay here."

Lucille wrinkled her nose. "No, that wouldn't be good."

"Maybe we could take the third floor of Grandfather's house," Katy mused. "That wouldn't be too bad."

"Or you and Jim could take my house."

"Your house?" Katy blinked. "I thought you were going to sell it."

"Well, I didn't intend to keep it. But I certainly wouldn't mind if you and Jim occupied it."

"Oh, Grandmother, that would be wonderful. You'd really let us live there?"

"Of course. I'm happy to have you live there. Although I've had some of the furnishings moved over to Mac's house. I hope it's not too barren for you."

"You won't hear me complain."

"And I let Sally stay on until the end of the month. But perhaps we should keep her on. She could be of help to you, after the baby comes. And I know she needs the work."

"I wish Sarah Rose could come with me instead."

"Excellent idea. Perhaps Sally would like to keep house for JD."

"Do you think she would?"

"It's work. I don't see why not."

"Well, I can think of a couple of reasons." Katy shook her head. "For one thing, she doesn't seem to like him much."

"And because JD can be a bit difficult?"

"Yes. Plus he might throw a fit to find out he's losing Sarah Rose."

"Sarah Rose is free to make her own choices." Lucille smiled. "And I have a feeling I know what that will be, darling."

Katy didn't know what to say. And, even though she felt happier, the tears came pouring out again.

Lucille didn't seem to mind. "Don't worry, darling, all women are a bit emotional when they're with child. It's perfectly natural." She pointed to an interesting dress design. "This would look lovely on you, Katy. After the baby arrives, of course. But with that loose design and higher waistline, you wouldn't even have to fret over not having your figure back."

Katy agreed it was quite attractive and before long they were making plans to put together a dress sample for the shop . . . and when the time was right, for Katy. Lucille promised to bring fabric swatches the next time she came. And she promised to handle the work situation with Sarah Rose and Sally. "Don't you worry about a thing, darling girl." She kissed Katy's cheek with a knowing smile. And by the time her grandmother left, Katy felt a real glimmer of hope. Life would go on.

CHAPTER 15

A nna frowned at the headline of the article that Frank had just handed to her. "You want this on the front page?" she questioned him.

"Well, it's pretty big news," he said defensively.

"Not good news." She shook her head. "Will this war ever end?"

"I'm sure that the Kaiser is hoping this new offensive will end it."

"That's grim."

"That's the truth, Anna."

"Germany is launching five major offensives against the Allied Forces?" she read aloud. "All at once?"

"The Germans call it the Ludendorff Offensive. The theory is that General Ludendorff has reorganized and redirected all the German troops from the Russian front to this. Apparently, the goal is to divide the Allied armed forces. To once and for all weaken and ultimately defeat them."

"Then why did you call it the 'New Spring Offensive'?" She scowled. "That sounds like a garden party or something."

"Because the offensive launched last week. On the first day of spring. And that's what the Brits called it."

"But spring is supposed to be a lovely, happy time—and this article is anything but, Frank."

"That's true. But are you suggesting we should shield our readers from it?"

"No, of course, not. I just wish we'd get some good news for a change."

"Well, unfortunately, if Ludendorff's plan succeeds, there will be nothing but bad news from here on out."

"Why are you being so gloomy?" she demanded.

"Because we're in a gloomy business just now." He shook his head. "It really makes me want to go over there and fight."

"Oh, Frank." She shoved the article back at him. "I can't believe you're still talking like that. Besides Ginger and your boys, think about Jim—coming home with only one arm."

He sighed loudly. "Yeah, I know. But that just gets me even more fired up. Jim's a good guy. He didn't deserve that."

"At least he's alive."

"When is he supposed to get home, anyway?"

"First week of April, if all goes well."

"That's coming right up. Think he'll get here before Katy has her baby?"

"We're all hoping he'll make it in time."

"Will he return to work here?"

"I hope so."

Frank nodded. "It'll be good to have him back."

"Yes, it will." She smiled as she pinned on her hat. "And it's a well-done article, Frank. It's just that it makes me fighting mad."

"You and me both."

"Well, if you can manage things here, I need to leave early. My mother is planning a little party to cheer up Katy this afternoon. Poor Katy had gotten so tired of being confined over at Doc Hollister's, she was practically climbing the walls. So Lucille arranged to have her moved."

"Not to the hospital, I hope."

"No. She's staying at Lucille's house for now. But she's still in confinement."

"Well, if you ask me, confinement agrees with Katy. The past few weeks, she's gotten her fashion column in on time every week. Sometimes it's been early. And this week's piece is about baby clothing and how she hopes to bring out a new line of children's clothing by next fall. I really think her fashion column is better than ever."

"I'll let her know you said that." Anna laughed as she picked up her satchel. "Not that it will bring much comfort coming from a man who wears plaid and stripes together."

He grinned at his interesting attire. "Well, tell your daughter that my wife adores her fashion column almost as much as Kathleen's Dress Shop. But reading the column is easier on the pocketbook."

Anna paused by Virginia's desk before leaving the newspaper office. "Are you sure you can't get away and come with me?"

"There's too much to do here." Virginia nodded to a pile of paperwork as she handed Anna a small parcel. "But I did get a little something for the baby."

"That's very thoughtful. Thank you."

"And tell Katy I'll pop in to visit her when it's not so busy."

"I know Katy will love that."

As Anna walked across town, she hoped Lucille's plan would be an encouragement to her impatient daughter. As Katy would say, waiting was not her strong suit. In fact, she was still waiting to get word from Jim. A Red Cross nurse had kindly written a short note, assuring Katy that Jim was recovering, but so far no real communication had come directly from Jim. And Anna hadn't heard any news from Daniel either. So she could relate to her daughter's aggravation. It was difficult to wait—and thanks to the Great War, the whole world seemed to be stalled . . . or perhaps it was simply holding its breath.

"Come in, come in," Clara said cheerfully as she answered the door at Lucille's house. "Welcome to the Stafford house."

"*Stafford* house?" Anna frowned as she removed her jacket. "Isn't that a bit presumptuous?"

"Not really." Clara lowered her voice. "You see, Lucille has a surprise for Katy."

"Our last guest is here," Lucille announced as she greeted Anna in the foyer. "I'm glad you could join us." She winked then lowered her voice. "I've hidden your baby carriage in the bedroom that Katy plans to use as the nursery. Katy hasn't seen it."

"Oh, good. I'm glad it arrived on time. Did it look nice?" Anna had ordered the wicker carriage from San Francisco several weeks ago.

"It's perfectly lovely. I'm sure Katy will be thrilled."

Anna set her hat down and looked around. "The house looks different."

"Yes. As you know I took quite a few of my favorite furnishing to your father's house. And Mac allowed me to bring some of his things back over here. Do you think it looks all right?"

"I like it." Anna smiled as they went into the living room where the other guests were already having tea.

"Mother." Katy struggled to stand up and then went over to hug her. "I'm so glad you made it."

"Goodness, you're bigger than ever, Katy. I can barely get my arms around you."

"Don't remind me." Katy rubbed her back. "And I still have about three weeks to go. I asked

Doc Hollister if there was any chance it could be sooner."

"What did he say?"

Katy shrugged. "He said it was unlikely, but you never can tell."

"I'm afraid this is your year of learning patience." Anna turned to greet the other women, and soon they were all visiting and enjoying tea.

After a while, Lucille stood. "As you all know, I planned this little get-together to celebrate the fact that our dear Katy will be a mother before long. And now we will allow Katy to lead us to view the baby nursery."

"Oh, dear. That's not a good idea." Katy frowned. "I haven't been able to do anything to prepare it for the baby."

"That's because I won't let her." Sarah Rose exchanged a knowing glance with Lucille. "Doctor's orders."

"Sarah wouldn't even let me rearrange a single thing in here." Katy looked around the living room. "But with Bernie and Mickey's help, I was able to direct where I wanted things positioned. Still, it takes great self-control to just sit and watch."

"Yes, and Miss Katy still tries to sneak around and rearrange things," Sarah told Anna.

"Well, I'm glad you're here to keep her in line," Anna said.

"And it's not easy," Katy confessed. "I can't

wait until this confinement period is over. I keep telling Doc Hollister that other than being big and clumsy, my energy is back and I feel fine. But he insists I'm not supposed to lift a finger or he'll put me in the hospital. So exasperating."

"Yes, but despite the doctor's warning, I still caught her rearranging pictures on the wall just this morning," Sarah tattled.

"And did I get hecky-pecky for that." Katy laughed.

"So on to the baby nursery." Lucille took Katy's hand. "You lead the way, little mother."

"I hope you ladies won't be disappointed. I'm afraid this room has been more for storage than anything, but I like that it's handy to the master bedroom." Katy grimly shook her head as she led the procession of ladies down the hall-way.

Lucille winked at Anna. She'd already confided that they'd been hard at work in the nursery. The painter came while Katy was napping several days ago. Mac had sneaked an heirloom cradle in, and Clara had sewn pretty bedding and lacy white curtains. The other women had slipped their various contributions to Lucille to tuck away and so far, it seemed, Katy was completely in the dark.

"Here you go." Katy's tone was lackluster as she cautiously opened the door. "What?" She rushed into the cheerful, sunny room, looking

187

around and gasping in wonder. "How on earth did all this happen?"

The ladies laughed and suddenly everyone was talking at once, sounding like a flock of chickens, as they examined and exclaimed over every corner of the well-outfitted and attractive nursery.

"It was Lucille's idea."

"She told us what colors you liked."

"Ooh, look at that sweet baby carriage from Anna. White wicker is perfect for summer strolls."

"And what an adorable cradle!"

"That was Mac's contribution," Lucille said. "He refinished it for Katy."

"It's all just perfectly perfect," Katy said with tear-filled eyes. "I don't know how you managed to do this without me knowing, but I'm so very grateful. I was worried that I'd have to use a bureau drawer for a bed." She examined a pretty bassinette by the window and a shelf holding a set of little Beatrice Potter books. "I love these."

"That was from me." Marjorie Douglas smiled. "I just love those little bunnies. I've put another set aside for little Larry's first birthday," she told Ellen.

Katy picked up a well-worn teddy bear. "Oh, I remember this."

"Yes. It was yours," Anna told her. "I saved it."

"And this!" Katy pointed to the christening

gown hanging on the closet door. "It is so beautiful."

"I made it," Ellen admitted. "It's even fancier
than the one you made for Larry."

"That's because Ellen wants you to have a
girl," Clara teased.

"And these lovely walls." Katy turned to
Lucille. "I remember now when you asked me
what I thought was a good nursery color and I
said buttery yellow because I wanted the room to
feel sunny and warm. And this is just delightful."
She sat down in the upholstered rocking chair
with a dreamy expression. Anna could almost
imagine her rocking her baby there.

"Oh, and I nearly forgot." Anna handed her the
parcel. "This is from Virginia. She was unable to
come but promised to drop in on you at a later
date."

Katy unwrapped the package and held up a
petite silver cup with a duckling engraved on the
front. "Isn't this darling!"

"Now all you need is the baby," Ellen told her.
"Speaking of which, I need to get home to mine.
I promised young Molly Bower that I wouldn't
be more than two hours."

"Well, I'm glad you came." Katy hugged her.

The other women began to say their goodbyes
and trickle out until only Lucille, Anna, Katy,
and Sarah Rose remained.

"Now, I don't want to be bossy, Katy, but I'm

afraid you've worn yourself out." Sarah Rose led Katy to an easy chair, insisting she sit and then laying an afghan over her lap. "Dr. Hollister will never forgive me if I let you overdo it."

"I'm so glad you're watching over our girl," Anna told Sarah.

"Yes, I don't know what we'd do without Sarah Rose." Lucille smiled.

"And you have outdone yourself," Anna told Lucille as she helped Sarah Rose clear teacups and dishes. "Katy couldn't have been more surprised."

"Or happier." Sarah led the way to the kitchen.

"Well, I have one more surprise." Lucille produced a large envelope.

"What's that?" Anna asked.

"The deed to the house. I'm giving it to Katy."

"Oh, Lucille, that's so generous. Are you certain?"

"Of course! I'd planned to leave it to Katy in my will, but I figure that's a long way off. And I don't need it anymore. So why should Katy have to wait?"

"She has been getting lots of practice with waiting lately." Anna smiled.

"I'll take care of this." Sarah Rose made a shooing motion. "You go back in there with Miss Katy. Tell her your good news. I'm sure she'll be thrilled."

Katy was completely surprised by her grandmother's unexpected and extravagant gift. "I—I don't know what to say. Are you sure you—"

"I'm absolutely sure." Lucille hugged her. "Of course, the house is for both you and Jim. But I've put it in your name, Katy. I hope that's not a problem."

"Oh?" Katy's face was hard to read.

"I think it's perfectly fine to put the house in Katy's name. She's part of a legacy," Anna said to Lucille then turned to Katy. "You're part of a legacy of strong women."

"Yes, that's true," Lucille agreed. "Even your great-grandmother was a very strong woman—sometimes too strong, if you ask me."

"That's true. And my grandmother had her own wealth," Anna told Katy. "Did you know that she claimed 320 acres of land for herself when she and her husband settled here in the 1850s? She sold the land after becoming widowed—then invested the money into modern improvements at the newspaper office."

"Yes, I remember Grandfather saying something about that." Katy stared down at the deed in her lap.

"Anyway, I hope that you and Jim and the baby will be very happy here." Lucille leaned down to kiss Katy's cheek.

"I'm already happy here. Thank you so much, Grandmother." Katy's eyes filled with tears again. "Now all I need is Jim and the baby."

"I wonder who will get here first," Anna mused.

"I hope and pray it's Jim." Katy sighed. "I want him with me before the baby comes."

"Well, even if he's not here by then, you've got a lot of family and friends to help," Anna reassured her. "Just the same, I'm praying he gets here soon."

Katy was still stunned as she sat in the rocker in the nursery. She knew she should be in bed. Sarah Rose had already turned in and assumed that Katy had done the same. But Katy was too keyed up to sleep. She tugged on the front of her dressing gown, trying to make it bridge the gap over her rotund middle, but it was useless now. And so she reached for a light blue baby afghan that she recently knitted, tucking it over her bulbous belly.

"I wonder which of you will make the first appearance," she whispered. "You or your father? I guess I'll have to trust that to God."

As Katy slowly rocked, she tried to imagine what life would be like when Jim came home. Would it be the dreamy imaginings she used to entertain—back when she'd imagined him returning to her whole and strong and looking ever so handsome in uniform? Or would he now be weak and defeated? Would he still be recovering from his missing limb? And how would that affect his psyche?

What if he was much changed? She desperately hoped not. Jim had always been so strong and cheerful and positive—he'd been her rock. Dependable and self-assured and generally happy. But what if he was different now? She'd heard stories of men who were not themselves after war. Would Jim be one of them? And if he were, what would she do? *What would she do?*

Katy suddenly remembered what her mother had said about the legacy of strong women in their family . . . but that strength had been born of disappointment. Katy was well aware of that. First of all, her grandmother had given up on her marriage to Mac and, as scandalous as it was, she'd left him and later divorced and married a wealthy older man who'd given her everything money could buy . . . but not too much in the way of true happiness.

And then there was Katy's own mother. Her marriage seemed doomed from the start. Grandfather had foreseen it, warning her that she was making a mistake. But she was a strong woman who'd gone her own way. As a result, it had driven a wedge between her and her father. And Katy had been deprived of her grandfather until she was nearly an adult.

Katy shuddered to remember the truth about her own father. Something Anna had shielded her from for most of her young life. But when Katy finally heard the real story, she'd been determined to never enter into marriage lightly, and she certainly wouldn't have children at a young age like her mother had done. Katy had intended to pursue a career in design. She'd planned to save marriage and children for later— much, much later. So much for those ideals. And, to be fair, the Great War had something to do with her changed plans. As had her love for Jim.

Katy thought back to how her mother had stepped up, proving herself capable and able to compete in a man's world at the *Oregonian* newspaper in Portland. But it hadn't been easy for her. And it hadn't been easy for Katy either. How many times had she explained to friends why she had no father or any other family to speak of—and how often had she envied those with a mother in the home and a father who provided for a houseful of brothers and sisters? It had seemed sweetly romantic to her . . . something she would want someday . . . perhaps when she was in her late twenties. But here she was, barely eighteen—married with a child on the way. And although she tried to accept this state of affairs, she sometimes had her doubts.

What if Katy's marriage was destined to follow history's lead? What if Katy was forced to be a strong woman in the way her mother had been? But she couldn't bear to imagine raising her child alone. Still, she wondered what she would do if Jim was greatly changed. What if it became necessary to part ways? She hated to think of it, but she knew it was a possibility. And, she reminded herself, they'd only spent one wedded week together. How well did they really know each other? And Katy had been very young—and impulsive. For that matter she was still very young. What if her impulse to become a soldier's wife had been a big mistake? She rubbed her hands over her swollen midsection. Would the baby be forced to pay the price?

Katy felt a lump growing in her throat and tears welling in her eyes. She didn't like to go to these dark places and seldom allowed herself to entertain such negative thoughts. But when Lucille had presented her with the deed to the house—in Katy's name only—it had felt like a bad omen. She prayed that it wasn't.

CHAPTER 16

Anna skimmed the front-page article that Frank had left on her desk. Germany had launched its second spring offensive and didn't appear to be backing down anytime soon . . . if ever. But underneath that piece was an AP article about what was now being called the Spanish Flu. Remembering Daniel's concern about a world-wide epidemic, she eagerly read. This disease had crossed the Atlantic and numerous cases had been reported in random regions, including the Midwest. Hopefully it was not as bad as Daniel had predicted, but Anna decided to mention it to him in her next letter anyway. She knew he'd be interested.

She was tempted to write him now but knew her letter would be more personal if she penned it at home . . . away from the stress and distractions of the newspaper. She hadn't heard from him for a couple of weeks and that had been a short letter. In answer to her queries about Jim and when he would be coming home, Daniel had sounded slightly vague, saying that every amputee patient recovered differently . . . and that it was hard to say when Jim would be discharged from the army hospital in England and returned to the US.

Anna had tried to gently relay this information to Katy, encouraging her to continue writing to Jim—even though she'd only received one short letter written by him. He didn't even mention a word about his lost arm, but the neat recognizable penmanship had convinced Katy that he was missing his left arm. That was something. Still, it seemed concerning—at least to Anna—that Jim, an excellent writer, wasn't communicating better with his wife. Naturally, she kept these worrisome thoughts to herself.

She jumped at the sound of her phone ringing, answering it to hear Virginia's excited voice. "Anna, it is happening."

"What is happening?"

"The baby! It's coming. Sarah Rose just called. Katy needs to go to the hospital."

"Call her right back and say I'm on my way. Tell Sarah Rose to lead her out to the front and I'll pick her up." Anna grabbed her hat and purse and hurried out to the car parked in front. She'd been driving the Runabout to work every day so that she could zip home and pick up Katy when her time came. And now it was time.

Anna's heart raced as she drove through town. When she got to Katy's house, Sarah Rose was just leading her out. They both helped Katy into the car and then Sarah hopped into the rumble seat with Katy's overnight bag—and Anna headed the car toward the hospital.

"How are you doing?" she anxiously asked Katy.

"I'm not sure. I felt the pains a little while ago, but I thought it was indigestion. Then Sarah Rose set me straight. But I'm really not feeling too— oh, my—I spoke too soon." She groaned.

"Don't worry, honey, we're almost there. I'm so glad we have this hospital now. You'll soon be in good hands."

"Sarah called Doc Hollister," Katy said after a moment. "So he should be there."

"Good." Anna turned at the hospital, pulling under the porte cochere.

"I wish it was Dr. Daniel instead."

"Yes, I do too, dear. But JD is very experienced."

Katy let out another yelp, and Anna jumped out of the car and ran into the hospital, calling out for help. Before long, they were wheeling Katy inside with Anna and Sarah Rose following.

"It won't be long now," Anna told Katy as they all rode up the elevator.

"I hope not." Katy looked scared. "But Ellen was here for hours. Remember?"

"It's different for everyone," Sarah Rose pointed out.

"We'll take her from here," a nurse informed

them as they exited the elevator. "Don't worry, she'll be just fine. Dr. Hollister is already up here."

"We'll be in the waiting room." Anna squeezed Katy's hand. "I love you, honey."

"Thanks." Katy had tears in her eyes.

"You'll be okay," Anna assured her. "And just think, the baby will be here soon. Your long wait is about to end."

Katy nodded, but then began to moan again.

Anna really didn't want to leave her daughter, but the nurse and orderly were insistent as they wheeled her away.

"She'll be fine," Sarah told Anna, leading her back into the elevator.

"Yes, yes . . . I'm sure she will." Anna took in a deep breath.

"This is so exciting." Sarah pushed the button.

"I guess it's exciting." Anna frowned. "Or unnerving. I'm not sure which."

"Don't worry, Katy's in good hands now. Dr. Hollister might be a curmudgeon, as your father likes to say, but he's a good physician."

"Yes, I'm sure that's true. It's just hard seeing Katy in such pain."

"I know."

"And I wish Jim could've been home by now." Anna led the way to the waiting area. "I know Katy's worried about him. It's a lot for a young woman to bear."

"Miss Katy is a strong young woman."

"Yes. I know you're right."

"There's your mother and father now." Sarah Rose nodded toward the front door and Anna waved to them.

"How is she?" Lucille asked eagerly.

Anna quickly told her. "But how did you know she was here?"

"Mickey saw you whisking her away earlier," Lucille explained. "Then he drove us over in my car."

"Is she really all right?" Mac asked with worried eyes.

"I'm sure she'll be fine," Anna told him. "We just have to wait now. But you two didn't need to come already. It could be hours."

"I told Mac that very thing, but I couldn't keep him from coming," Lucille said.

"I just want to be sure everything is all right," Mac said.

"I need to call the dress shop since Clara was expecting me this afternoon." Lucille glanced over to the reception desk. "I assume there's a telephone here."

"Just tell them to close the shop," Mac said. "It's a holiday."

"A holiday?" Lucille frowned.

"Yes. Our great-grandchild's birthday." Mac chuckled. "That's a holiday, if you ask me."

To everyone's relief, Katy's baby arrived much

more quickly than Ellen's had last fall. After less than three hours, Doc Hollister found the small crowd of family and friends in the waiting room and, with a broad grin, made his announcement.

"Katy Stafford has just delivered a seven pound, six ounce, baby girl."

"It's a girl," Lucille said happily.

"A girl?" Mac looked slightly disappointed but then smiled.

"What will she name it?" Anna asked. "She was so certain it was going to be a boy. She was already calling it Jamie."

"Could a girl be called Jamie?" Mac asked.

"Oh, no, I don't think so." Lucille shook her head.

Doc Hollister cleared his throat. "The baby's name is Lucy Ann."

"Lucy Ann?" Anna and Lucille repeated together, exchanging happy glances.

"That's right." Doc Hollister nodded. "A healthy infant girl. And the little mother is doing just fine too." He pointed to Anna. "You can visit her in her room in about an hour. The others will have to wait a bit longer. But the baby should be ready for viewing in the nursery window before then."

"Do you have Jim's address at the hospital?" Mac asked eagerly.

"Yes, I'm sure I do." Anna dug in her purse, finding her little address book.

"We'll send him a telegram with the good news."

"Yes." Anna handed him the booklet. "That's a wonderful idea."

"I'll get this telegram right out." Mac grinned. "And then I'll go get some celebratory cigars."

After half an hour, Anna slipped away from the crowd of well-wishers to sneak upstairs and take a peek in the nursery window. But only one baby was there, and it was a boy. She was about to leave when she saw a nurse wheeling another bassinette up to the window. The card in front said *Lucy Ann Stafford*, along with the weight and birth date.

"Welcome, little one," Anna mouthed to the window. "What a little darling you are." She admired her for a few minutes and then went to the nurse at the desk, asking her to send a message to her parents and friends waiting downstairs. "Please, let them know they can come up and view the baby now."

"And you can go say hello to your daughter." The nurse told Anna the room number. "But don't stay long. And no other visitors for a while. She needs rest."

"I understand." Anna thanked her then eagerly went to check on Katy, happy to see that they'd given her a private room with an ocean view. "How are you, honey?" Anna asked quietly.

"Oh, Mother." Katy looked relieved as she

reached for Anna's hand. "Did you see her?"

"I did. She's absolutely lovely."

"But she's a girl." Katy frowned.

"Yes. A beautiful little girl. You should be proud."

"But I wanted a boy."

"I know you did, honey. But she's truly lovely. I don't think I've ever seen such a pretty baby. And Lucy Ann—what a sweet name. Your grandmother and I both feel very honored."

"Do you think Jim will approve?"

"Of course. Why wouldn't he?"

"Because I kept telling him his son little Jamie was coming. I never mentioned a Lucy Ann."

"Mac is sending him a telegram right now," Anna told her. "Jim will soon know about his beautiful little girl. And I'm sure he'll be thrilled."

"I wish he were here." Katy sighed.

"I know you do. We all do. But in time. Daniel said he didn't think it'd be too much longer. He said early June at the latest."

"That's a month and a half from now."

Anna nodded. "I know. But think of it this way, Katy. By that time, you'll be stronger and you'll have time to adjust to motherhood."

"I suppose." She didn't look convinced.

"And you might even fit into some of your pretty summer dresses by then."

Katy brightened. "Yes, that's true. I guess that's something to look forward to."

"And who knows, maybe the war will end by then—and life will return to normal again. Wouldn't that be wonderful?" Even as Anna said this, she didn't think it was terribly likely. But if it helped raise Katy's spirits, she didn't care.

"That would be nice." Katy nodded sleepily.

"The nurse told me not to stay too long. You need your rest."

"Yes . . . thanks to the baby, I haven't had a good night's sleep in the last couple of weeks."

"Well, sleep well now, sweetheart. Your waiting time for the baby is finally over." She leaned down to push an auburn curl from her daughter's brow then kissed her forehead.

Back at the nursery window, a small crowd was gathered, oohing and awing at pretty little Lucy Ann.

"Did you ever see such a beautiful baby?" Lucille asked Anna.

"I don't know . . . I thought Katy was awfully pretty, but then I was the mother. All mothers think their babies are beautiful."

"The nurse said it was because Lucy was born so quickly," Ellen told Anna. "I was in labor for so long that poor Larry looked like he'd been in a battle."

"But he's cuter than ever now," Clara pointed out.

"How is our little mother doing?" Lucille asked Anna.

"She's a bit worn out. And a little discouraged."

"Discouraged?" Lucille's brows arched.

"She wanted a boy," Anna said quietly.

"Not me." Ellen laughed. "I hoped she'd have a girl so that she and Larry can be sweethearts."

"Well, don't start planning the wedding just yet," Lucille said.

"Here comes Great Grandpa," Lucille called out. "Come and meet the pretty little princess."

Mac came over and peered into the window. "Oh, my. She's so tiny."

"They all are to start with," Lucille reminded him. "But isn't she beautiful?"

"I guess so." He frowned. "But she doesn't have much hair."

"Yes, she does," Lucille argued. "It's just that it's reddish so it blends in with her scalp. She'll probably have beautiful auburn curls like the rest of the women in her family."

"She looks bald to me," he said dourly.

"Oh, Mac." Lucille frowned. "Just you wait and see."

"Did you get the telegram sent?" Anna asked.

"Yes. I sent one to Jim, and then I saw Daniel's address and sent one to him as well." He pulled some cigars out of his jacket pocket. "And I even got these. But there's no menfolk around to share them with, so I guess I'll have to smoke them myself."

"Why don't you give one to JD?" Anna suggested.

"Yes, that'd be a nice thank you for delivering such a beautiful baby girl," Lucille told him.

Mac grumbled but headed off in search of the doctor just the same. Anna turned back to look at her granddaughter, watching as the tiny baby sucked on her fist. Hopefully Katy would come around to the idea of a little girl before long. And hopefully Jim would soon be home to see her too.

CHAPTER 17

K aty knew she had much to be thankful for—
Sarah Rose reminded her of it almost daily.
And, for Sarah's sake, Katy tried to keep her
feelings of discontent to herself. But it wasn't
easy to pretend that all was well and that she was
happy as a clam. It was hard to act like she wasn't
disappointed that her baby was a girl instead of
a boy. Or that she wasn't missing Jim more than
ever. And it was difficult to hide her discouragement over the fact Jim had only written one short
congratulatory note about the baby's birth.

Still, Katy was grateful that Sarah Rose was
so patient and understanding. And although she
didn't let Katy wallow in her misery, she didn't
seem to judge her for it either. That alone made
Katy want to try harder to return to her old positive self.

"Miss Lucille is bringing the photographer
today," Sarah Rose reminded Katy at breakfast
time. "She said to have you ready around ten
o'clock. She thinks you and the baby should still
look well rested and refreshed by then."

"I wish she'd wait on the photograph."

"But don't you want one to send to Jim?"

"Yes. But I'd hoped to have my figure back before the photographer came."

"Oh, you look perfectly fine, Miss Katy. And little Lucy gets prettier every day."

"I know, but I wanted to fit into one of my spring frocks."

"Maybe you can put one on and just leave it unbuttoned in back."

Katy considered this suggestion. "I suppose I could do that. No one would see it, would they?"

"No one, but you and me." Sarah chuckled. "I can pin something behind you if you like."

"You probably think I'm terribly vain." Katy set down her coffee.

"You're still young enough to care about such things. I understand."

"I just hope I look better by the time Jim comes home."

"If what Dr. Daniel said about early June is right, it's not too far off . . . only a few weeks away."

"I try not to get my hopes up too high." Katy sighed. "Just in case."

"I hear the little princess." Sarah stood. "You finish your breakfast. I'll go fetch her."

As Sarah went to the nursery, Katy reminded herself of how aggravated she got with Ellen when she'd lived with her. It seemed Ellen had complained about everything. Katy didn't want to be like that. For Sarah Rose's sake, she would have to try harder.

By the time Grandmother and the photographer arrived, Sarah had pinned a handkerchief over the back of Katy's favorite spring dress to hide the gap that couldn't quite be buttoned. And Lucy in her christening gown and cap couldn't have looked sweeter.

"The photographer suggested that you should sit in the wicker chair out on the porch," Lucille told Katy. "The light out there is just perfect, and he's already setting up his equipment." She lifted the baby from Katy's arms. "Come to Great Granny, little Lucy. Time to get your picture taken."

"She just ate, so she should be happy," Katy told her.

"Oh, this little girl is always happy, isn't she?"

"I'll admit she's a much happier baby than Ellen's Larry was at this age." Katy reminded herself that was just one more thing to be thankful for. "Hopefully she won't get too sleepy while he's taking the photograph. It's almost morning nap time."

"It won't take too long," the photographer called out from where he was positioned at the end of the porch.

Katy sat in the wicker chair, smoothing her skirt as Lucille placed the baby in her lap. "I hope this is worth the effort. I really felt we'd both look better in a month or two."

"Nonsense." Lucille stood back to look. "You both are pretty as a picture." She chuckled. "And you'll make a lovely picture."

"What about your idea for four generations in the photo?" Katy asked.

"We can do that next time." Lucille patted Katy's curls into place. "Anna was too busy at the newspaper today. In the meantime, you'll have a nice photograph to send to Jim."

"I wonder if he'll even get it in time. Remember that Dr. Daniel thinks he'll be discharged in early June."

"Just imagine how encouraging it will be for him to get it while he's still in the hospital, Katy. It will make him want to get well quickly and come home."

Katy wondered about that. So far, she hadn't gotten the impression he was that eager to return to her. That worried her more than she cared to admit to anyone.

"You need to stay quiet now," the photographer called out. "And keep the baby as still as possible."

"You both look lovely," Lucille said from the sidelines. "Just think about your dear husband and how pleased he'll be to get this photo from you."

Katy tried to think about Jim . . . tried to

imagine him being pleased to be a father. But it had been so long—nearly a year. Sometimes it was hard to even remember what he looked like.

Anna cringed at what Frank had just presented to her for today's front page headline. *German U-boats in US Waters.* Well, this was definitely a first. But it was not good news. Not for the United States. Just when everyone had hoped that Germany had become worn down and that the Allied Forces were making real progress, the German Navy had the audacity to move submarine boats nearer to the US. It was truly maddening. And Anna did not even want to run the headline.

"Here we go again." Frank sounded weary. "Are you really suggesting we keep this news from our readership?"

"No, no . . . of course not." She handed it back to him with a tired sigh. "I just wish it was happier news."

"Maybe the next paper will be about how the US Navy has torpedoed and sunk all those U-boats to the bottom of the sea."

"I guess they're asking for it."

"And I don't want to add insult to injury, but the AP just reported that Germany is launching its Third Spring Offensive."

"Oh, good grief." She let out an exasperated

sigh as she unfurled tomorrow's editorial from her typewriter and handed it to Frank.

"Happier news?"

"Afraid not."

Frank quickly scanned the piece then looked at her with a furrowed brow. "You sure you want to run *this?*"

She nodded glumly. "People need to know."

"But you were just complaining about bad news, Anna. This piece about the Spanish flu epidemic sounds terrible."

"Our readers need to be warned," she grimly told him. "This epidemic is not going away. Not in the least."

"Where did you find this information?"

"From Daniel. I just got a letter yesterday. This flu is spreading like wildfire. All over the world . . . and the outcome is getting worse. People are dying by the thousands in Europe. And by the hundreds in other places. They're not even sure how it spreads exactly. And it doesn't appear to be limited only to war regions. Even the climates are different—it's in the tropics as well as cold northern regions like Alaska. But the medical experts believe it's the same flu."

"Frightening."

"And young children and old people are usually the most vulnerable." Anna cringed to think of her sweet infant granddaughter being exposed to this deadly disease. "I know it's not here—

not yet anyway, and hopefully it won't get here. But from what Daniel says, no area can assume they will escape it. But he does believe that care and prudence can help. So, as you can see, I'm warning people to take any illness seriously. I'm encouraging them to immediately report any flu-like symptoms and to quarantine before it has a chance to spread."

"I see that."

"And Daniel has already written to his father about having areas ready for quarantine at the hospital, just in case."

"Do you really think it will be that bad? I mean here in Sunset Cove?"

"According to Daniel, it could make it here. Hopefully not. But if readers take heed to warnings like this, the outcome might be better for everyone."

"Tomorrow's paper is going to be rather dark and gloomy." He gathered the papers and slowly shook his head. "Just glad it's midweek and not Saturday."

"Maybe that old saying is true," she said. "You know that it's darkest before the dawn."

"One can hope."

Fear and anxiety rushed through Katy as the messenger boy parked his bike on the sidewalk in front of her house. She'd been out on the porch with Lucy, lifting her spirits with a bit of late

213

May sunshine. But as the uniformed boy strode toward her, her spirits plummeted.

"Telegram for Mrs. James Stafford," he formally announced.

"Thank you. That's me." She reached for the telegram and, clutching it and the baby to her chest, hurried into the house, slamming the door behind her.

"What is it?" Sarah Rose asked with a furrowed brow.

"It's a telegram. Here, Lucy. You rest for a minute." She eased the infant into a bassinet and, with shaking hands, tore open the envelope and read. "It's from Jim!" she cried. "He's on his way home right now."

"Thank God." Sarah came over to look.

"It says he'll arrive at our train station on—oh, Sarah—it looks like it's today! He says he'll be on the afternoon train." She thrust the telegram to Sarah. "Read it for me—make sure I'm not just imagining this."

"You're right, honey. It says Tuesday, May 28, afternoon train."

"Oh, I can't believe it." Katy was pacing back and forth. "I need to bathe and fix my hair and—"

"Calm down, Miss Katy. It won't do you any good to go into fits."

"Yes, yes. I know. But Jim will be here in less than three hours."

"That's plenty of time to get pretty."

"And we need something special for dinner. Do we have anything nice?"

"While Lucy naps and you make yourself pretty, I'll run to the store."

"Thank you—thank you!" Katy hugged her. "What would I do without you?"

Sarah Rose smiled. "I'm just glad your man is coming home, Miss Katy. It's a happy day indeed!"

"And when you go to the store, please, don't tell anyone that Jim's coming home. I don't want a lot of fanfare. Not at first. I want Jim all to myself."

"That seems a good plan."

"I don't even want Mother or my grandparents to know just yet."

Sarah Rose nodded. "I'm sure Jim will appreciate a quiet homecoming. I expect he'll be worn out from the traveling."

"Yes. We'll make sure he's well rested before we tell the others our good news."

By three o'clock, Katy felt that she'd managed to put herself together fairly well. Her hair was pinned up and she had on one of her favorite spring dresses—and not one of the military-influenced styles. This one was pale pink with ribbons and flounces—and showed off her feminine curves. She felt certain Jim would appreciate it.

As she got into the Runabout, she took in a deep, calming breath. There was no need to hurry since the train wouldn't be there for forty minutes yet. The baby had been fed, and Sarah Rose had promised to dress Lucy in a pretty gown. And she'd gotten a nice roast to put in the oven for tonight's dinner. Jim's homecoming was destined to be just about perfect.

Katy took her time driving through the spring countryside. Everything looked even more beautiful than usual. Maybe it was just her, but the world looked picture perfect. The grass and trees were so many lovely shades of green, and the wildflowers along the road's edge bloomed so perfectly, and the bright blue sky . . . she wanted to get out her paints and replicate this scene. But that would have to wait for another day. Perhaps she and Jim could take a romantic picnic together.

To her relief, no one from town was at the train station. She really didn't know what to expect when Jim arrived, but she suspected he might be somewhat uncomfortable about his changed condition. But she felt ready for this. She'd rehearsed all afternoon the various ways she would calmly take the absent arm in stride. She would act as if nothing had changed for him, as if he still had two strong arms. The important thing was that he was alive and that he was coming home. That was all that mattered to her.

She got out of the car and, after removing her

car coat, she secured her favorite wide brimmed summer hat. Hearing the whistle of the rapidly approaching train, she took in a deep breath, smoothed her skirt, and strolled into the terminal.

Despite her placid outward demeanor, Katy's heart pounded at the sound of hissing train brakes. She silently prayed for strength as the big black engine slowed down for the platform, watching as a porter leaped out and got the step into place then hopped back inside, emerging with a brown duffle bag, followed by a uniformed officer. For a moment, she didn't believe it was Jim. This man had a dark beard and looked older and thinner. He also had on dark tinted glasses. But it was the man's two arms that convinced her it couldn't be Jim. So she looked beyond him, hoping to spy her beloved emerging.

But suddenly the train was leaving, and the thin soldier was the only other person on the platform besides her. Feeling rude for staring, she glanced away. And that's when she heard him call her name.

"Jim?" She turned back, staring in shock at this stranger.

With the duffle bag in his right hand, he hesitantly approached. "It's me, Katy. I'm home." Even his voice seemed different. But she said his name again—and when he nodded, she ran toward him, blinking back tears. As he dropped his bag, she ran into his arms, but as he embraced her, she felt the difference in him. His body seemed rigid and board-like, and not as muscular as she remembered. But it was the hardness of his left hand that reminded her . . . the missing arm was replaced with a prosthetic. Doc Hollister had explained about such devices when she'd been in the hospital with Lucy. He'd even shown her disturbing photographs in a medical catalogue in an effort to prepare her for what was to come.

"Oh, Jim," she sobbed softly into his chest. "I'm so happy you're home."

He held her back and looked down at her. "I'm glad to hear that." His tone sounded oddly flat. "I'm glad to see you too, Katy. You are even more beautiful than I remembered."

"You must be exhausted from your journey." She stepped back as he picked up his bag. "I drove the Runabout. And I didn't tell anyone else you were coming today. Well, except for Sarah Rose. She's home with Lucy. But no one else will be around just yet, and we'll go directly home."

"Good. That sounds good."

As she led him to the parked car, she chatted nervously, telling him about Lucy's latest developments, the roast Sarah was making, about what a lovely drive she'd had through the countryside. "And I'll drive us home. I know you must be tired."

"Thank you." Again his tone sounded stiff and stilted.

Relieved that he didn't protest not driving, she got into the driver's seat. She knew her grandfather was unable to drive without the use of two hands, but she wasn't sure about that prosthetic. Was it only for appearances, or did it actually function like a real hand? She was embarrassed to ask. As she drove, Katy pointed out the verdant green trees and colorful spring flowers, but she stopped when she realized Jim wasn't even looking. Instead, he stared down at his lap. At least he appeared to be looking down. It was hard to tell due to those odd tinted glasses.

"Are your eyes all right?" she asked as they came into town. "I mean because of the glasses. Were they injured somehow?"

"My eyes are fine," he said curtly.

"Oh." She nodded. Why did he sound like that? She wasn't sure exactly what the emotion behind that tone was, but it sounded slightly angry or irritated. Had she done something wrong? Or perhaps he was simply tired.

"Well, here we are." She pulled up to the carriage house and tugged on the parking brake. "Home sweet home."

"*What?* Where is this?" He sounded confused. "Where are you taking me?"

"This used to be Grandmother's house. Remember, I wrote to you about how she gave it to me? I mean to *us.* Sarah Rose and Lucy and

I have been living here for a couple of months now. It's very comfortable."

"Oh." He pursed his lips as they got out of the car. "I guess . . . I forgot."

"I'm sure you've had plenty to think about." She waited as he got his bag then led him up to the house. "I can't wait for you to meet your daughter, Jim."

"My daughter?" He paused in front of the door, waiting for her to open it.

"Yes, you'll have to get used to that. You're a daddy now."

"Yes . . . of course. A daughter."

"Lucy Ann is a darling. I hope you don't mind that I named her after Mother and Grandmother." She felt uneasy as they went inside, but she kept her voice bright and cheery. "Well, here we are. Excuse me a minute, while I check on something." She ducked into the kitchen to find Sarah slicing vegetables. "Jim's in the living room," she whispered nervously. "But he's acting, well, a bit strange."

Sarah Rose simply nodded. "I'm sure it feels strange for him to be home. He's been away for so long, Miss Katy. Might be an adjustment."

"Yes, of course. That must be it. Anyway, I'll introduce him to Lucy now."

"I just put her down for a nap. She'll probably be sleeping."

"That's okay. He can just get a quick look at

her." Katy went back to find Jim standing in the middle of the living room, still holding onto his duffle bag, and still wearing those strange tinted glasses. "Do you want to see the baby?"

"The baby?"

"The baby, your daughter—Lucy Ann." Katy tried not to sound aggravated at how disconnected he seemed in regard to their child. "Sarah said she's asleep right now. But we can take a peek at her."

"Yes. The baby. Of course. I'd like to see her." He still clung to his duffle bag.

"Right this way." She led him down the hallway, stopping by the nursery door. "Can you see with those dark glasses on?" she whispered.

"Oh, yes, I forgot." He set down the bag then carefully removed and folded the glasses, slipping them into his chest pocket.

"This is the nursery," she whispered as she opened the door. She reached for his hand, realizing it was the prosthetic. Although it was covered in a leather glove, it felt hard and cold. But instead of reacting, she continued to lead him over to the bassinette where Lucy was peacefully sleeping. She waited as Jim stood there, gazing down upon her, his face void of expression. He made no move to touch her or kiss her or anything. It was as if she was a stranger.

Finally, Katy tugged on him. "You'll see more of her later."

Back in the hallway, she closed the nursery door then pointed to the master bedroom. "This is our room, Jim. I had your clothes and things moved out of storage from your old boarding house. I put them away as best I could." She showed him his closet and bureau. "Feel free to rearrange them as you like. But everything you need should be here."

He just nodded.

"Maybe you'd like to lie down and rest before dinner," she suggested. "You do seem tired."

"Yes. I am tired. I will rest." Again, he sounded mechanical. As if he'd rehearsed those words. And when he walked over to the bed, he reminded her of a windup toy soldier, just going through the steps.

"I'll let you know when it's dinnertime." She closed the drapes to darken the room and then turned to watch him sitting on the chair by the bed. "It's so wonderful to have you home again, Jim. I've waited so long for this. I hope you're as happy as I am that we're back together again."

But he didn't respond. Instead, using his one good hand, he meticulously unlaced and removed one shoe, letting it fall to the floor with a dull thud. And then he went to work on the other. She was tempted to offer help but didn't want to insult him or treat him like a child. When she finally paused by the door, Jim was already starting to lie down.

"Rest well," she whispered.

He said nothing—simply leaned back and closed his eyes, almost as if he wanted to shut out everything around him. Including her. As she quietly closed the door, she told herself her poor husband was understandably exhausted after his long days of travel. But as she walked through the quiet house, she knew something more was going on. Something she couldn't understand.

CHAPTER 18

Anna waited as Mac finished reading her editorial piece about preventing the growing epidemic. "Is the Spanish Flu really as bad as you've made this sound?" He frowned as he laid down the paper and picked up his coffee cup.

"According to Daniel, it is very serious." Anna spread marmalade on her toast.

"Let me have that newspaper," Lucille said. "I want to read about it."

"Hello in the house?" Katy called out from the front room. "Anybody home?"

"We're in the dining room," Anna called back. "Having breakfast."

"Want to join us?" Lucille offered.

"No. I just need to talk to someone—about something." Katy's eyes looked troubled and she was actually wringing her hands.

"What is it?" Anna asked with concern. "Is Lucy all right?"

"Yes, yes. Lucy is fine. I came over to tell you that Jim is home."

"Jim is home?" Lucille dropped the paper.

"You mean home in the United States?" Mac clarified.

"I mean home next door." Katy pulled out a chair and sat.

"How on earth did that—"

"Yesterday. The afternoon train. But something is wrong with him. He's not the same as—"

"He's home—in your house *right now?*" Anna interrupted.

"Yes. That's what I just said."

"Is he with the baby?" Anna asked.

"No. He was still sleeping. He fell asleep yesterday afternoon. He didn't even wake for dinner. He was so tired—"

"He's in your bedroom?" Anna demanded.

"Yes, Mother. We are married, after all. Why are you being—"

"Has he been with the baby?" Anna asked.

"Barely. He saw Lucy yesterday, but it was only for a—"

"Katy, you don't understand." Anna stood. "I just wrote about this in today's paper. You probably haven't seen it yet."

"Wrote about what? That Jim came home? How did you—"

"No, that's not it," Mac intervened. "Anna wrote about the Spanish Flu and how the epidemic is spreading like wildfire. It's extremely dangerous."

"According to Daniel, it can hit anyone of

any age—including you and the baby," Anna clarified. "The war is the big the reason for this epidemic. Servicemen get sick, are hospitalized, sent home, and the disease spreads."

"And Jim was in the hospital," Mac reminded her. "It's possible he was exposed."

"Or even while he traveled by train," Lucille pointed out. "Your mother is right to be worried, Katy. Jim could very well be carrying the deadly germs that spread this disease."

"And you said Jim is acting strangely." Anna stood. "It's possible he's ill."

"And he could be like Typhoid Mary!" Katy's eyes grew huge. "My baby!"

"Go back home," Mac told her. "Keep Jim away from the baby."

"I'm calling JD right now." Anna hurried to the hallway telephone and called JD's home. When he didn't answer she called the hospital, telling them it was an emergency.

"I need to speak to Dr. Hollister immediately." When he came to the phone, she quickly explained the situation.

"I'm sending an ambulance."

"Is that necessary? Katy or I could drive—"

"Everyone needs to avoid contact with him, Anna. You should know that. You wrote that piece and—"

"Yes, yes. I'm sure you're right. I'll let Katy know."

"And tell her to stay away from him. The driver and attendant will handle Jim. But tell Katy to call me as soon as Jim is removed." Anna agreed to that then hurried to call Katy, explaining that JD was sending the ambulance.

"The ambulance?"

"Yes. He insisted. And he said for you to avoid Jim. Is he still asleep?"

"Sarah Rose thought she heard him get up."

"What about the baby? Is she safe?"

"Sarah's in the nursery with Lucy. She read your editorial, Mother. She understands the danger—she assured me Jim hasn't been near Lucy this morning."

"Good. Oh, dear, I think I hear the ambulance siren."

"I do too. I don't like it. Do they have to use it?"

"They're probably enjoying themselves. You better go let them in. But don't be around Jim, Katy. Let them handle Jim. And JD said you're to call him after Jim is taken to the hospital." As Anna hung up, she silently prayed. First of all she prayed that Katy and Lucy and Sarah would remain healthy . . . and then she prayed for Jim. Poor Jim . . . to come home to such a welcome.

Katy's feelings were mixed as she watched the oversized vehicle leave the house. She couldn't erase that frightened look in her husband's eyes.

Still wearing his uniform from yesterday, he'd been rumpled and disoriented. He clearly didn't understand what was happening. But all she could do was stand by—at a distance—and watch. She felt like she'd betrayed him somehow . . . and yet she was relieved to have him gone.

Remembering her mother's instructions to call Doc Hollister at the hospital, she went to the telephone. First he questioned her, similar to what her mother had done.

"How much contact did you have with Jim?"

"Hardly any. We hugged at the station. But he seemed different. I even wondered if he wasn't well."

"Did you sleep in the same bed?"

"Actually, I slept in the spare room. He was tossing and turning and moaning and groaning. I just couldn't bring myself to sleep—"

"Good for you. And the baby. Did he hold the baby?"

"No. He just looked at her."

"Did he see anyone else? Your family or—"

"No. He didn't even see Sarah Rose."

"That's all good. Now I need you to do a few things. Let Sarah Rose mind the baby since she's not been exposed. Since you've been exposed, you'll have to manage these tasks yourself." He began to list the chores. "Remove all the bedding and any clothes Jim used or brought with him. I'd tell you to just throw them away, but we don't know for sure that Jim is ill. For now, get them away from the house and everyone."

"In the garden shed?"

"Yes. That's fine. Do the same with any clothing you wore while with him. And wash down any surface that Jim touched. Hot soapy water. And then you take a hot bath and wash your hair."

"Is that everything?" Katy felt tired just thinking of all that work.

"Don't use the bedroom that Jim slept in. Open the windows in there, but shut it off from the house. You will have to sleep somewhere else."

"That's fine. What about Lucy? Is there anything I should do to protect her?"

"First of all, you'll have to avoid all contact with her. This means she'll have to be bottle fed from now on. I'll send some information over for Sarah Rose. And I think it would be wise for both Sarah Rose and the baby to move elsewhere for the time being. And they shouldn't be exposed to anyone."

"Is that really necessary?"

"If Jim has the Spanish Flu, it's not only necessary, it's required."

"I guess Sarah and the baby could be at my grandparents' home. They could have the top floor to themselves."

"Yes, that's a good plan. And if Jim really does have the Spanish Flu, he will need to be quarantined until he's well. And then you'll have to remain quarantined at home. But we'll need to watch you for symptoms. If symptoms develop, you will be hospitalized and quarantined here as well."

"How long until we know if Jim is sick?" she asked helplessly.

"That depends on if and when he was exposed. I'll know more after I examine him. In the meantime, you get to work on that house, Katy. And then stay out of the way while Sarah Rose moves the baby out."

By noon, Katy had completed her list of cleaning chores and now, isolated in the guest bedroom, she waited for Sarah Rose to relocate herself and Lucy Ann to her grandparents' house. Mickey and Bernice were helping move things, and Lucille was clearing out one of the top floor bedrooms for the temporary nursery. And since she was alone and tired and discouraged, there was no one to see her crying. So she let her tears flow freely.

Life as she knew seemed to have ended yesterday. It was as if Jim's arrival in Sunset Cove had turned her whole world upside down. Oh, she felt sorry for him. He was very pathetic . . . and lost. But she also felt a bit of anger toward him. If he'd been around sick people and exposed to this horrible disease, why had he brought it home to his loved ones? If they were his loved ones. Katy hadn't felt particularly loved by him.

"I'm all done here," Sarah Rose called through the closed door. "Lucy Ann is all set up in her new nursery. Don't fret about her, Miss Katy. She looks perfectly healthy to me. But I'll watch her closely and keep you advised if I'm concerned."

"Thank you." Katy choked back a sob.

"And Bernice already mixed up some of the formulated milk that Dr. Hollister sent over. And Lucy took to the bottle with no problem. She's fast asleep now. So don't you worry about her. And if you do feel worried, you just pray, honey. That's better."

"I'll try to keep that in mind." She reached for her handkerchief.

"Bernice plans to bring your meals over for you. She'll leave them in the kitchen."

"Tell her thanks." Katy blew her nose. "And thank you, Sarah Rose. I know my baby is in good hands."

"And it probably won't be for long. We're all praying for you and Jim to be well."

Katy thanked her again . . . and then Sarah left and Katy felt more alone than she'd ever felt in her life.

She knew it was time to pray.

Chapter 19

When she realized how distressed her daughter had become, Anna took it upon herself to communicate with JD regarding Jim's condition. She spoke to him every day and so far, for nearly a week, he had assured her that Jim was showing no flu symptoms.

"He's just very worn down from his amputation and not fully recovered," he explained over coffee. "I got his army records and discovered he hadn't been officially released from medical care."

"How did that happen?"

"He'd been shipped over with a lot of other patients. Apparently, he was one of the few ambulatory cases so, while the patients were being transferred to a train headed for the Walter Reed's Clinic in Washington DC—and the medics were occupied—Jim simply wandered away. When no one was looking, he bought himself a ticket for a westbound train and left."

"Does that mean he must return to Washington DC?"

"No. I secured permission for him to continue his treatment here."

"Did you find out if Jim was exposed to the Spanish Flu?"

He shook his head. "They wouldn't commit to anything, but it's no secret there are servicemen under quarantine in various parts of the country. Probably DC too."

"Yes. Daniel even mentioned some places were keeping it under wraps."

"So I plan to have Jim in isolation here for another week . . . possibly longer. If no symptoms develop and he's strong enough, he can go home."

"Strong enough?"

"He is greatly debilitated, Anna. He's underweight, and I feel fairly sure he's suffering from shell shock."

"Shell shock?" Anna had read about this puzzling condition but found it hard to believe that a brave man like Jim Stafford could succumb to it. "What makes you believe Jim has shell shock?"

"He's not himself, Anna. He doesn't sleep well. He's shaky and distraught. His speech is stilted, and he's full of uncertainty. From what I can see—and based upon my research—he is likely suffering shell shock. Or what more modern doctors are now calling battle fatigue."

"Then you believe it's an actual physical

disorder? I've read a bit myself. And I know that some people consider it an excuse for cowardly soldiers, in order to escape active service." Anna glanced around the café, anxious that no one was eavesdropping on this rather personal conversation.

"I've no doubt that some spineless soldiers resort to such deceitful measures. But Jim was already discharged due to his amputation. He wouldn't need to pretend to have shell shock or battle fatigue."

"Yes, that's true. But can you tell me more about this malady? I'd like to understand it better." Anna wanted to grasp this as much for Katy's sake as her own.

"Well, some experts view it as a weakness in nature or character. A psychological defect of sorts. I suppose I'm inclined to agree."

"But Jim has never been weak. He stood up to rum-runners and bootleggers and was even shot while helping me with a news story." Her defenses rose, setting down her coffee cup with a loud clink. "I really can't understand how a man like Jim could possibly have shell shock."

"He's been through hell, Anna. According to the records I received, his unit suffered a horrific ambush by the Germans. Many of the men in his charge died right in front of him. He nearly died himself from blood loss, but medics got him out in time. Not soon enough to prevent a nasty infection. That's the reason he remained in the British hospital for so long. His infected wounds nearly killed him."

"Oh . . . I didn't know. So that could contribute to his . . . uh, shell shock." She said the last words quietly as the waitress came to them with a fresh pot of coffee.

"According to my research, there are numerous theories about the disorder. I believe modern artillery could be to blame" He paused as their cups were refilled. "Some leading psychiatrists believe that loud explosions and speeding projectiles create a psychological change to the human brain—and that leads to the symptoms of what we call shell shock."

"How strange. I've never heard of that theory. I suppose it makes sense." She stirred a bit of sugar into her cup.

"Not many people understand shell shock, but there's a disorder called *railway spine* that's similar. Victims of train wrecks experience the same symptoms."

"Is there any treatment for shell shock?"

"There's electric shock therapy."

"Oh, dear, that sounds dreadful."

"Also I've read about psychological analysis and what they call *talking cures,* but I don't buy into that kind of softness. My recommendation would be for Jim to return to his old way of life. He should go back to work at the newspaper. He needs routine and good hard work to occupy his mind—and in time, this disorder will fade away."

"You really think work is the answer?" She studied his creased brow as he sipped his coffee. Although he was playing the expert, she wondered how much real experience he'd had with this disorder. Still, his suggestion made sense.

"That's how the Brits are treating it. And they've got plenty of cases since they've been at war much longer than the US. England has created *work villages* for veterans who suffer from shell shock. The men live and work in a controlled environment, and they get better . . . over time."

Anna sighed. "That's a lot to take in. I wonder how much of this I should relay to Katy. She's already distressed."

"No need to tell her anything about the shell shock. Not yet."

"And what about Katy being quarantined? How soon until she can return to her regular routines? She misses her baby fiercely."

"If she shows no symptoms by the end of the week, I think she can be reunited with her baby. I checked on both mother and child only yesterday, and they both appeared healthy."

"Can I tell her that?"

"Yes. Maybe it will lift her spirits."

Anna thanked him and then hurried back to her

office in order to use the telephone to call Katy. She quickly communicated this bit of good news to her. "Just think, honey, in a few days, you'll have your baby back in your arms."

"Yes. That's wonderful. But what about Jim? How is he doing? Doc Hollister never says much of anything to me. I get the feeling he's trying to protect me from something. But I'm his wife, I should have a right to know."

"JD wants to keep Jim for another week, or maybe longer. Just to observe him." Anna told Katy a bit about the severity of Jim's battle injuries. "He hadn't even been discharged from his medical care at the military hospital, but he just got on a train and came home anyway."

"That might explain why he was acting so strangely. Poor Jim. He just wanted to come home. Well, we'll help him get better."

"Yes. I'm sure we will." Anna bit her lip.

"Do you think he'll be back to his old self by the time Doc Hollister sends him home?" Katy sounded hopeful.

"I don't really know, honey. I guess we'll just have to wait and see. But JD did recommend Jim return to work at the newspaper. And I'll certainly be happy to have him back."

"Oh, that sounds great. Jim loved writing for the paper. I'm sure he'll be happy to hear about that."

"Yes. I think it'll be good medicine for him."

But as Anna hung up the phone, she wasn't so sure. Would work really be enough? JD's concern for Jim had surprised her. And shell shock? Was that the right diagnosis? Anna had never seen Jim Stafford acting weak about anything.

By the end of the week, Katy's world returned to normal. Sarah Rose and Lucy were back home, the house returned to order, and best of all no one had gotten sick. Including Jim. According to Doc Hollister, Jim did not have the Spanish Flu. "And I am fairly certain that he never had it," he told Katy after he stopped by to check on her and the baby on Friday afternoon.

"So when can he come home?" she eagerly asked.

"He needs to remain in my care for at least another week. Maybe longer."

"Why?"

"He needs to gain weight. If he hadn't snuck away to come home, he would be in the Washington DC hospital right now."

"Yes, my mother told me about that. But couldn't he put on weight here at home? Among other things, it would be cheaper."

"The army is covering his hospitalization."

"Oh." Katy ran her hand over Lucy's fuzzy head. "But it seems that Jim would recover more quickly if he were home with us . . . with his loved ones. Don't you think?"

Doc Hollister frowned. "Not necessarily. Right now, Jim needs peace and quiet and good medical care. And we'll see he gets it."

"But what if we gave that to him right here?" She waved to the pretty living room behind her. "Wouldn't Jim prefer this to a stark hospital room? And you know what a good cook Sarah Rose is."

"Yes, I'm well aware of what a good cook she is. Much better than that silly woman you stuck me with." He scowled. "That was a sly move on your part."

"Sarah Rose is a free woman," she reminded him. "She makes her own choices."

"As I know." He softened a bit. "Don't tell her I miss her."

"But back to Jim. Couldn't you see your way to let him come home, dear Dr. Hollister?" She gave him her most beguiling look.

"Like Sarah Rose, Jim is a free man. I will let him decide which is best." He stood, closing his doctor's bag and picking up his hat. "But here's the truth, Katy. I think he would prefer to remain in the hospital."

"I find that hard to believe." She walked him to the front door.

"Jim is not well." He put on his hat. "And he knows it."

"Oh?" Katy felt confused. "But you said he doesn't have the flu."

"Yes. But he does have a condition. And the best treatment for the time being is to keep him in the hospital. If he puts on enough weight and gets enough good rest, I am happy to discharge him in a week or so."

"Oh, well, a week then." She brightened. "That's not too long. And can I visit him now that he's not in quarantine?"

"That is up to you. And your husband." He tipped his head. "Good day."

As Katy closed the door, she couldn't quite make sense of the old doctor. Unless she was imagining things, it seemed he was trying to keep her and Jim apart. But why? Was he just being persnickety and opinionated again? Whatever the case, she intended to pay Jim a visit. But that could wait until visiting hours. Right now she just wanted to enjoy having her baby and Sarah Rose back at home. That was enough for today.

Chapter 20

Katy dressed carefully on Saturday. It was the first time she'd been out of the house since her quarantine, and her plan was to visit her husband at the hospital then go to the dress shop to visit with her friends there. But when she got to the hospital, asking for Jim's room number, she was informed that Jim wasn't allowed visitors.

"Are you sure about this?" she asked politely. "I realize that was true while my husband was under quarantine, but Dr. Hollister told me just yesterday that his quarantine was over."

"It's doctor's orders," the receptionist told her. "No visitors."

"Is the doctor here?" Katy didn't hide her irritation.

"Only Dr. Myers. And he's seeing patients right now."

"Do you know when my husband *will* be allowed visitors?"

She shook her head. "I'm sorry, Mrs. Stafford. But I suggest you call ahead next time."

"Thank you, I'll do that." Katy turned and

marched out. What was wrong with those people? What right did they have to keep a wife from seeing her husband? She fumed all the way to the dress shop and then, after going through the back door and into the privacy of the workroom, she poured out her disgruntled story to her grandmother and Clara.

"I would think they'd want you to spend time with Jim," Clara said. "To help him get better."

"I agree." Lucille nodded eagerly. "And you look so pretty, dear. That alone should make poor Jim feel better."

"Do you think it's a mistake?" Clara asked as she finished off the hem on a dress. "Maybe you should call Dr. Hollister."

"I don't know. He was treating me oddly yesterday. I almost got the impression he didn't want me to see Jim. Do you suppose he thinks my presence would be upsetting?" Katy paused to check on little Larry, who was contentedly sleeping in the crib in the corner. That meant Ellen was probably working out front.

"I don't see how." Lucille pinned a silk rose onto a straw hat and held it up. "Everyone knows how much Jim adores you. I still remember his face on your wedding day. I never saw such an enormous smile as when you came walking down the aisle."

"You were such a pretty bride," Clara added.

"And your time in quarantine hasn't hurt you

any." Lucille patted Katy's cheek. "You look well rested and prettier than ever." She looked at the back of Katy's dress, where the gap had been closed and neatly buttoned. "And you seem to be getting your waistline back too."

"I didn't have much appetite last week."

"Well, don't fret about not getting to see Jim today." Lucille made another adjustment to the hat. "Just be glad that your man is home, Katy. And that no one here has the Spanish Flu."

"Yes, that's plenty to be thankful for." Clara smiled. "Now, you better get out there and say hello to Ellen, or she is likely to throw a fit."

"Here." Lucille handed Katy the hat. "Why don't you take this out to Gladys Rollins. She's waiting for it."

Glad for the distraction of working at the shop, Katy carried the pretty hat out, presenting it to the police chief's wife and helping her to try it on. "That looks lovely on you," she told her.

"And it's perfect with your rose-colored dress." Ellen smiled.

"Just don't you girls tell my husband how much it cost," Gladys said in a conspirator's tone.

"Your secret is safe with us," Katy assured her.

"Yes. Husbands don't need to know everything." Ellen giggled.

"Speaking of husbands, did I hear that yours is home?" Gladys's brows arched.

"Yes. But he's still in the hospital."

"Oh, dear, is he all right?"

Katy felt relieved that she wasn't questioned about the Spanish Flu. She'd asked her family to keep that information quiet until they knew for sure what was going on. "Jim is still recovering from the wounds he got in the war. Doc Hollister is taking excellent care of him and refuses to let Jim out of the hospital until he gains some weight." She frowned. "My poor husband was skin and bones when I picked him up at the train station. I know I will feel much better when he fattens up a bit."

"I wish my husband had that problem. I keep telling Harvey he needs to tighten his belt—and I'm not talking about our budget either." She laughed as she paid Ellen for the new hat. "Put my dowdy old hat in the box and I'll just wear this one out."

After Gladys left, Ellen hugged Katy. "I'm so glad you're okay. Mother told me to tell no one about your quarantine, and I didn't let out a peep. But I was worried for you and little Lucy. And Jim too, of course. I was praying for all of you."

"Thank you." Katy adjusted the collar on a blouse on a mannequin.

"So he doesn't get to come home yet? That's too bad."

"And they wouldn't even let me visit him today."

"Well, at least your husband is home . . . or

almost." Ellen frowned. "I haven't heard from Lawrence in weeks."

"But do you keep writing to him?"

"I try. But I'm not as good at it as you were."

Katy considered this. Did all those letters she'd sent to the hospital mean nothing to Jim? He'd seemed oblivious to everything from the baby's name to where they'd been living. Had he even read those letters? And if not, why not? Katy had heard stories of soldiers who'd gotten involved with French women, but surely Jim wouldn't do anything like that. She knew he wouldn't. And yet . . . something was definitely wrong. And it wasn't just the missing arm either.

When Anna learned that Katy had been denied access to Jim at the hospital, she decided to do a little investigating herself. On Monday morning, she went to see JD, demanding to know what was going on.

"It was Jim's request."

"He doesn't want to see Katy?" Anna blinked. "Why not?"

"I don't know. He says he's not ready." He looked down at the clipboard he was studying.

"When will he be ready?"

"I don't know. Maybe you should ask him."

"Am I allowed to visit him?"

"Sure. He didn't say he wouldn't see anyone else. Just that he wasn't ready to face Katy."

"Face Katy?" Anna frowned. "What does he think she will do?"

"I didn't mean it like that." He held the clipboard up. "I need to go check on this patient. But you can go talk to Jim if you like." He told her the room number.

As Anna walked down the long hallway toward Jim's room, she braced herself for what she might find. Katy had already told her about the beard and tinted glasses, the wooden hand, and how emaciated he was. But when she peeked through the open door, she was pleasantly surprised to see he was clean shaven and without dark glasses. From this angle, she couldn't even see his left side—the missing arm.

"Hello?" she called out cheerfully.

He narrowed his eyes and then nodded. "Come in, Anna." His tone wasn't unfriendly, but it didn't sound like him.

As she went closer to his bed, she sensed that he was uncomfortable. "I don't mean to intrude, but I wanted to see how you're doing."

He shrugged then held up his left arm. He didn't have on the prosthetic hand that Katy had told her about, and the wrapped stump ended just below his elbow. Not as bad as she'd imagined . . . but still hard to see.

"You look better than I expected." She smiled. "I see you've shaved."

He rubbed his chin. "Yes. I had forgotten about

that. I didn't shave on the ship. Or on the train. Poor Katy."

"Well, we're just glad you don't have the Spanish Flu. That was quite a scare."

"So I heard."

"How are you feeling?" She pulled up a chair and, not waiting to be invited, sat down, closely studying him.

"I think . . . I feel better."

"JD—Dr. Hollister—told me he wants to keep you awhile."

"I need to gain weight."

She nodded. "You look very thin."

"Yes."

"Dr. Hollister also mentioned you may have shell shock."

He looked surprised but nodded.

"I hope that was okay. I think he wanted to tell Katy, but it seems he—or maybe it's you—are trying to protect her. Is that right?"

He nodded again.

"Well, that's admirable. But I think Katy is a lot stronger than you think."

"It is . . . it's a lot. She's young."

"That's true. But, as you know, Katy has always been old for her years. And she is very strong. She's proved that again and again."

"I know."

"And you're very strong too, Jim." Anna began to remind him of the brave things he'd done while helping her with news stories. How he'd chased down criminals and even taken a bullet. "I bet you were just as brave on the battlefield."

He barely nodded, but his eyes were sad.

"I know you lost a lot out there, Jim. And your men too. I can't even imagine what that must've felt like for you. We cover war stories in almost every issue of the paper, and it never gets easier."

"Yes."

"Well, I just want you to know that I understand. I mean, I don't understand everything, of course, but I understand how this must be very hard on you. And losing your hand. That can't be easy either."

"It's not that bad."

She tried not to look surprised.

"Compared to others. It's not that bad."

"Yes, of course." She glanced over at the darkened window. "Do you want me to open the blinds for you—and let some light and fresh sea air in here? I'll bet you have a good view from this room."

"No. Leave it."

"Oh?"

"The color . . . it hurts my eyes." He reached for something on the bedside table and then put on the tinted glasses that Katy had told her about. "I need these."

"The color hurts your eyes?" Anna was confused. Did he mean the light?

"In battle. In the trench. It's all brown. Many shades of brown."

"Oh?" She tried to imagine it. "Like the news photographs we get?"

"Yes. But there's no smell in the photos."

"It must have been horrible, Jim." Her heart went out to him.

"Yes."

"I did some reading about shell shock. Some people feel that talking about it helps."

"I don't know."

"I can understand that you might not want to tell these things to Katy. In fact, I'm not sure that would be good."

"I agree."

"But you have other friends. And I can listen."

"No, you can't." His brow creased. "Not you."

"Maybe a man would be easier to talk with. There's Mac. He is no stranger to war stories. You could talk to him. Or there's Frank at the newspaper office. I think he would be a good one to—"

"I don't want to talk about it to anyone."

"But I've been watching you just now, Jim. You seemed to relax just a little when you were talking. Maybe it's good to get some of this out."

"No." He firmly shook his head.

"Maybe in time."

He said nothing, just stared down at the sheet.

"I don't want to wear out my welcome." She

smiled. "Assuming I was welcome at all. I did sort of burst in on you."

"It's okay." He looked up and almost smiled. "You're a friend."

"And I'm your mother-in-law," she reminded him. "And although I wanted to visit you as an old friend, I also came on behalf of Katy. She is brokenhearted that she can't come visit you. I hope you'll reconsider keeping her away. You'll be surprised at how much she can bear. She's a lot stronger than she looks."

"I know."

"And wouldn't it be better to spend some time with her here than to wait until you get home? You two need to get reacquainted, Jim."

"I know."

"Katy is actually worried that you have stopped loving her. She didn't want me to tell you that, but it's the truth."

"I love her." His tone sounded more like the old Jim. "I do."

"I thought you did. But she needs to know it. She has never stopped loving you."

"Are you sure?"

"I'm positive. But she's confused, Jim. She doesn't know where she stands. And she knows that you've changed. She just doesn't know why. You're going to have to be honest with her."

He pursed his lips and shook his head.

"I don't mean you have to tell her all about the

war and how horrible it was. I think you're right, she doesn't need to know all about that. But she does need to know what you're struggling with. I haven't mentioned anything about shell shock to her. But she needs to know. Otherwise, she might come to the wrong conclusions. She might assume you don't love her."

"Yes." He sighed. "I think you're right."

"Good. Besides being your mother-in-law, I'd still like to be your boss. JD thinks you can return to work soon. After you've regained your weight and feel stronger. I know I'd love to have you back. It hasn't been the same without you."

He brightened. "Really?"

"Absolutely. So I hope you'll do all you can to get well enough to get kicked out of here. And I hope you'll talk to Katy."

"I will. Ask her to come."

"Thank you!" She stood and reached for his good hand. Grasping it in hers, she patted it.

"Thank you," he said quietly.

"Now I'll let you rest." She squeezed his hand. "And I want to hear that you're cleaning your plate at every meal."

He mumbled, "Yeah," and she told him good-bye. She felt slightly encouraged as she left, but she also knew Jim had a huge mountain to climb. She prayed he was strong enough to start taking the first steps . . . and that he'd let his loved ones help him.

CHAPTER 21

A fter more than a week of daily afternoon visits, Katy still couldn't figure out her husband. Some days he would be up and about and almost seemed like his same old self, and she would leave the hospital feeling light and hopeful. But on other days, Jim would still be in bed and barely able to string a sentence together. But at least he'd gained enough weight to be discharged. Hopefully, that was a good thing.

"Are you nervous?" Anna asked on Saturday morning.

Katy nodded, carefully rearranging the roses she and her mother had just cut. "I suppose it doesn't matter, but I want everything to be perfect."

"I think that's nice." Anna looked around the living room. "I'm so impressed how you've taken Mac and Lucille's castoffs and merged them into something so beautiful. But then, you've always had the touch. When Daniel comes home . . . and if we marry and share a home . . . I want you to come help me set it up."

"I'd love to do that. But first you must let me help with your wedding."

"Speaking of weddings, have you heard Clara's news?"

"No—what is it? Did Randall finally pop the question?"

"Yes. She is over the moon."

"Oh, wonderful. I've already told her I want to help with her wedding. When is it going to be?"

"Soon. She wants to be married in June."

"Just like Jim and me." Katy sighed.

"That's right. You're approaching your first anniversary."

"I have no expectations." Katy frowned.

"Oh, that's not fair. You never know what's around the next corner. I miss my optimistic girl."

"I'm sorry, Mother. I'm still here. And thinking about Clara and Randall's wedding does cheer me up. Nothing like a good wedding to lift our spirits." She pointed at Anna. "And then we'll start planning yours. It can't be too far off now. Grandfather keeps saying the war is going to end soon. Maybe you can have an autumn wedding with golden chrysanthemums and red roses and—"

"Slow down." Anna laughed. "And just so you know, we only want a very simple wedding, honey. Maybe just close family at City Hall. That's what Daniel said he'd like."

Katy frowned. "That's no fun. A marriage should be a celebration, Mother."

"Tell you what." Anna clipped a rose stem. "You can plan a lovely wedding dinner for us after we get married." She handed Katy the salmon colored rose. "But perhaps I'm jumping the gun . . . goodness knows what will happen by then."

"Mother." Katy turned to look at her. "You're not worried that it won't happen, are you? That you and Dr. Daniel won't get married when the war ends?"

"I have to admit, it seems rather far off and distant . . . like Daniel. And it's possible with all that's gone on, well, he could change his mind."

"Oh, Mother." Katy put a hand on her shoulder. "I've seen him talk about you and the love in his eyes. I still remember the day he asked me how I'd feel about having him for a stepfather."

"Really?" Anna brightened. "You never told me about that."

"I was on my way to marry Jim when we crossed paths on the train. And he was very fatherly and concerned."

"That's right. He sent me the telegram reassuring me about you. I almost forgot that."

"Well, if you'd seen him talking about you, you'd have no doubts about how much he loves you. I've had a lot of lessons on waiting this year. I guess you're still getting yours."

Anna smiled. "I'll just have to be more patient."

"To be honest, I will too. Just because Jim is coming home doesn't mean that he's back to normal."

"I know. Mac has been visiting him too. I hear Jim has good days and bad days."

"Doc Hollister told me that, among other things, he believes Jim suffered a concussion when he was injured. That may have something to do with his ups and downs."

"Yes, Mac mentioned that to me. Mac's theory is that Jim's brain can heal. Remember what bad shape Mac was in when we first got here? After his stroke?"

"Other than his bum leg and paralyzed arm, Grandfather is doing so well now that I sometimes forget how he could barely speak."

"But you helped him through that time, Katy." Anna sighed. "Maybe you'll have to do that again with Jim."

"Yes . . . but I think it's something more too. I think it has to do with all the horrors of war. Sometimes I look into his eyes when he's not aware, and I feel like I can see fear and trauma there. Like he's reliving it."

"I'm sure you're right about that. There's a condition called shell shock . . . something that a few veterans bring home with them. It's possible Jim has that." Anna looked away.

"You know something, don't you, Mother?

Did Doc Hollister tell you Jim has shell shock?"

Anna sighed. "I think it's difficult to diagnose, but yes, JD mentioned that Jim could be suffering from it."

"Then what can we do?"

"Probably just what you're doing now, honey. Talk to him when he wants to talk. Create a beautiful, peaceful home. And JD says Jim should return to work."

"Yes, we've discussed that, and Jim thinks he's ready. He wants to start back up on Monday. Do you think that's wise?"

"According to JD." Anna handed Katy a piece of fern for the arrangement.

"Well, it sounds good to me." Katy turned. "And I think I hear the baby—Sarah Rose is doing the shopping this morning."

"When do you pick up Jim?"

"After lunch." Katy put the last rose in what had turned into a gorgeous bouquet. "Tell Mickey thanks for the extra flowers, and thank you for the encouragement."

"Call us if you need anything. And let me know how it goes."

Katy promised to keep her mother informed, then went to check Lucy. Even though she wasn't quite two months old, she seemed so much more like a little person now. "I hope your daddy appreciates what a jewel you are," she said as she changed her diaper. "Even if you're not a boy." She put her face down close. "And you, my darling, have convinced me that baby girls are much nicer than boys. And today, you are going to look like a little dolly in your pretty pink gown and bonnet." Katy dressed Lucy in one of the baby ensembles she'd designed and held her up to admire her. "Pretty as a picture."

Hopefully by late fall, in time for Christmas shoppers, they would have a full line of pretty baby and children's clothing. And since a number of babies had been born during the past year, and a number of young brides were still expecting, Katy felt sure that Kathleen's would have plenty of customers. Well, if this war would end. According to Grandfather, it couldn't last much longer. But every time Katy glanced at a headline, it seemed that the Germans were pushing even harder.

Katy and Sarah sat down to a light early lunch, but neither of them spoke much. Katy was too nervous, and Sarah was probably just trying to be thoughtful. "I really don't know how this will go," Katy told Sarah as they carried the plates to the sink. "Like I've told you already, Jim is a bit unpredictable. He can be like his old self one moment and then become dark and moody the next."

"Miss Katy, I don't want to speak out of line here, but I have a suggestion."

"Yes?"

"Well, I wonder if—for the time being—you should consider sleeping in separate rooms. I've already freshened up the spare room and, being that it's farther from the nursery and in the back of the house, it's quieter than the master. Would your husband be more comfortable there?"

"You could be right." Katy frowned. "Jim told me he still has bad dreams. And he's been used to a quiet, darkened room. It might be a better way for him to get used to being home."

"While you're picking him up, I could move his things to the spare room. So he'd feel at home there. And if he needs a quiet place to gather his thoughts or just sit, there's that easy chair in there. And I can put some books in there for him. In case he feels like reading."

"Yes. That's an excellent idea. If Jim doesn't like having his own room, we'll just change everything back. But I have a feeling he'll appreciate it. Just until he gets better. But like Doc Hollister said, being home will be a transition for him." Katy hugged Sarah Rose. "I don't think I could do this without you."

"I'm thankful I can be of help." Sarah smiled. "And here's the truth—I've never been happier here in Sunset Cove than I've been living here in this house and helping you."

"Really?" Katy blinked. "But I know how much you liked working for Dr. Daniel."

"I did enjoy that, but it was hard work—and

truth be told, I'm no spring chicken. And besides that, well, there were some obstacles. Working at the hospital was never a very comfortable fit for me. And keeping house for old Dr. Hollister?" She just shook her head.

"Yes, I know how that goes. But I never told you how the old curmudgeon complained about me stealing you from him."

Sarah laughed. "You didn't steal me. I came happily. And the truth is, I've felt more at home here than anywhere. And I love helping with Lucy."

"Well, you are a treasure. And I hope you never leave." She looked at the clock. "Speaking of leaving, I better get going. Jim might already be waiting."

Jim's homecoming was quiet and peaceful. Lucy was down for her afternoon nap, and Sarah was puttering in the kitchen. During the ride home, Katy had explained Sarah's suggestion that he use the spare room, and he had looked relieved.

"You go in and get settled. Take a nap if you need to, or maybe you'll want to read. Sarah put some books in there." Katy smiled. "I need to check on the baby." Of course, she didn't really need to check on Lucy, but it was an excuse to give him some time to adjust. Seeing that Lucy was sweetly sleeping, Katy went to speak to Sarah Rose.

"So far so good," she said quietly.

"And I'm making chicken soup for dinner." Sarah checked the pot. "I thought a simple meal might be better."

"Perfect." Katy looked out the window toward the beach. "It's such a beautiful day—I wonder if I can encourage Jim to go for a walk with me." She remembered some of their previous romantic walks, holding hands, exchanging a kiss . . . maybe this would be the medicine he needed.

"It's worth a try." Sarah chopped a carrot.

So when Jim emerged from the spare room, Katy mentioned a beach walk with Lucy in the baby carriage.

"I think the baby is too little to go on the beach," he said woodenly.

She started to argue this point, wanting to declare she'd taken Lucy for walks there before—but stopped herself. "Then how about if you and I take a walk? Sarah will be here with Lucy."

Jim agreed, but it felt reluctant.

By the time he put on his old corduroy jacket and felt hat, and they slowly made their way down the beach stairs, Katy's hopes for a pleasant walk were dwindling. On the beach, with Jim in his tinted glasses, Katy positioned herself on his right side, hoping that he'd take her hand. When he didn't, she reached for his. But like his prosthetic hand, his "good" hand felt stiff and lifeless too. And even though she pointed out the sights he used to love, he didn't seem the least bit interested. Plus the brisk sea breeze and sound of the crashing waves clearly disturbed him.

"Was it always this bright and loud?" he demanded.

"Well, the sun is out, and the ocean is acting a bit frisky today." She peered out past the surf. "Looks like the white caps are growing. But it's not—"

"I want to go back inside."

And so they turned back. Once they were in the house, Jim disappeared into his room and Katy, seeing Lucy was awake, put her in the baby carriage and strolled down the street. This was not going to be an easy transition . . . for any of them.

Anna hid her surprise to see Jim at the newspaper office on Monday morning. Katy had already told her that he wasn't settling in too well at home, and Anna had assumed that he might not be ready for work either. But wearing a suit and tie, which looked a little too large for his still-thin frame, he sat down at their editorial meeting with a notepad.

"Welcome, Jim," she said brightly as Frank, Ed, and Reginald took their seats. "We've all been looking forward to having you back on the team." The other men greeted him too, shaking hands and slapping him on the back.

"Thanks," he mumbled. "Might take time to get back to snuff."

"No worries," Frank told him.

Jim held up his prosthetic hand. "I'll be slower on the typewriter."

"You obviously forgot about how Ed types," Anna teased. "Hunt and peck."

"But I get the job done," he reminded her.

"And Jim will too," she said. "Now let's start the meeting."

Frank began. "As you all know, the Allied Forces had a good victory last week. More information just came in about the Battle of Cantigny. The 28th Regiment of the 1st Division really—"

"I know that division," Jim said suddenly.

"Maybe you'd like to take that story." Anna glanced at Frank, hoping he wouldn't mind and, to her relief, he nodded.

"I, uh, I guess I could." Jim looked uncertain.

"Anyway, it's good news," Frank continued. "On the sixth of June—late last week—US forces captured Bouresches and South Belleau Wood."

"That's great news." Anna smiled.

"Here you go." Frank handed his notes to Jim. And now they went over the other assignments and news stories. Fortunately, because of the extra summer tourists and traffic, there seemed plenty of stories to go around.

"And I'm following up on those bootleggers that got caught by the lighthouse," Frank finally said. "I don't think they caught all of them, so I plan to go sniffing around this morning."

"Maybe you should take someone with you," Anna suggested, glancing at Jim who was staring down at the notes in front of him. "Well, you be careful, Frank. If you find anything too interesting, get out of there and call Chief Rollins."

As they went their separate ways, Anna felt concerned for Jim. Still, she knew she had to let him be. Either it would work or it wouldn't. And JD had claimed getting back into routines would be best. Plus, Katy had been so relieved that he was going back to work. Yesterday evening, when she and Katy took a quick walk on the beach, Katy had admitted that living with Jim was like constantly walking on eggshells. Hopefully working with him wouldn't be. And hopefully her staff would be patient and understanding. Because Anna had a feeling it was going to take awhile for Jim to get up to speed. As she went to her office, she prepared herself for the possibility of having to rewrite Jim's piece on the recent Allied victory. Unless his return to reporting ignited him. Now wouldn't that be a victory!

CHAPTER 22

Katy had no idea what to expect when Jim arrived home from his first day back at the newspaper, but she did feel hopeful. She'd thought he'd come home for lunch earlier, but he'd called to say he wanted to remain at work and that Virginia had run out to get him a ham and cheese sandwich. But he'd sounded happy, even joking about how Virginia wanted to "fatten him up."

So when he came home in good spirits, even smiling, Katy thought old Doc Hollister must've been right after all. Working and routine were probably just what Jim needed. As just the two of them sat to dinner—because Sarah had insisted—Jim told her about the news story he was working on. "It feels good to write about a victory. If the Allied troops keep fighting like this, the war will soon end."

"Wouldn't that be wonderful."

"Thanks to my slow typing skills, I'm not done with it yet." His smile faded slightly. "But I will finish tomorrow."

"Good for you. I can't wait to read it. How nice to have good news about the war for a change."

"Yes . . ." He looked down, and Katy realized she should keep their conversation lighter. And so she told him about Lucy's latest development. So far, he had shown very little interest in his infant daughter. Katy knew she had to be patient, but at the same time she felt that Lucy's cute smile and twinkling eyes could breathe life into her daddy. If he'd only let her.

"Speaking of Lucy, I want to take her out for an early evening stroll." Katy picked up their empty dishes. "Just out front along the sidewalk. But I think she could use the fresh air. Fresh air is good for babies."

Jim didn't respond, so she simply took the dishes to the kitchen. But when she returned, she smiled and patted his cheek. "It'd be lovely if you could join us. I think fresh air is good for daddies too."

"I suppose you're right." He nodded. And before he could change his mind, Katy asked him to get out the baby carriage while she got Lucy ready and before long, they were strolling down the sidewalk. At first, he resisted pushing the carriage, but when he discovered he could manage it with his prosthetic hand, he didn't seem to mind. Meanwhile, Katy tried to keep a cheerful conversation going.

"Look, Jim." Katy paused to point at Lucy. "She's smiling up at you."

He leaned down to look. "By golly, she is."

"See, she knows her daddy."

By the time they got home, Katy felt very hopeful. Jim was more like his old self than ever. "Look," she pointed out the ocean view window. "It will be a gorgeous sunset tonight. Want to watch it with me?"

He looked uncertain. But as Sarah came to get the baby ready for bed, Katy hooked her arm in his, leading him back outside. "We don't have to go down to the beach," she assured him. "We can watch up here. Remember how we used to watch sunsets together? Sometimes we even danced. Right down there on the beach. Remember?"

He shrugged.

"Come let's sit," she suggested. "We can snuggle to stay warm against that cool breeze."

He reluctantly agreed, and soon they were on the beach, looking out over the ocean, but Jim was fumbling in his chest pocket. Finally, he removed his glasses case and put on the tinted glasses.

"Is the light bothering your eyes?" She tried not to sound irritated, but she didn't like it when he put those detestable glasses on. He just nodded, and she decided to ignore it. "Well, it's going to be a beautiful sky tonight. Already there's coral and gold."

Again he nodded.

"What do you think of our little daughter?" she asked. "Isn't Lucy precious?"

"The baby is very small."

"Of course, she's small. Lucy Ann is barely two months old."

"Uh-huh."

She turned to stare at him. "Are you disappointed, Jim? I know I promised you a little boy—and I had wanted to name him after you. Little Jimmy. Or Jamie. I never could quite decide. But is that troubling you? Did you hope for a son?"

"No, no." But his denial wasn't convincing.

"Then is it her name that bothers you? Did you want to call her something different than Lucy Ann? I suppose we could still have it changed. She's so little, she would never know."

"No. Her name is fine."

"But you wish she were a boy," Katy declared. "I'm sure you did. You are disappointed. I can tell."

He turned to look at her. "I'm glad she is a girl, Katy. I did not want a son. I swear I did not."

Katy just shrugged. She still didn't believe him.

"I am glad she's a girl, Katy. A girl will never have to go to war."

"Oh . . ." Katy nodded. "I thought this war was supposed to ensure that the world never goes to war again. That's what President Wilson keeps telling everyone."

Jim let out a long, tired sounding sigh then rubbed his temples.

"Oh, Jim. I'll bet you're worn out after your first day of work. I shouldn't keep you out here to watch this. Let's go back inside."

"Yes. That would be good."

Her arm linked in his, she led him around through the back door. Sarah was cleaning up the kitchen. "I just gave Lucy her bottle and put her down, but you can go in and say goodnight." She smiled at Jim.

Katy thanked her and, hoping that Jim would join her in the nursery, led them down the hallway. But he went straight to his room. Katy sighed and continued to the baby's room. "Goodnight, little princess." She kissed the rounded cheek, tucking the baby blanket up to her chin. "Someday your daddy will tell you goodnight too."

As Katy went on to her own room, she reminded herself of the progress Jim had appeared to have made—and in just one day. She couldn't expect him to return to his old self overnight. She needed to be more patient. Tomorrow would probably be even better.

On Tuesday afternoon, Anna was relieved to see that Jim had finished his front page article about the Allied victory. And, other than a few typos, which she'd marked and the typesetter had changed, it was really quite good. His experience in the army had given him a deeper understanding of the war and those in it—and it showed in the article. Perhaps he could be put in charge of all the war related stories from now on.

She just hoped Frank wouldn't feel bad—or as if he'd been replaced. Although he seemed intrigued with the bootleg story he was working on. Hopefully he'd finish it by press time. She glanced at the clock to see that it was nearly press time now. Maybe she'd better go check on Frank.

As Anna strolled through the busy office, she felt a surge of hopefulness. With Jim back, they were fully staffed again. And based on the story going into tomorrow's paper, it really did seem the war was drawing to a close. Wouldn't it be great if life returned to normal? Hearing the chatter of typewriters and the clunking noises of the press cranking up was like music to her ears. Life at the *Sunset Times*—just like the presses—was merrily rolling along.

"Just finished it." Frank rolled the page out of his typewriter, waving it at her.

"Thank you." She snatched it, giving it a fast read and only finding a couple of things to mark. "Looks good, Frank. And I'm curious to hear how it all turns out."

"I'll keep following it."

"Take it to be set. I know page two is waiting." She continued back and, pausing by Jim's desk, she noticed that he was gone. But since he'd worked through lunch again, he was probably overdue for a break. As she turned to go in her office, she noticed a shadow down the hallway and, peering to see who was lurking back there, she was surprised to see it was Jim. Pinned against the wall, almost as if someone were pointing a firearm at him, his face was pale with fear.

Anna gasped, looking to see if perhaps one of the bootleggers or rumrunners had cornered him a gunpoint, but she saw nothing. Jim was alone in the hallway. She cautiously approached him. "Jim?" she said loud enough to be heard over the clattering press machinery. "Are you okay?"

He didn't answer but kept staring straight at the wall across from him. Suddenly, Anna understood. The noise of the press cranking up had caught him by surprise. It had probably reminded him of the battlefield. "Jim." She gently touched his shoulder and he jumped. "Jim," she said again. "Come to my office."

When he refused to move, she tugged on him, pulling him into her office and shutting the door, which only muffled the pressroom noise. "Sit down." She gently but firmly shoved him into the chair. "The noise reminds you of the battlefield, doesn't it?"

His good hand was shielding his eyes now and

his head was shaking, it seemed uncontrollably. Anna didn't know what to do. Should she call JD for help? But he might send an ambulance. And that might be humiliating for Jim. Suddenly she remembered the secret passageway that Mac had built into his office years ago. She used it occasionally to duck out without drawing attention, but mostly it remained locked and forgotten.

"Come on, Jim." She grabbed his good hand, tugging him to his feet. "Let's get out of here." She pulled him through the secret door and out onto the sidewalk, where it was much quieter. "Take some deep breaths," she told him and, to her relief, he did. "And now, let's walk." She hooked her arm into his and began to move them down the street. After a block or so, she felt him starting to relax just a bit.

"I'm sorry," he mumbled.

"Nothing to be sorry for," she said lightly. "I know the noise in the pressroom was what did it. I forget how loud it is. I'm sure it sounds a bit like artillery."

He simply nodded then fumbled for his tinted glasses, shoving them on with a trembling hand.

"I'll walk you home and you can—"

"Not home." He turned to look at her.

"Why not?"

"Katy. She'll be worried."

Anna thought for a moment. "Then we shall pay

Mac a visit." And she continued on home, talking soothingly to Jim with each step, reassuring him that it was all perfectly understandable. "Even people who haven't been on the battlefield often react when the presses start up," she said as she opened the front door. "It's startling."

"Hello?" Lucille smiled as Anna led Jim into the front room.

"Jim's going to visit with Mac." Anna continued through.

"I'll have Bernie bring an extra teacup." Lucille nodded as if she understood and hurried away. Anna moved into Mac's sitting room.

"Jim is having tea with you today," she told Mac. "You should see the fine article he wrote for tomorrow's front page." She led Jim to a chair. "Perhaps you can tell Mac about it."

Mac glanced curiously at Anna and then nodded as if, he too, understood.

"The noisy press started up," Anna said casually. "I forget how loud it sounds. And it took Jim by surprise." She leaned down to look at Jim. "Why don't you chat with Mac about it over tea? Explain to him how it made you feel. I know Mac would be interested."

"That's right." Mac nodded. "I am interested, Jim. We talked about some of your battle memories in the hospital. And I'm eager to hear more. I've never been the right age to go to war, but it's always fascinated me."

"I'll see you fellows later," Anna told them and, letting herself out, she went to find Lucille, quickly explaining the situation.

"I thought it was something like that."

"Maybe you could let Katy know that Jim is here. But not right away. I think Jim and Mac should have a good talk first. A good man to man talk. I think Mac is just the person to understand him."

As Anna walked back to the newspaper office, she prayed a silent prayer for Jim. His condition was obviously worse than she'd imagined. And working at the newspaper no longer seemed a good option. Although he could work from home. At least on the days the press ran. After all, Mac had been working from home for the last few years. Yes, she decided as she slipped back through the secret entrance, she would ask Virginia to have his typewriter and a few things sent home so he could write there.

Anna knew it wasn't ideal—and Katy might be disappointed to have him underfoot again—but it seemed the only viable solution. Hopefully, it was only temporary. And in the meantime, she was going to write Daniel. She chided herself for not thinking of this before. Daniel, over there in the thick of war, he must have some good advice for dealing with shell shock. She sat down at her desk and immediately penned a letter, describing the situation with Jim and asking for Daniel's professional opinion. His father might have more years of experience, but Daniel had a healer's heart. Oh, if only he could come home and help them.

CHAPTER 23

Katy hid her dismay at her mother's suggestion that Jim should write for the newspaper from home. She'd seen how disturbed and anxious Jim had been when he came home on Tuesday afternoon, pacing the floor and shaking his head. And she understood how the printing press noise could've upset him. She'd been unsettled by the clanking and banging herself the first time she'd experienced it.

The next morning, while Jim was still sleeping, Katy and Sarah Rose set up a quiet workspace in a small second floor bedroom. And not the one that overlooked the sea, since the ocean made Jim uneasy. To make him even more comfortable, Sarah sewed up heavy curtains to darken the usually sunlit room. Katy wasn't sure how he would react since he'd refused to even talk about this idea the previous night, but to Katy's relief he seemed to appreciate his new office.

So it was that they were both working from home. Although Katy had been drawing her designs for women and children's clothing in

275

the living room, and she often worked on her weekly fashion column from the rocker in Lucy's room while she slept, after seeing Jim's nice new space, she considered setting up the other sunny upstairs room for herself. Except she didn't want to be too far away from Lucy.

The next few days passed relatively peacefully and quietly. Jim pecked away on another war news story and consequently spent most of his time upstairs in his office. Katy, Lucy, and Sarah returned for the most part to their routines. But by the end of the week, Jim seemed irate and disturbed over something.

"Is your piece for the newspaper done?" Katy asked him on Friday morning. "Because I can take it over there with mine. They need them by noon."

"I guess it's done." He frowned. "Such as it is."

"Great," she said brightly. "I'll pop upstairs to get it before I go." Katy tried not to be too concerned over Jim's disposition. By now she knew that it changed as quickly as the weather. And sometimes with the weather. Instead, she got dressed for going out then went upstairs to get his piece. But seeing him sitting in the dark, gloomy room, glowering down at his typewriter with his prosthetic hand lying nearby . . . well, it was not a pretty picture.

"Is this your article?" she picked up two type-written pages, and he simply nodded.

"Okay then." She leaned over to peck him on the cheek, something she'd been reminding herself to do, trying not to cringe at his unshaven bristles. Hopefully he'd take care of that before she got back. "I'm going to run by the dress shop after the newspaper. But I'll be home by the time Lucy wakes from her afternoon nap. If you need anything, just call for Sarah." Again he just nodded, but his brow was creased and his good hand was balled up in a fist.

As she went downstairs, she wondered if writing for the newspaper was too much to expect from him. Maybe they were pushing him too hard. She started to tuck his article into the valise where hers was waiting then decided to sneak a peek. Perhaps it was writing this war story that had disturbed him like that. But as she quickly skimmed his article, she was shocked. Oh, the writing was good . . . but the content was unnerving. Instead of a news piece, Jim had written a strongly opinionated editorial that was decidedly opposed to the Great War. And even though Katy personally hated the killing and destruction going on over there, she knew that expressing such views was not only frowned upon—it was illegal. She'd overheard her mother and grandfather discussing this very thing more than once.

Even so, she took Jim's piece, along with her own to the newspaper office. But instead of turning them in to Frank, she went straight to her mother's office.

"Hello, darling." Anna smiled, waving her in. "What brings you here?"

"Jim's article." Katy pulled it out. "You need to see it before anyone else."

She reached for it. "Is it not well written?"

"Oh, the writing is very good. But you need to read it." Katy sat down as her mother read. When Anna looked up with widened eyes, Katy simply nodded. "You see what I mean."

"Oh, dear." Anna laid the objectionable piece down. "We can't print this, Katy."

"I know."

Anna got up to close her office door. "I don't necessarily disagree with some of Jim's conclusions, but the Sedition Act makes it impossible to run this piece. We would be shut down so fast it would—"

"Not only that, Mother, Jim could be arrested for simply writing those words."

"Or speaking them." Anna sat down with a loud sigh. "I hope he hasn't voiced any of this— do you think he has?"

"This is the first I've heard of it. But, really, who could blame him for feeling this way?" Katy tapped his article. "Like he says in this, he witnessed the senselessness of war firsthand. He watched his men bleed to death in muddy fox-holes. Saw the mistakes commanders made that cost even more men their lives. Even though I hated hearing these atrocities, it helps me understand Jim better now."

"Yes, and that's a good thing. But Jim—and you—need to keep quiet about this."

Katy nodded. "I considered burning the piece."

Anna frowned. "Oh, don't burn it. It's well done. But it needs to be locked up in a safe place. And I'm afraid we can't have Jim work for the paper if he wants to write pieces like this."

"I know."

"But it might be helpful to Jim to write about his experiences," Anna said slowly.

"Really? Do you think so? He seemed to get so agitated when he wrote this peace."

"Well, he was already agitated, Katy."

"That's true."

"Maybe he needs to get those memories out of his system. Sort of like purging."

Katy frowned. "They're such horrid stories."

"I know. But is it better for him to hang onto them, hide them away inside of himself—or to get them out?"

"That does make sense. But what if he doesn't want to?"

"Well, you obviously can't force him." Anna drummed her pencil, clearly trying to think of a way to encourage her troubled son-in-law.

"What if he was writing a book?" Katy said suddenly.

"Yes! It could be a memoir. A soldier's story."

"And if he thought of it like that, as if it was something that might someday be published—he might be more willing. It would be kind of like a job." Katy liked the idea of Jim working in his little office every day.

"Exactly. But he'd need to understand that no one could know about the content. He could tell people he was writing a book, but nothing else."

"That's how I am about my clothing designs," Katy said with enthusiasm. "I try to keep them to myself until they're being transformed into actual dresses. I could tell Jim that his book should be like that."

"And who knows. Maybe when the war is done . . . maybe the government won't be so hardnosed about anti-war opinions."

"Let's hope so. In the meantime, I will keep this—and anything else Jim writes—in a very secure place." Katy reached for the piece.

"I'm glad you understand the severity of the Sedition Act. Even though Chief Rollins is a family friend, he has to enforce this law. And it would be horrible to see Jim in prison."

Katy shuddered and then let out a slow sigh. "Although he's already in a prison of sorts. A self-enforced one." She blinked back angry tears. "He doesn't even like the ocean any-more, Mother. And he avoids Lucy and barely looks at me. It's like he wants to shut himself away from anything alive or beautiful or happy."

"Has he told you why he wears those tinted glasses?"

"Not really. Although I think the light hurts his eyes."

"That's part of it, Katy. But he admitted to me that color hurts his eyes."

Katy blinked. "Color? How is that possible? Color is so beautiful. I adore color. How can it possibly hurt his eyes? That makes no sense whatsoever."

"He said it's because everything was so dark and dreary on the battlefield. The mud, the trenches . . . even the sky. I believe he said it all looked brown."

"Oh." Katy slowly nodded. "I guess I can sort of imagine that. How awful."

"And, as you know after reading what Jim wrote, it wasn't just the visual bleakness."

"Don't remind me." Katy shuddered. "Some of those words feel indelibly stuck in my brain now. I'd like to erase them."

Anna held up her pencil. "In fact, that's a very good reason you shouldn't read Jim's writing. Not now anyway. But it would be good if someone else could read it—a way for him to know that his story was being heard."

"Not you, Mother." Katy shook her head. "I don't think you need to hear it any more than I do."

"Well, I read stories about war and hardships all the time."

"I know. But what about Grandfather?"

"Yes. That would be perfect. And Mac is a good writer and respects good writing. He could be like a mentor to Jim."

"And it's handy having him practically next door."

"This is turning into a great plan." Anna smiled.

"If we can get Jim onboard." Katy stood. "I should probably turn my column in to Frank. He's appreciated that I've been on time lately."

"Yes. You do that. Just keep Jim's safely out of sight."

"Believe me, I will." Already Katy was making a plan for a place to hide Jim's writings away. Hopefully, he'd understand the need to keep his opinions about the war to himself. And perhaps Grandfather could help persuade him of the dangers of speaking out. Because, despite Jim's need for isolation these days, she didn't think he'd fare too well in a real prison. She hoped and prayed that never happened.

Katy had barely left Anna's office before Anna began to second guess herself—and what might turn out to be a harebrained and disastrous plan. What if she'd given Katy bad advice? Encouraging Jim to write about his war experiences—and to express such negativity . . . What if it blew up on them? The Sedition Act had only been adopted a month ago, and already arrests were being made across the country. Tomorrow's paper included a piece about a group in Portland that had been rounded up for questioning.

But she didn't have time to think about that now. She'd promised to meet JD for lunch. She knew he'd been feeling blue lately and suspected he was lonely. As she walked to the diner, she knew she couldn't tell him about Jim—at least not about his anti-war views. The fewer people who knew about that, the better it would be for all.

JD was already seated, and before long their orders were taken. As usual, he began the conversation with his hospital news. One of the nurses had needed reprimanding this morning. Most of the patients didn't seem to appreciate the modern medical care provided there. And perhaps worst of all, Dr. Myers was not measuring up to his expectations and JD had decided to let him go. "After all, Daniel will be home when this blasted war ends. That can't be too far off now. I don't need that stupid young doctor bungling everything in the meantime."

Anna wanted to point out that JD's negative experiences might be impaired by his negative perspective, but she knew that was pointless. So she told him a bit about Jim, describing his reaction to the noisy press machines earlier in the week.

"Well, that's not surprising. I could've predicted as much." He casually sipped his coffee.

"But you had recommended him returning to work."

"Yes. I think he needs to work. And I also think it's good for him to be around that noise."

"But he was frozen with fear," Anna argued. "How can that be good?"

"He needs to face his fears."

Anna wasn't so sure but said nothing.

"How can he get past this if you and Katy mollycoddle him?"

"Mollycoddle?" She felt her hackles rising.

"Jim needs to stand up to this neurosis."

"I respect your professional opinion," she said calmly, "but as you told me, there are a number of varying opinions on the care and treatment for shell shock."

He nodded. "Yes, that's true."

"In fact, I've written to Daniel about it. I'd like to hear what he thinks since he's actually treating soldiers—some who in all likelihood are experiencing these same symptoms."

"Excellent idea, Anna. Have you heard back from him?" He brightened.

"No." She glumly shook her head.

JD's countenance softened. "I miss him too."

"You do?" She studied him closely.

"Of course I do. Oh, I know Daniel and I don't always get along or see eye-to-eye on everything professionally, but he is my son."

"And he's a fine doctor too."

"Yes . . . and probably getting better every day." He salted his soup. "When he does write back to you, as I'm sure he will, I'd be interested to hear his thoughts on shell shock."

"I'll be sure to tell you. In the meantime, we are taking your advice about the need for Jim to work and have a routine. We're encouraging him to write a book on his war experiences. A memoir of sorts. It will keep him busy. And who knows, he's a good writer . . . perhaps someone will want to publish it someday." She had no intention of mentioning Jim's anti-war views.

"That's not a bad idea." He got a thoughtful expression. "I've often thought of writing a book of my own. In retirement, of course. I think I have an interesting story."

Anna wasn't surprised by this. People like JD often believed they had fascinating tales that others were dying to read. But based on the way people shied away from JD's longwinded lectures, she had her doubts. Still, she tried to encourage him and even offered to give him some writing suggestions when he was ready for it. She could tell he was lonely and, like her, missing Daniel. He might be an old "blowhard," as Mac liked to say, but he was human . . . and getting older . . . and Daniel's father.

CHAPTER 24

Anna was relieved to hear from Daniel the following week. And eager to share his suggestions with Katy, she agreed to help her daughter with flower arrangements for Clara and Randall's wedding. As Katy drove them to the church, Anna began to tell her about Daniel's letter.

"He does agree with his father that having some sort of work or routine is good. But he agreed with me that the noisy atmosphere at the newspaper was definitely troublesome. He shouldn't go back there—not until he's well. Daniel suggested you maintain a quiet, peaceful environment."

"And I'm trying to do that, Mother."

"I know. You've created a wonderful home, Katy. Daniel also recommended things like gardening or wood carving—quiet activities where Jim can have some control and see some results. He said that seems to work with other soldiers."

"What about writing?" Katy asked as they

carried buckets of flowers into the sanctuary.

"Yes. Daniel said that writing therapy has been helpful too."

"So we're on a good track then?"

"It seems like it. Jim has had a pretty good week for the most part." Anna picked up the scissors. "I'll snip stems for you."

"And I'll arrange." Katy took the first bloom.

"Daniel also mentioned what they're calling the Three Truths Shattered philosophy."

"Three Truths Shattered? That sounds a bit ominous." Katy set a rose in the vase.

"The shattered truths are, first, seeing the world as meaningful; second, seeing the world as comprehensible; and third, seeing oneself in a positive light."

"I'm impressed you memorized that, Mother."

"Well, I decided to write an editorial on this very thing. I find it very interesting and, if and when our soldiers come home—which hopefully will be sooner than later—I think people need to be aware of what to expect."

"So explain it to me." Katy threaded a strand of ivy between the roses.

"Well, the war—and I believe this refers to power-hungry, greedy aggressors who started the whole mess—has made the world feel meaning-less."

"I can see that. It's like living in peace feels meaningful. But this horrible war and the loss of lives and good men like Jim coming home so broken . . . well, it does feel meaningless."

"You need to be careful who you say that too, Katy."

"I know. And I'm keeping Jim's writing under lock and key. We call it the Secret Project. And he seems to enjoy that."

"Perfect."

"So what about the other two shattered truths, Mother? This interests me."

"The next one is seeing the world as comprehensible. Again, it's the consequence of war that makes us unable to comprehend—especially for those in the midst of the battles."

"I'm not in the midst of those battles that Jim went through, but I can't comprehend it either. Honestly, I can't begin to understand how things got so bad—or how it just kept going—and seems to be never-ending. I sometimes feel so angry about it, I want to scream." She shoved a rose into the vase so hard the stem broke. "Blast it!"

Anna sighed. "So maybe you understand this better than most people."

"I feel like I'm living it. What is the third shattered truth?"

"I think this is more for the veterans—the survivors of war. They can't see themselves in a positive light."

"Well, that certainly describes Jim. Not always,

of course. But often I'm just staggered by how negative he is—about himself and everything and everyone. It's like he has no hope whatsoever."

"According to Daniel, that's not unusual."

"But what can we do about it, Mother?"

"Probably just what you're doing. And be patient. Daniel says it takes time, but he feels hopeful for Jim. He says Jim is made of the right stuff to get past this."

"I hope you're right because sometimes—like last night when I wanted him to hold Lucy for a bit while Sarah and I cut flowers for today—he refused. He gave no reason, just walked off. Then he secluded himself in his office all night. For all I know, he slept there. He wasn't even up when I left this morning. I told Sarah Rose to just let him sleep." Katy paused to look at Anna. "But here's the honest truth, Mother, sometimes I get really scared . . . when he doesn't get up in the morning . . . or he's too quiet upstairs and I can't hear the typewriter."

"Scared?" Anna was almost afraid to ask.

"I worry, Mother. What if he did something . . . to take his own life?"

"Oh, Katy, I can't imagine Jim would do that. Despite his troubles, I know he loves you and the baby. I just know he does."

"I'm not so sure. I don't like to tell people this, but we don't share the same bedroom." Katy's eyes got teary. "And he's never even kissed me. Not once since he's come home."

"Oh, Katy." Anna put an arm around her. "I'm sorry. That must be hard."

"It doesn't even feel like we're truly married. Not like I thought it would be. It's more like we share a house. I think Sarah Rose knows how it is, but she doesn't say anything. And I'm too embarrassed to admit how I feel to her."

"I think she'd understand, honey. But I'm glad you told me. And I agree with Daniel, I believe it's going to get better. It'll just take time . . . and patience on your part."

"You know me, though." Katy shook her head. "I've never been patient. Not with myself or anyone."

"That's not entirely true." Anna handed her a peach colored rose. "I remember how patient you were with Mac when we got here. You'd play chess with him and encourage him to talk."

"Grandfather called me a slave-driver. He still teases me that I used a bullwhip to get him to speak again."

Anna laughed. "I guess I mistook your perseverance as patience. I suppose it will take a bit of both to get through this." Anna checked her watch. "I promised Clara I'd go over there before the wedding—to help her dress. Do you think you can handle the rest of this on your own?"

"Of course. In fact, I shall take my time and

enjoy the quietness of the sanctuary. I asked Sarah to remind Jim he needs to dress for the wedding. He promised me that he'd go several days ago. And I'm hoping the ceremony will remind him of our own . . . a year ago."

"Oh . . . I hope you're not expecting too much."

Katy waved her hand. "It'll be what it'll be. And Clara needs you, Mother. I already helped her with the last fitting of her dress, so I know she will look perfect, but she'll need you by her side today. And you're going to look lovely too, being her attendant in your sea green dress. Clara put it in her apartment after we finished it yesterday." Katy frowned. "Too bad Daniel can't be here to see you in that dress. He would swoon."

Anna laughed and patted her back. "Well, if it the gown is that wonderful, perhaps I'll wear it when Daniel and I get married . . . someday."

"You mean your wedding at City Hall?" Katy teased.

Anna sighed. "If that's what Daniel wants, that's what I want." But as she walked over to Clara's, climbing the stairs to the apartment above the dress shop, Anna wondered what it would be like to have a bigger wedding. Although she wasn't really looking forward to today's celebration. Not because she wasn't happy for Clara and Randall, but because she felt certain that witnessing their nuptials would be a harsh reminder to her that Daniel—and her wedding day—were far, far away.

Clara was just slipping into the cream-colored silk dress that Katy had designed for her. "You look like a young girl," Anna said as she fastened the satin covered buttons down the back. "Very beautiful."

"Oh, Anna." Clara exclaimed suddenly. "I don't know if I can go through with this today."

"Why ever not?" Anna went around to face Clara, seeing her tear-filled eyes. "Whatever is wrong? Is it Randall?"

"No. It's not Randall. It's AJ." Clara nervously fingered the pearls around her neck. "When I got these out of my jewelry box—pearls from my mother—I found AJ's Medal of Honor there. I've been thinking about him all morning long."

"Oh." Anna didn't know what to say.

"He should be dressing up, Anna. For his wedding day. Not me. Did you know he would've been twenty-one next month? He should be the one standing in the church—waiting for the girl of his dreams to walk down the aisle. And instead it's just—" She choked back a sob.

"Oh, Clara, Clara." Anna hugged her, holding her tightly. "I'm so sorry. And I'm not entirely surprised you feel that way."

"Then you think I should call the whole thing off too?" Clara stepped back, reaching for her handkerchief.

"No, no. I don't think that's the answer. AJ wouldn't want you to—"

"But I feel so guilty! I shouldn't be happy like this. My boy's only been gone just over six months. And here I am getting married and—"

"Clara—you need to remember AJ's last letter to you. It seemed as if he was prepared for what happened, as if he knew he was going to a better place. He wanted to be where he was, and he loved his soldier buddies. And he died a hero." Anna tried to think of something more comforting.

"I know he died a hero, but he's still gone. And this should've been his big day—not mine. I'm old and he was—"

"I don't know about all that. But you need to ask yourself something." Anna looked into her friend's eyes. "How would AJ feel right now if he thought his death was about to ruin this day for his mother? You know how much he loved you. How would he feel if you denied yourself happiness because of him? Would he like that, Clara?"

Clara blinked. "I—uh—I don't know."

"He wouldn't. You know he wouldn't. It would hurt him to think you were sacrificing your happiness because of him. And what could he do to make you see that?"

"I don't know."

"You know what I think?" Anna grasped Clara's hand.

"What?"

"I think AJ will be dancing up there in heaven to see you marrying Randall today. Just think of how much Randall helped AJ through his troubles while he was in jail. Randall visited him and represented him in court and fought to get him the second chance at an honorable life. Remember how proud AJ was to wear that uniform—to serve his country? Especially when he could've easily been wearing stripes instead."

Clara somberly nodded. "That's true. He was so glad to go into the army."

"So, even though it's understandable to miss your son today, you need to remember AJ is celebrating with you." Anna went over to the still-opened jewelry box and removed the shiny Medal of Honor. "And I think AJ would be proud to have his mother wear this on her special day. Don't you?"

"Oh, Anna, I would love to do that." Clara took the medal tenderly in her hands. "But where will I pin it?" She looked down at her pretty dress.

"We probably need Katy's advice, but I know she's busy." Anna stepped back to survey the fashion situation and pointed to the satin ribbon belt at Clara's waist. "What if we pinned it right here—in the center of that bow?"

Clara checked it out in the mirror. "That's perfect. It's like a pretty piece of jewelry . . . but so much more." She turned back to Anna. "Thank you! Now it's time you got dressed."

Clara and Randall's wedding was surprisingly sweet. And the only tears shed seemed to be happy ones. But as everyone gathered at the Grange for a reception of food and dancing, Anna found herself missing Daniel. She watched Randall and Clara on the dance floor along with number of other older couples—including Lucille and Mac, who moved a bit more slowly due to his bad leg. She hated to admit it, but Anna longed to be out there with them . . . in Daniel's arms. Instead, she was sitting at a table with Ellen and her baby and Randall's mother, Marjorie.

"How do you feel to see your son married?" Anna asked Marjorie.

"I suppose I have mixed feelings."

"Why is that?" Anna was worried that Marjorie didn't fully approve of Clara.

"Well, you know what they say. A son is a son till he takes him a wife, a daughter's a daughter the rest of your life. I feel I've lost my son."

"Oh, I don't think that's true," Anna reassured her. "Clara doesn't have her mother, so I'm sure she will be glad to have you step in. My daughter relies on me more now that she's married than before."

"Speaking of your daughter, where is she?"

Ellen asked. "I haven't seen Katy and Jim since the wedding."

"Katy wanted to drop Lucy home. Sarah offered to watch her during the reception. But I'm sure they're coming for the reception."

"Lucky Katy. I couldn't find anyone to watch Larry."

"He looks so adorable in that little blue suit, I think you should be proud to have him as your escort." Anna smiled at the double-chinned baby. "He's growing up so fast."

"He looks huge next to Lucy," Ellen said. "But she'll catch up."

"Well, I must admit it was a lovely wedding," Marjorie said. "I really didn't think Randall would ever get married. But I can't deny how happy he looks."

"And my mother is happy too." Ellen sighed. "And I can't believe I feel jealous."

"Jealous?" Marjorie's brows arched.

"Having her husband with her. I haven't heard from Lawrence in over a month."

"Sometimes no news is good news," Anna reminded her. She spotted JD sitting by himself in a corner. "If you ladies will excuse me, I should probably go say hello to Daniel's father."

"Good luck with that," Ellen teased.

"Oh, Ellen." Marjorie frowned. "Old Doc Hollister isn't that bad."

"That's right," Anna agreed as she stood.

"There's more to him than you know." Of course, Anna knew that JD hardly showed his softer side to anyone, but she'd been privy to it a time or two. She smiled as she greeted him and even asked him to dance, preparing herself for his rejection.

"Don't mind if I do." He stood and politely bowed as he took her hand. To Anna's surprise, he was a very good dancer. But then Lucille had mentioned it before—and she remembered how Mac had been envious . . . since his own fine dancing skills had been stolen by his stroke.

"You dance well," she told JD as the song ended.

"My wife taught me." He stepped back. "May I get you some punch?"

Anna smiled. "That would be nice."

With their punch glasses in hand, they sat back down in the corner JD had been occupying. "That's interesting that your wife taught you to dance. I don't know much about her. Daniel never said much." Anna sipped her punch, waiting.

"I'm not surprised at that. I'm sure that Daniel didn't approve of the way I treated his mother."

Anna tried not to look surprised. "Why is that?"

"Don't get me wrong. It's not that I mistreated her. My wife never wanted for anything . . . materially. But I suppose I neglected her. According to Daniel, I was married to my job—

and the hospital. I suppose, looking back, I can admit that is mostly true."

She simply nodded.

"But I felt I needed to work hard . . . to prove myself."

"Why did you need to prove yourself? I would think that just being a successful physician in such an impressive hospital would be proof that you'd succeeded in your profession."

"It would seem that way. And I did succeed in my profession. I was widely esteemed through-out Boston—and along the Eastern Seaboard."

She nodded again.

"Yes, and I can see it in your eyes, Anna. You are thinking you've heard all this before."

She grimaced. "Well, yes, I have heard that before. But I've not heard much about your wife or why you felt the need to prove yourself. And I find that very interesting."

His faded gray eyes twinkled ever so slightly. "Would you like to hear my story?"

"I doubt we have time for the whole story, but as much of it as you care to tell."

"The wedding today took me back. I remem-bered my own wedding day long ago—and how nervous I was to take my bride."

"You, nervous? I can't imagine it."

He chuckled. "That shows how adept I've become at disguising myself. But I was nervous that day. You see, Daniel's mother was from a very well-off family. They had higher aspirations for their daughter."

"But you were a doctor. Wouldn't that impress them?"

"A country doctor."

She blinked. "You were a country doctor?"

"At first. You see, my father was a farmer in upstate New York. And not a very successful one, at that. I worked hard to put myself through medical school. My first job was in a small town not far from my family's farm. A town even smaller than Sunset Cove."

"So how did you meet your wife?"

"I practiced medicine in that Podunk town for about a year, mostly setting bones, occasionally helping to birth babies, and more often than I care to admit, I was treating livestock. But if you repeat that, I will deny it."

Anna couldn't help but laugh.

"So when I was asked to serve as the physician for a fancy seaside resort during summer season, I eagerly accepted. I hoped that I might make some connection that would help me land a better job in a bigger city. Instead, I met Abigail."

"Your wife."

He nodded. "She was a beauty who never would've given me a second glance—except that she fell and broke her ankle."

"And you treated her."

He nodded. "And I gave her the best treatment possible. And then I checked on her daily. Multiple times. While her family and friends were out having fun at the seaside, poor Abigail was laid up in her parents' cabin. So I would stop by and take her books or candy. I would sit and visit with her, or carry her outside to sit in the sun. And somehow by the end of summer, I had won her over. I proposed, and she accepted."

"That is a really sweet story, JD." Anna was truly surprised.

"Her parents didn't think so." His expression turned grim. "They were against the union. But the more they opposed it, the more convinced Abigail became. Her parents finally agreed, but only on the condition that I would further my education at Harvard Medical School first. And since Abigail's father had connections with the school, I was admitted that fall. I think Abigail's parents thought it would put an end to our relationship . . . that I would either fail in my studies or Abigail would grow weary of waiting. But that didn't happen."

"So you got married." Anna smiled.

"Yes. And I was determined to make Abigail and her family proud of me. As a consequence, I probably devoted more time to my work than to my marriage." He sadly shook his head. "I regret it now."

"Well, I'm glad you told me about that part of

your history." She patted his hand. "It explains so much."

"If I had it all to do over again, I would do it differently."

"I'm sure you would. And there must be some consolation in that Daniel is living his life differently."

JD sighed. "But you saw how, despite knowing better, I tried to control his choices. I wanted him to follow in my footsteps with an impressive medical career. I can see now—after spending time here in Sunset Cove—that was a mistake."

"It's good that you can see that now."

"I suppose. But it does fill one with regret . . . and loneliness." He stared out to the dance floor where couples, including Lucille and Mac, were now waltzing.

"You're not the only lonely person here." Anna nodded to where Marjorie was now sitting by herself. "I think Randall's mother is a bit blue about her son getting married. He used to spend a lot of his spare time with her . . . and now she'll be alone more."

"Marjorie Douglas." JD's brow creased slightly. "A handsome woman. Not as beautiful as your mother. But she's a good conversationalist. We often chat when I go to her store."

"Why don't you ask her to dance?" Anna suggested.

His eyes lit up. "Don't mind if I do."

Anna watched as the old gentleman stood up straight and, squaring his shoulders, strode over to Marjorie. He bowed politely—and for a moment, Marjorie appeared speechless. Anna hoped and prayed she wouldn't refuse him. Then Marjorie gracefully stood and, with a demure smile, accepted his hand. Just like that, they joined the others on the dance floor. Victory!

Although Anna felt happy for them, she felt more alone than before now. She glanced around the busy room, hoping to spot her daughter, but she couldn't see Katy or Jim anywhere. Katy had so been looking forward to this reception, hoping the romantic occasion would touch Jim . . . and that he would want to dance with her. But apparently Katy's plan had failed. Anna felt sorry for her frustrated daughter . . . and even more for Jim. Hopefully nothing serious was wrong. Probably just a disagreement over attending the festivities. Would the young couple ever be able to get past this? Or was it something they were destined to live through—like their wedding vow promises just a year ago—until death did them part?

CHAPTER 25

At first Katy was so angry, she was tempted to go to the wedding reception without him. But she knew that would ultimately be embarrassing. It would require explanations and excuses—and she didn't want to have to lie to cover the fact that Jim wasn't ready to be out in a noisy social gathering. Still, she was aggravated as she removed her pretty shell pink dress and silk stockings. She sadly hung it up and then put on a pale blue cotton dress and went to the nursery where Sarah was just putting the baby down.

"Why did you change?" Sarah asked as Katy bent over to kiss Lucy's forehead. "What about the reception?"

"Jim." Katy tipped her head toward the door as if it explained everything.

"I'm sorry."

"It's such a pretty day, I think I'll take a walk on the beach while Lucy is napping."

"Yes, you do that." Sarah Rose smiled. "Fresh air and sunshine will be good for you."

Katy nodded and, without even getting her shoes, went outside, down the beach stairs, and onto the beach in her bare feet. Despite the beautiful day, there were few people strolling in the sand. They were probably all at the reception. But determined not to dwell on that—or feel sorry for herself—Katy just walked and walked, soaking in all the beauty around her.

On her way back, with her spirits lifted and restored, she prayed for Jim—begging God to do something to make him better . . . to bring him back to her. She felt certain it would take a miracle. As she got closer to home, she noticed a figure slowly descending the stairs. He moved so slowly, she assumed it was an old gentleman. But as she got closer, she recognized her own husband. Wearing his dark tinted glasses and his favorite corduroy jacket, he lifted his hand in a tentative wave.

"You've come to the beach." She happily went over to him, grasping his right hand. "Come walk with me."

"Okay." He nodded and, although his gait was stiff, he didn't drag his heels.

"I was just recalling the time I taught you how to do the turkey-trot down here. Do you remember?"

"I do."

"And what about that walk we took down here after our wedding?"

"I remember that too. I was worried you would spoil your dress, but you didn't even care."

"I was just so happy to be with you, to be your wife."

"Are you still happy?"

Katy didn't know what to say.

"I know you're not." He stopped walking to look down at her. "You couldn't possibly be."

"I'm happy that you came home," she said. "But I'm sad that not all of you is here." She looked down at his left arm. "And I'm not talking about that."

"I know."

"But I'm determined to be patient." She peered into his face, trying to see his eyes behind the tinted lenses. "And I believe my old Jim is going to return to me . . . in time."

"I'd like to believe that."

"But you don't?"

He shook his head.

"Then I will just have to believe big enough for the both of us. For all three of us, because Lucy is in this too."

"Thank you." He gently squeezed her hand. "I'm sorry I couldn't go to the reception with you. I thought you'd gone alone."

"No."

"I wouldn't blame you. I know how much you love that sort of thing."

She smiled. "To be honest, I loved being down

here maybe even more than being in a loud, stuffy room with a bunch of people."

"I wish I loved being down here." He looked nervously toward the ocean.

"You used to."

"I know."

She turned them around, trading places, so that he now looked toward shore and she faced the sea. "Is that better?"

"I guess so."

"What is it about the ocean that bothers you? The waves aren't very noisy today."

"I'm not sure exactly. But when we were transported back to the US aboard the Red Cross ship, I couldn't stand to see the ocean. I already felt terrible, but something about those end-lessly churning waves, that deep water that was painfully blue . . . it just made me feel worse."

"In what way? You weren't seasick, were you?"

"No. But the ocean made me feel even more helpless and . . . hopeless too."

"Oh." Katy wanted to understand.

"I did like the wedding today." His tone had just a hint of hope.

"You did? Why?"

"It reminded me of when we got married. Wasn't it about this time of year?"

"Yes . . . I thought of that too."

"A year ago, we had no idea where we would be now."

307

"Oh, we knew you were going to war . . . and I hoped you'd come home."

"But we didn't know I'd be like this . . . or that there'd be a baby."

"That's true." She reached up to push a dark curl away from his forehead, noticing he needed a haircut.

"I know you wanted to dance at the wedding reception." He held up his prosthetic hand with a nervous smile. "Want to try it down here?"

"Really?" Before he could change his mind, she grasped the hard, wooden hand and, waiting for him to put his other hand against her back, reached for his shoulder. "We don't have real music, but when did that stop us before?" Without really thinking, she began to sing "A Bird in Gilded Cage." She knew it was a sad song, but one that she knew all the lyrics to. And so she sang it all the way through.

"Is that how you feel?" Jim asked. They had stopped dancing, but he continued to hold her. "Are you my bird in a gilded cage?"

She tried to think of the right answer—because it had startled her how some of the words sounded not only melancholic, but strikingly symbolic. She hadn't intended it to be like that. "Well, no one can say I married you for your money, James Stafford," she said lightly. "News writers are not exactly rich."

"That's true."

"But I suppose I can relate to parts of that song . . . a bit. People in town probably look at me like that. They may assume that because I live in a pretty house, wear pretty clothes, I must have a pretty life."

"But they don't know the half of it?"

"Oh, Jim." She embraced him fully. "Everyone has their troubles. If they don't have them now, they will surely have them later. And I am not a sad little bird trapped in a pretty cage. I love you, Jim Stafford. I never stopped loving you. I never will."

And then he leaned down to kiss her.

During the next week, Katy felt like Jim had turned a real corner. Oh, it wasn't the sweet fairy-tale life she'd dreamt of, but it was definitely better. Jim still spent most of his time in his darkened office, madly pecking away at the typewriter. And sometimes he would take his pages over to discuss them with Mac.

One of the best changes was that Jim had decided to share Katy's bedroom. But it wasn't all good. Some nights Jim would leave in the middle of the night and she would awaken with worry that something was wrong, only to find him sleeping in the spare room again. And a couple of nights, when he'd remained with her all night, she'd been awakened by the terrifying sounds of him suffering through a nightmare. But by the second time, she realized that she could gently nudge him awake. At first he was alarmed, shaking and wet with perspiration. But she urged him to sip some cool water, take some deep breaths . . . and he eventually calmed down and returned to sleep.

In her mind, Katy thought it was like the old proverbial saying of two steps forward and one step back. But at least they were moving ahead. That was encouraging. And it was encouraging to see him taking a bit of interest in his daughter. She sometimes caught him talking to her while she was in her bassinette. And he'd even held her a few times. But if she started to cry—like all babies were bound to do at times—he couldn't get away from her quickly enough.

By Independence Day, Katy felt they'd really made some good progress. And as she helped Sarah Rose put the last bits and pieces into their picnic basket, she could hear Jim playing with the baby. "Isn't it wonderful?" Katy put the bottle of lemonade in a corner. "Jim and Lucy together."

"Yes." Sarah nodded as she closed the basket. "I hope you three have a lovely day today."

"Aren't you coming?"

Sarah shook her head and smiled. "I'm going to enjoy a nice, quiet day to myself."

Katy nodded. "Yes, I'm sure that sounds nice. But how about the fireworks show tonight? You'll watch that, won't you?"

"Of course. I wouldn't miss it. But I'll watch it from the house. I can stay with the baby while you and Jim enjoy yourselves."

Instead of driving to the city park, they walked. Katy wheeled the carriage and Jim carried the picnic basket. And they looked, Katy felt sure, just like a normal little family. But she knew that looks were deceiving, and she just prayed they would make it through the day without any drama.

But not long after settling into the park with family and friends all around, the band began playing in the gazebo. And Katy could tell Jim was troubled by the boisterous horns and drums. "Is it too loud for you?" she whispered into his ear. When he nodded, she suggested he take a stroll around town. "Maybe you'll get used to it from a distance. Or wait until it's over and come back to walk home with us."

He agreed and, while everyone else was watching the band in the gazebo, he slipped away. One step back. Still, Katy consoled herself by remembering Jim wouldn't have even come to an event like this a couple of weeks ago. Two steps forward.

As things wound down at the park and the band finally broke up, Jim returned. And acting completely normal, he helped her put the picnic things away, told their friends and family goodbye and, with him carrying the basket and her wheeling the carriage again, the little family walked home. But they were barely in the house when Lucy began to howl. She was hungry and sleepy and loud. Once again Jim disappeared. But Katy gave it no concern as she tended the baby, putting her down for a nap.

After a pleasant afternoon, with everyone quietly reading or napping, they had a late dinner and, as Sarah cleaned up, Katy put the baby down for the night. Then after getting her warm shawl for the cool night air, she went to see if Jim was ready.

"I think I'm too tired to go," he said with reservation.

"But it's the Fourth of July—don't you want to come celebrate? It'll be just you and me tonight. Sarah wants to stay with Lucy." Then she remembered his sensitivity to noise. "Or maybe the fireworks would be too much for—"

"You're right. I do want to celebrate. And with my best girl too."

Katy felt a bit uncertain now. Had she talked him into something he wasn't ready for? But before long, they were strolling toward the bluff in the dusky light. And Jim was even whistling. "What a beautiful evening," he said with his good arm linked with hers. "And romantic too."

When they reached the viewing area where others were already waiting, Jim laid down the blanket, and they both sat down to wait. But as soon as the first sky-rocket shot into the sky and exploded, Jim leaped to his feet—and Katy realized how mistaken she'd been.

"You stay and enjoy this," he said. And before she could stand up he took off.

Of course, Jim would hate the fireworks! What had she been thinking? But instead of chasing after him, and drawing even more attention to themselves, she decided to stay and enjoy the show. Hadn't Jim told her to? Katy felt certain he'd go straight home, probably barricade himself in his quiet office. She imagined him typing away on his book, blocking out their town's festivities.

The display didn't last long since, as they all knew, fireworks were greatly limited due to the war. But the sparkling blasts had looked pretty reflected over the incoming tide and, like the rest of the crowd, Katy had clapped and cheered at each new burst of colorful light—trying not to think about Jim.

As she folded her blanket, Katy gave Jim credit for at least trying to be out here with her. She could imagine how it would all be much better by next year—if the war ended like people were predicting. By then, Jim would probably be able to enjoy the whole show, and perhaps Lucy would be old enough to be thrilled by the pretty lights too. Little Larry had seemed to enjoy it. She told her friends and family goodbye and then, with her blanket draped over one arm, strolled home in the gentle evening air. The sky was so clear that the stars shone brightly over the ocean. Maybe she could entice Jim out to admire them. That would be romantic too. Maybe even better than fireworks.

But when she got home, she couldn't find Jim anywhere. And Sarah hadn't seen him come into the house at all. So Katy went outside again, looking all around the house and down the street. She even asked a few trickling parties going home from the fireworks if they'd seen her husband. But no one had.

Back in the house, she didn't know what to do. Should she call someone . . . or just wait for Jim to come home? And where had he gone? Sarah offered to sit up with her, but Katy pretended to be nonchalant. "I'm sure he just wanted to take a walk," she said lightly. "To clear his head. You go on to bed."

Sarah looked doubtful but said goodnight. And then Katy waited . . . and waited . . . and waited. By three in the morning, she felt desperate and worried. Where was he? When was he coming home? But Lucy was waking and would need a diaper change and a bottle. Katy warmed the bottle then discovered Lucy in need of a complete changing. By the time she had her cleaned and fed and soothed, it was half past three. As she rocked Lucy back to sleep, Katy silently prayed for her missing husband. Once she finally tucked Lucy back into the bassinette, it was almost four.

It wasn't long until the sky was turning gray, and she knew sunrise was only an hour off. But Jim had still not come home. She considered calling her mother for advice, but that would wake the whole house. She thought of calling Chief Rollins, but did she really want to get him out of bed this early? Finally, she decided to go outside and look for Jim again herself. Leaving a quick note for Sarah, Katy pulled on Jim's worn corduroy jacket, slipped into her old beachcombing boots, and headed out. Although it seemed unlikely that he would be on the beach—since he still disliked the sound of the waves—that is where she headed.

CHAPTER 26

The sun was just coming up when Katy spied a lone figure down the beach—just outside of the caves. A rush of fear surged through her. She knew there'd been recent rumors of rumrunning along this particular stretch of coastline. In fact, her mother had warned against walking down this far—especially alone. The last thing Katy needed right now was to come upon a criminal stashing illegal alcohol in the caves down there. And since the tide was just going out, it seemed a realistic possibility.

She slowly turned around, trying not to draw attention to herself and hoping to spot another morning walker or beachcomber meandering along—someone she could walk with. But aside from her and the man by the caves, the beach was deserted. She kept her back to the lone figure to avoid the appearance of staring and, trying not to appear frightened, slowly walked toward home. But then she wondered—could it have been Jim?

Strange as it was to imagine him down here

like this, she had come down to look for him. She wished she'd thought to bring the binoculars Grandfather had given her. Just in case, she bent down, pretending to pick up a shell and looking over her shoulder. By now the figure seemed to be purposely striding toward her. And it appeared he was wearing a gray suit—just like Jim had worn yesterday. And then the man lifted his hand in a friendly wave—calling out her name.

"Jim!" She stood up straight, hurrying toward him. As she got closer, she could see that not only was it her very own husband—he looked happy. And now he was smiling and running, swooping her up in a big one-armed hug.

"Oh, Katy. It's so good to see you. So very good!"

She couldn't help herself as she sobbed relieved tears into his shoulder—clinging tightly to him. "I was so worried, Jim. I—I know the fireworks must've upset you. I don't know why—why I didn't think of it before we went. I'm sorry."

He let her go and, still holding onto her hand, looked into her eyes. "You're right. The fireworks were too much. I wanted to believe I was stronger than that, but as soon as they hit the sky—the flashes of light and the loud blasts—I felt like I was back in France . . . in the trenches again. It all seemed very real at the time. And I had to get away from it."

"I understand." She sighed as they slowly

walked toward home. "I never should've pushed you last night. I'm really, really sorry."

"It's not your fault." He squeezed her hand. "And I think it was a good thing."

"A good thing?" She glanced at him. "But you were gone all night, Jim. What happened? Where were you?"

"I took off running last night, trying to escape the artillery—I mean the fireworks. I honestly don't remember how I even got down on the beach, but when I found myself here, I just kept running like I was being chased by the devil himself."

"How terrible."

"I ran hard and fast, and I must've gotten well beyond the caves, although I really don't remember that. I could hardly breathe. And yet I could still hear the booms in the distance—and see the flash of light over the ocean. So I stopped and closed my eyes and covered my ears, trying to block everything out. Not just the fireworks. Because the battle memories kept coming at me. I felt as if I were still there, crawling from one filthy trench to the next, and the enemy was still firing."

"Oh, Jim." Her heart ached for him.

"But the whole while, I kept telling myself, *It's not real, it's not real. You are home. You are home.* Over and over again. I know it probably sounds silly to you, but—"

"It doesn't sound silly. I've heard you having nightmares some nights. And I read that piece you wrote for the newspaper. I know you've been through hell—and that you're still tortured by the memories. But you're right, Jim, it's *not real* and *you are home.*"

"I know." He nodded. "Eventually I realized the fireworks show was over. For all I know it might've been over for a while. But I wasn't ready to go home yet. I just sat there in the sand . . . listening to the sound of the waves and staring out into the darkness . . . and praying. I'm not sure how much time passed. But I had a strange sense of peace. I can't even explain it. It felt sort of like the relief you feel when a headache or an illness goes away."

"Like I felt after Lucy was born."

He smiled at her. "So I stood up and started to go back home. But when I reached the caves, the tide had come all the way in and I couldn't get past without swimming, and that didn't seem a good idea. I even attempted to scale the rocks, but it was so steep, and the rocks were wet and slippery. I didn't like the idea of falling and being swept out to sea . . . leaving you and Lucy alone."

"No, I'm so glad you didn't do that." Katy remembered how fearful she'd been last night— worried she might never see him again.

"So I found a protected spot and I dug a bed

in the dry sand and I went to sleep." He sighed. "And I slept like a log. No nightmares. I woke up as the tide was going out and headed for home. And there you were." He hugged her again.

"Yes, here I am."

"Now I realize I might not be completely over this thing, Katy—what Doc Hollister calls shell shock or battle fatigue. But I feel like I made some progress last night."

"Of course you did."

"It occurred to me that it's been about six months since I was injured. And I never told you . . . didn't want you to know, but I was a mess at first. Even worse than when I came home. Looking back, I can see how far I've come since then. It gives me hope that I can beat this thing . . . if I can just keep moving forward."

"But you have to be patient with yourself," she said—as much to herself as to him. "And I don't want to push you either. Just keep working on your book and stick to your routines . . . and I'm sure you'll get beyond it. And I'll do all I can to help you."

He thanked her, and as they went up the beach stairs, Katy knew this battle wasn't over, but she also knew they needed to fight together.

Anna was pleased to hear of Jim's breakthrough and progress during the past month, but she was glad that he was taking his time about returning to work. And now, besides working on his war memoir, which Mac was helping him with, Jim had recently begun to write some non-war-related articles for the newspaper. And he made a point to deliver them himself, eventually scheduling his stops to coincide with the running printing press. He felt it was therapeutic to expose himself to the noise, although he only stayed a few minutes the first time. But each subsequent time since he stayed a bit longer. And today, he had even sat down at his old desk for a while.

"Does this mean you're considering returning to work here?" Anna asked on her way back to her office.

Jim stood with a smile. "I'm always thinking about it. But like my sweet wife keeps telling me, let's not push things." He pointed to the papers in her hand. "Got an assignment for me in there?"

"Come into my office," she told him. After they sat down, she explained that there were a number of news stories all coming in at once. "But mostly related to the war. How do you feel about taking one of them?"

"I think I'm ready." He nodded. "And I promise not to editorialize it into an anti-war piece."

"Yes, you have to give me your word on that." She studied his face, pleased with how much more relaxed he seemed than when he'd first come home several months ago. "By the way, how is your memoir coming along? Mac keeps telling me how impressed he is with your writing. He hopes that someday—when the war is over, and the government remembers the First Amendment—it might even be published."

Jim waved a hand. "Oh, I doubt that. But I must admit it's been helpful to me to write about my experiences. But I'm sure it won't interest anyone else."

"Don't be too sure."

"Well, I am sure of this—no one beside Mac will see it until the Sedition Act is behind us and we regain freedom of speech. But in the meantime, what can I help with?"

Anna fingered through the pages. "This is actually a positive story for the Allied Forces. The Amiens Offensive. It just came through. But I want it to make Saturday's paper." She handed the notes to Jim, waiting as he skimmed it.

"We forced all German troops back to the Hindenburg Line," he declared happily. "That is fabulous news."

"I know. Real front-page stuff. Do you want to handle it?"

"Sure. And look, here's quote from General Ludendorff." Jim chuckled. "He's calling the eighth of August a black day for the German army. I'd call it a red-letter day for the US and our Allied Forces."

"We can make that the headline." She made

note of this. "So if you're comfortable with this, I need it by tomorrow afternoon."

"You got it."

As he left, Anna wondered if she should have a backup plan for this important story. If nothing else, she could work late . . . or ask Mac to take a stab at it this evening. But instead, she decided to simply trust Jim. Worst case scenario, she could whip something short out in time for press tomorrow. Hopefully, that wouldn't happen.

Katy had pages of sketches and designs ready for the infant and children's line she wanted to feature in the shop by late fall. And now that it was mid-September, it seemed there wasn't a moment to waste. Not only that, but she was itching to return to the dress shop—and not just for short visits like she'd been doing.

"Do you think it would be wrong for me to go in to work two or three days a week?" she asked Sarah Rose over lunch. "I long to be back there, around the fabrics and notions and trims, so much easier to put the floor samples together." She closed the sketch book she'd been showing Sarah. "And to be honest, I would love not feeling so housebound all the time. I love my baby and don't want to miss anything, and yet . . ." She sighed.

"I don't think it's wrong that you want to be more involved in your dress shop. But I wonder if you need to be there for full days. What if you started out with a few hours a day—perhaps during Lucy's naptime?"

"Yes, that's a good idea. I just hope Jim will agree."

"Speaking of Jim, he's barely stuck his nose out of his office since yesterday. Even when I took him up his lunch earlier, he barely said two words." Sarah looked concerned. "Is he feeling all right?"

"Yes. I think so." Katy wondered though. She'd been so busy finishing her fashion column and revising sketches, she'd barely noticed.

"Well, he must be wrapped up in his book." Sarah began to clear the table.

"It's not his book. He's working on a war article for the paper." Katy frowned. "I hope it's going well. I suppose I should check. He promised to take my piece along with his by one."

"Well, it's nearly one." Sarah tipped her head. "And I hear the baby."

Katy stood. "You check Lucy and I'll check Jim." She hurried up the stairs, knocking on his office door. "It's just me," she called out cheerfully. "It's time we got our features into the paper." She paused to look at him, surprised to see that he was unshaven and still wearing his pajama top. "Are you okay?"

He looked up from the typewriter with an uncertain expression. "I guess so."

"Is it the war article?" she asked. "Was it too soon?"

"I don't know. I've been over it so many times, I can't even think straight." He rolled it out of the typewriter. "I'm afraid it's no good."

"Well, Mother will be the judge of that. And it's nearly one right now. So I better run this and my piece to the paper."

"I don't know." He frowned as she picked up his article. "Maybe I should just throw it away."

"Sorry." She leaned down to kiss his bristly cheek. "Too late."

"But Katy, I—"

"Don't worry, Jim. Mother won't print it if there's anything wrong. But I don't have time to discuss it now. I need to get going." She pointed at him. "And you need to clean up and shave."

As she hurried downstairs, she was worried. Had this article set him back? He had seemed genuinely excited about it yesterday. But now? She was tempted to skim the article herself, but if she was going to town, she needed to fix up a bit. And now she had a good excuse to stop by the dress shop too. She would get her grandmother and Clara's opinions about her returning to work a few hours a day. Hopefully they'd be supportive of the idea.

September was usually one of the good months for weather in Sunset Cove, and today was no different. As Katy strolled through town, breathing in fresh sea air, it was hard to believe there was a nasty war still raging on the other side of the globe. Again, she wondered about Jim's story. Was it possible she was now carrying a piece of seditious news—something that could land both her and Jim into serious trouble? She hoped she didn't look too suspicious or guilty as she hurried into the newspaper office.

"I'm here to see my mother," she quietly told Virginia.

"You know where to find her." Virginia narrowed her eyes. "Are you all right, Katy?"

"Yes, yes, of course." Katy held the valise closer. "I'll just go find her now." She hurried past the other reporters, entering her mother's office without even knocking. "Sorry to burst in on you," she said quickly. "But I'm worried about Jim's article."

"Oh, dear." Anna set down her editing pencil. "Trouble?"

"Maybe. He was acting a bit strangely."

"I hope the article didn't set him back. It was meant to be a positive, victorious story."

"Yes, that's what he told me yesterday. But today, well, I'm not sure. He was very worried. He didn't even want me to take it." Katy felt slightly sick as she handed it to her.

"Did you turn your piece in to Frank yet?"

"Not yet."

"You go do that right now. He needs to get it

to typesetting. Meanwhile, I'll do a quick read on Jim's article. Come back and I'll tell you the verdict."

Katy hurried out to Frank's desk. "Here you go." She forced a smile. "Hope you like it."

"I'm sure I will. Ginger always looks forward to your pieces. It's the first thing she reads in Saturday's paper." He looked at her article.

"I'm glad she likes it." Katy looked nervously toward her mother's office.

"Anything wrong?"

"No, no . . . I just need to speak to my mother again. If you'll excuse me." She turned and hurried back to Anna's office. "So?" she asked eagerly. "Is it seditious—should we burn it?"

"No." Anna's smile seemed amused. "It's not like that at all."

Katy sank into the chair with relief. "Then why was Jim so worried?"

"I think it's because he's handled it a bit differently."

"Differently how?"

"He wrote this piece from his own point of view, like a veteran's take on the victorious day. Almost like he was there. And, of course, he was there last winter. But the way he handled this piece, well, it's quite different."

"Will you be able to use it?"

"I wondered about that myself. But it's so good, Katy. I can't *not* use it."

"May I see?"

"Yes. But hurry. I want to get it to typesetting."

Katy quickly read what turned out to be a surprisingly compelling story. "My goodness, Mother, this is encouraging!"

"Isn't it a nice piece for our readers to enjoy over their Saturday morning coffee?"

"Yes. It's wonderful. But is it really true, is the war really turning around, is Allied victory truly around the corner?"

"Well, I suppose that's a matter of opinion, but I'm inclined to agree with Jim on this. I believe we've reached a turning point. Germany has been pushed way back, and their resources and manpower are so depleted. I honestly don't see how they can hold out much longer."

Katy held the article up. "Want me to take it to typesetting for you?"

Anna nodded. "Thank you. And thank Jim too."

"I was going to stop by Kathleen's before going home, but maybe I should go back and let Jim know the good news."

"Better yet, I'll call him right now. I want to congratulate him on a very well-done article."

Katy let out a relieved sigh. "Thanks, Mother." As she left the newspaper office, Katy felt like a heavy weight had been lifted from her. Jim's article was okay. No, it was better than okay. It was great!

CHAPTER 27

The newspaper received such a positive response to Jim's personalized news story that it was agreed he should continue to cover big war events in a similar fashion. And the stories continued to roll in. The following week, Jim wrote about the greatest air assault of the entire war—launched by the United States. And it turned out he actually knew at least one of the pilots personally, which made his story even richer. Anna couldn't have been more pleased. And, according to Katy, Jim was feeling more and more comfortable in this new role.

By late September Jim returned to working at the newspaper office. "I think it's time," he told Anna when she questioned if he was pushing himself too hard. "There's an energy here that I need."

"I understand," she said. "I've always thrived on the hustle-bustle. I don't think I'd do well working at home. But then, I was raised on all this." She waved her hand toward the noisy press room.

"Yes, I know . . . printer's ink in your veins."

She laughed. "Third generation."

"Does that mean Lucy will be fifth?"

"If she wants it."

"Well, according to Katy, she's going to be an artist."

"Speaking of art, how do you feel about Katy going back to work at the dress shop? She said you two were discussing it."

"I'll admit it was hard at first, and I started to put my foot down. I thought she needed to be home, taking care of the baby." His smile looked sheepish. "And taking care of me."

"So I heard."

"But she reminded me of our agreement before marrying. I promised her that I would be supportive of her career." He shook his head. "I even promised to take her to Paris."

"Well, even if the war ends soon, I don't think travel to Paris will be advisable for a while."

"That's what I told her, but she's holding me to it . . . someday. Maybe when Lucy is old enough to enjoy it."

"Would you enjoy it?"

He shrugged. "Maybe I would by then. I'm sure that France will be nothing like I remember it. It might be refreshing to see it restored to peace." He held up the story he was just turning in. "And according to my sources, peace is on its way. This is the fifth and what is predicted to be the final attack at Ypres."

"Amen to that." She took the pages. "But it does give me cause to wonder."

"Wonder?"

"What will we write about when the war is over?"

He laughed. "Well, maybe we can focus on more local stories and good news."

"And, thanks to prohibition, we'll always have the rumrunners and bootleggers to chase after."

"They do make for some interesting stories." He grinned. "I wouldn't mind following up on some leads myself."

"Well, let's focus on getting the war wrapped up first. And then perhaps our readers will enjoy a brief reprieve from serious news. I think our first editorial meeting—after the war is officially over—we should brainstorm the happiest stories around and have at least one paper be nothing but good news."

"I like that." He nodded. "Hopefully it won't be long."

After he left, Anna realized that the hospital had been opened for a year now—why not do a piece about that? And since she was overdue for a JD coffee date, she arranged to stop by the hospital for an afternoon visit.

"You're looking rather dapper," she said as she sat down across from him. "Special occasion?"

His lips curled up in what seemed a self-conscious smile. "I'm having dinner at Marjorie Douglas's home tonight."

Anna tried to hide her surprise. "Well, that's nice to hear. Marjorie is a lovely person and a very good cook too."

"So I've heard." He picked up his coffee. "Lonely old men enjoy a home-cooked meal now and again."

"Is that all it is?"

"Are you interviewing me for the paper right now?"

"No, this is strictly off the record." She smiled.

"Well, I find Marjorie to be good company. She's a warm woman and a natural conversationalist."

Anna nodded. "I couldn't agree more." And now she turned back into a journalist, asking about the hospital's first year of operation.

"As you know, the hospital has never been full, but that's not surprising. We don't even have the staff it would take to run at full capacity."

"Yes, especially after you let Dr. Myers go."

"That's true. But so far I've been able to handle the patient load and, with the war drawing to a close, Daniel will soon be here."

She smiled. "Yes. I'm sure you're looking forward to that."

He nodded. "And as the population of Sunset Cove and the surrounding regions expands, and the need for professional medical care increases, the hospital is large enough that—with additional doctors and staff—we should easily accommodate the growth." He told her about some of the modern equipment he hoped to see added to the hospital after the war's end. It was interesting to hear him speaking in a more positive way about their town and hospital. Was Marjorie Douglas having a good influence on the old doctor? Anna hoped so!

As soon as Katy walked into the dress shop on Friday afternoon, she could tell something was wrong. Clara and Ellen were huddled together in the back of the workroom, and Lucille had a deeply furrowed brow.

"What is it?" Katy whispered.

Lucille tipped her head toward the door. Leading Katy into the showroom, which was devoid of customers, she began to explain. "A telegram for Ellen."

"Oh, no." Katy covered her mouth with her hand. "Not Lawrence—is he—?"

"Not dead. Not that they know of, but he's—"

"Been injured like Jim?"

Lucille grimly shook her head. "No. Missing in action."

"Missing in action? When? Where?"

"He was involved in a battle near Ypres. Apparently they don't know much of anything specific."

"Jim was just writing about that battle. It sounded as if the Allied Forces were winning."

"Just because our side is winning doesn't mean our soldiers won't suffer."

"No, of course." Katy nodded. "I know that."

"All we can surmise is that Lawrence has somehow been separated from his unit. He hasn't been listed as wounded or dead—not yet anyway. Though how they keep track of such things in all that chaos is beyond me. But the telegram clearly states he is missing in action. And promised a letter to follow."

"So now it's the wait. Poor Ellen. I should go talk to her."

"Yes. I felt it would be easier to hear it from me. Ellen is very upset."

"And it looks like customers coming." Katy nodded to the front door and then ducked into the workroom.

"Did you hear?" Ellen asked with teary eyes.

"Yes." Katy went to hug her. "I'm so sorry."

"I just don't know what to think."

"The word *missing* is so vague," Clara said sadly.

"Yes," Ellen agreed. "What does it *really* mean?"

"I honestly don't know," Katy told her. "Except that he's missing."

"Could he be in prison?" Clara asked quietly.

Katy shrugged, keeping one arm wrapped around Ellen.

"I wish there was someone I could ask, someone who could explain. Do they say a soldier is missing, but he's really dead and they just don't know it yet?"

"I'd like to know that too," Clara said. "It seems cruel to stretch something out longer than necessary."

"What is the point of sending a telegram like that?" Katy frowned. "Why don't they just wait until they find him?"

"Because he had been missing for a week," Clara said glumly.

"Do you think he ran away?" Ellen asked with wide eyes. "Is that what missing in action really means? I mean, I was so surprised when he decided to enlist. You remember how he felt about the war. The way he used to talk. If he had talked like that nowadays, he'd have wound up in prison."

"Yes, but he changed," Katy reminded her. "He really turned around. He was proud to go serve. I don't think he would've run away."

"Then, tell me, what does *missing* mean?" Ellen was starting to cry again.

"Do you think Jim would know?" Clara said eagerly. "His articles in the paper sound so well informed. And he was in the army over there."

"He might be able to explain," Katy admitted.

"Can we go ask him?" Ellen asked.

"I don't see why not. He's at work, but since

335

it's almost press time, he can't be too busy. Let me give him a call."

After Jim agreed to meet them for tea at the hotel, Katy hoped it wasn't a mistake. What if missing did imply that a soldier had turned coward and run? And if so, what were the consequences? She thought she remembered hearing that a soldier could be shot for desertion. Or was that just in the olden days?

"Good afternoon, ladies." Jim stood as the three of him joined him at the table which was already set up for tea. He turned to Ellen as they all sat down. "I hear you've had some disturbing news."

"Yes." Ellen handed him the now rumpled telegram. "Can you tell me what that means?"

Jim studied the communiqué, then sighed. "I'm sorry to hear this about Lawrence."

"But what does missing in action *really* mean?" Ellen demanded. "Do you think it's just a fancy of way to say that he turned cowardly and ran?"

"No." He handed her back the telegram. "Missing in action means that he was involved in a battle but didn't report back to his unit when they regrouped. He went missing."

"So he isn't a deserter?" Katy asked quietly.

Jim shook his head. "I really don't think that's what happened. And if his commanding officer had any reason to suspect desertion, I doubt you'd have received this telegram."

"Then why did they send it?" Ellen demanded. "What good does it do to tell me this?"

"Lawrence had been missing long enough that his commanding officer was responsible to report it. It's just standard practice. Whether a soldier is wounded or killed or missing, it must be reported. It's not always easily done, but they have to keep track of such things."

"The fact Lawrence didn't return from battle . . . could that mean he's dead?" Clara asked with wide eyes.

"Not necessarily." Jim sighed. "Oh, it's possible. Anything is possible in war. For instance, Lawrence could be wounded and unable to return to his company. He could be simply lying low and hoping he'll be rescued by some Allied troops. And then, of course, there's another possibility."

"What's that?"

"He could've been captured. But it seems unlikely. The telegram says he was at the Battle at Ypres. And the Germans are clearly losing. Everyone predicts the war is just days away from ending. I can't imagine the Germans would be eager to take any prisoners now. What would be the point?"

"But you're certain he didn't run?" Ellen asked again. "I don't think I could bear it if he became a coward."

"Here's the truth, Ellen. Lawrence has been there through the thick of this war. He would know that the Allies are closing in, and that the Germans are very close to surrender. Everyone over there knows that by now. I think it's highly unlikely he would desert when he knows the war will soon end. Why would he do that?"

Ellen barely nodded. "He wouldn't, would he?"

"I agree," Clara told her. "It would make no sense."

"What Jim said about Lawrence being wounded makes sense," Katy said. "If he couldn't make it back, he could be hiding out . . . waiting for help. I can imagine that."

"Yes, I can too," Clara said. "We all need to be praying for help to come, and for Lawrence to make it home."

And sitting right there in the hotel restaurant, they all bowed their heads and prayed for Lawrence's safe return. As they prayed for Ellen's missing husband, Katy sneaked a quick peek at her own husband. She felt so proud for the way he'd handled this situation . . . so glad that he'd made it safely home.

CHAPTER 28

Victorious war stories continued to pour in to the newspaper office, including reports in early October that Germany and Austria had written to President Wilson, requesting an armistice. This was definitely good news, but the war was not over yet. Anna suspected the Allied forces wouldn't easily accept a peace prescribed by the warmongers who'd started the war in the first place.

But when German U-boats backed out of international waters, and then the notorious General Erich Ludendorff resigned, the proverbial writing seemed to be on the wall. It was hard to dispute the Great War was drawing to its close.

But even as the *Sunset Times* ran these pieces of encouragement and hope, Anna observed a dark, frightening cloud on the nearby horizon. Something so foreboding and deadly that, according to Daniel, it could bring as much distress and heartache as the Great War.

"Is something wrong?" Jim handed Anna his

front-page story about Ludendorff's resignation. "You look upset."

She glanced at his story then sighed. "It's the Spanish Flu."

"Yes. I know we did that piece last week—about the case in Portland earlier this month and the precautions they're taking."

"The flu is even closer than Portland now and—"

"How did you hear that? I haven't seen anything come through on the wire."

"Dr. Hollister just called me. Apparently there are certain people in high places who want to keep the lid on it. But JD knows how I've tried to use the newspaper to warn citizens. I wrote a piece about influenza prevention steps shortly before you came home. And I suppose we jumped the gun by quarantining you, but you'd been overseas and seemed ill."

He nodded somberly. "Well, I probably needed the quarantine for other reasons."

"So we took it seriously then . . . and I think we need to take it even more seriously now—now that it's in Oregon."

"Is it because the war is ending—the troops are coming home?"

"Yes. And some returning soldiers are already being contained on army bases. But it's not limited to the armed forces. JD said there have been several civilian cases in Coos Bay. And now

340

he's treating a sick fisherman—at our hospital. This fisherman had just come from Coos Bay."

"Did Doc Hollister say it's really the Spanish Flu?" Jim looked concerned.

"He thinks it's a realistic possibility. The fisherman is in quarantine and under observation right now."

"Are you going to write about *that?*"

She sighed. "I have to, Jim. I don't want our readers to panic, but they need to be aware. If anyone else has been to Coos Bay or Portland, they need to be cautious. And Portland has taken steps to avoid spreading the disease. We might need to do the same."

"Well, I hope JD is wrong. I hope the fisherman just has a bad cold."

"I do too. But what if he's really sick? We don't know who he's had contact with . . . or even if he has a wife or family."

"That's a good point."

"And even if it's a false alarm—and I hope it is—our readers need to be reminded to take caution. Especially if they're traveling to an infected area or cross paths with someone who has come from there. This disease spreads like wildfire. Already tens of thousands have died from this. It takes young and old—and those in between—with no respect to social status or wealth."

"I don't like to be reactionary, but it makes me want to take extreme measures to protect my household. Maybe Katy shouldn't be working at the dress shop right now. What if a customer came in from Portland or Coos Bay? What if she got exposed and brought it home to Lucy?"

"That's a legitimate concern. Businesses in Portland have shortened hours and some stores have closed altogether." She rolled a sheet of paper into her typewriter. "So I need to get busy. I want to write this piece, and then I plan to write Daniel a letter. He'll be interested to hear about these outbreaks so close to home."

"Do you think the army would possibly let him go?"

"I doubt it. Every time he writes, which isn't often, he sounds so terribly busy over there. But he might have some good advice for us." As she started to type, Jim let himself out. Anna paused for a moment. Would it be selfish to pray for Daniel to come home quickly—especially when there were so many soldiers in need of good medical care? Still, she reminded herself, having Daniel come home wouldn't be just for her. JD had sounded worn down and weary when he called. He would never be able to handle an epidemic on his own. And he probably regretted dismissing Dr. Myers now. These were things she would write to Daniel.

Katy was surprised to see Jim coming into the dress shop shortly before closing. "Did you come to ride home with me?" she asked pleasantly. And then she noticed his overly somber expression. "Is something wrong?"

"Maybe."

Katy glanced at Ellen, who was helping with a fitting. "Is it Lucy?" she asked as she hurried Jim to the workroom where they could talk openly.

"No, it's not Lucy. Not yet anyway." He glanced at the table where Clara and Lucille were finishing a winter coat for Thelma Morris. "I have something to say that I think you all should hear." He quickly explained what Anna had just told him.

"A case of Spanish Flu, right here in Sunset Cove?" Clara's brows arched.

"Doc Hollister doesn't know for sure, but he's got a fisherman in quarantine. Just in case. And we don't know yet if the fisherman has family in town or if anyone else may have been exposed. But Anna and I were talking about precautions Portland is taking. Perhaps you read the article in last week's paper. Anyway, this dress shop is a public place . . . anyone can walk in here. Even a sick fisherman's wife." He pointed to Ellen's sleeping baby in the crib in the corner. "Besides you ladies, little Larry could be exposed."

"Oh, dear." Clara looked horrified.

"I can't tell you ladies what to do," Jim said to Lucille and Clara. "But I am going to ask Katy to remain at home with the baby until we know more." He looked into her eyes. "Do you mind very much, Katy? I know how much you wanted to be back at work and—"

"You know I wouldn't do anything to put our Lucy at risk." She smiled.

"I think we should close the shop until we know whether or not there's an active case of Spanish Flu in town," Lucille said with authority.

"I agree wholeheartedly." Clara nodded.

"Then it's done. We can take things to work on at home. And perhaps even hire someone to deliver garments." Katy pointed to the table. "Like Thelma's winter coat and the dress I'm working on for Mrs. Knopf. And the children's line." Katy turned to Jim. "How about if you help me load things into the car?"

As Katy pointed out the things she wanted to take home, she wondered if they were being overly cautious. But as she thought about the vulnerability of Lucy, she knew it was the right thing to do. Hopefully there would be no epidemic here, but she'd read her mother's article last week . . . and the ones before. She understood the dangers of this disease.

As Katy drove them home, Jim asked if she was disappointed about this change in plans. "I know how you were looking forward to having more business with the war's end in sight. And before Christmas."

"That's true. But it's not worth endangering our child."

"I'm glad you see it like that. And if there is no sickness here and Doc Hollister feels we're not in real danger, I don't see why you can't reopen the dress shop."

"I think I'm looking forward to being at home more." She sighed as she pulled up to their house. "It's more tiring than I expected to go to work—even just a few hours a day. And I miss seeing Lucy waking up from her afternoon nap." She turned off the car. "And I've been thinking, Jim, Lucy needs a little brother or sister."

"You're not—"

"No, no, not yet." She shook her head. "But maybe next year. You and I were both only children. I don't think we want that for Lucy."

He leaned over to kiss her. "No, Lucy definitely needs a brother or sister—maybe even three or four."

"Well, I don't know about that." She laughed. "I guess we'll have to wait and see."

Anna had just started writing to Daniel when the phone rang. Again, it was JD. "I'm sorry to bother you, but you asked me to keep you informed."

"Yes. I'm just writing to Daniel now. I'd like to know what's going on. Anything definitive yet?"

"I'm afraid this is it, Anna. This patient has all

345

the signs and symptoms of Spanish Flu—and he is quickly growing worse."

"Oh, dear. What does that mean? Will you have to quarantine your entire staff? Does the man have family around that have been exposed? What about you—will you be quarantined as well?"

"Those are all questions we're addressing right now. I don't have time to say more, but I just felt you should know. The public must be made aware. It's time to take all precautions."

"Thank you. I'm on it." Anna hung up the phone then ran out to the press room, yelling. "Stop the press! I mean it. *Stop the press!*"

As the machinery clunked to a stop, she explained. "We need to change the front-page headline. And we need to move the story about Spanish Flu from the third page to the front." And suddenly they were all working, making the changes, and the *Sunset Times* was ready to print. Yes, it was grim news, but it was necessary. Everyone in town would know about the possibility of an epidemic by morning.

CHAPTER 29

S unset Cove was a bustle of activity the next
morning. But by late afternoon, Main Street
resembled a ghost town. Anna knew there were
now two patients in the hospital under quarantine
and, according to JD, there could be more. The
fisherman wasn't doing well, and his home and
fishing partner were under mandatory quarantine.
If symptoms developed on his contacts, those
people would have to be hospitalized too. Lists
of possible contacts were being made and
they would be told to remain under voluntary
quarantine. The nurses who'd been exposed to
the illness would remain at the hospital. And JD
was already trying to locate another doctor to
come help in case it grew worse.

"I don't think it's likely I'll find a doctor to
come here," he told Anna on the telephone a few
days later. "And we now have seven active cases
of influenza and the first one has died."

"How are you holding up?" she asked with
concern.

"As well as can be expected."

"I'll continue to caution our readers in tomorrow's paper," she promised. "I think the advance warning could help to keep this under control. At least I hope so."

"Hard to say. One of the patients here thinks she got exposed at the mercantile."

"Oh, dear." Anna knew everyone in town went to the mercantile.

"Yes, I already spoke to Marjorie about it. Thankfully, she is fine. But as you know she's keeping her doors closed except for telephone orders and deliveries."

"Yes. Most of the other businesses, as well as Katy's dress shop are doing the same."

"I haven't actually been in town, but that's what I've heard." He sighed. "Did you write to Daniel about this?"

"Yes. I sent the letter. And the next day, I sent a telegram as well."

"Thank you."

"I hope you're not overdoing it, JD. I know I don't have to warn you, but isn't it the very young and the older folks who are the most effected by influenza?"

"The fisherman who died was only twenty-six."

"Oh."

"And we now know that all ages are at risk. Young healthy people all over are being struck down by this gruesome disease. It defies the usual medical rationale."

"Yes, but your heart condition, JD—shouldn't you take that into consideration?"

"Be assured, I'm a physician and know to take all precautions. Don't worry about me."

"It's just that I care."

"Thank you, Anna. I appreciate it."

"Let me know if there's anything I can do."

"Short of teaching my housekeeper how to be respectful or cook a decent meal, I can't think of anything."

Anna chuckled, but as she hung up, she got an idea. She would ask both Bernie and Sarah Rose about the possibility of making some wholesome dinners for JD. Maybe they could take turns. And she would willingly use the Runabout and drive them there herself. Of course, she knew she'd need to avoid contact with JD since he was at the hospital every day. But she could leave them on the front porch shortly before dinnertime.

During the next week, there were a few more cases of Spanish Flu, but it wasn't exploding like in some locations—particularly the big cities. JD attributed this to the forewarning the *Sunset Times* had given. Anna attributed it to the hospital handling it right.

"Thank you for orchestrating my dinners," JD told her on the second week of the outbreak. "But that's not why I'm calling."

"Is there news?" She hoped that he was going to say it was getting better.

"Yes. I'm sorry to say we've taken in several more patients today. Not from in town, thankfully. These are from White Rock. That means we're up to fourteen active cases now. And that's after we've lost three."

"Two more deaths?"

"Yes." His tone was somber. "And, I hope I'm wrong, but I'm afraid there will be at least three more." He let out a weary sigh.

"Oh, dear."

"Any word from Daniel?"

"No. I haven't heard a thing. But according to all the AP reports we've received, the Armistice is fairly certain to be next week. We've heard that it might be signed on the eleventh of November at eleven in the morning."

"Well, it's about time."

"So maybe that means some doctors will be coming home."

"We can only hope. From what I hear, between the war and this epidemic there will continue to be a real shortage of doctors for a while."

"Hopefully that will change after the armistice is signed."

"And not a moment too soon. By the way, you don't need to bring me dinner tonight."

"Oh? Did Sally learn to cook?"

"Marjorie wants to bring a meal over."

"Do you think that's safe? I mean for Marjorie?"

"I always take all precautions before coming home. And Marjorie doesn't seem concerned."

"And I'm sure you could use the company." Anna actually felt relieved to know that JD would have Marjorie's companionship . . . and she wondered if something romantic might be developing.

On November 11, the day the Great War armistice was signed, the fire station blew its whistle at eleven o'clock, and a few people honked their vehicles horns or other noise devices, but other than that, the town which was putting itself under a mandatory quarantine was quiet. The hospital now had two dozen active cases and there had been eight deaths.

In an effort to be cautious, Anna had cut the newspaper office to bare bones. Anyone with family was now on leave or working from home. The newspaper was reduced in size and volume, and the office was primarily manned by Anna and the pressmen. Because Anna was coming and going to work, she was driving the Runabout and picking up groceries and running errands and delivering meals to JD's house on the nights when Marjorie wasn't visiting.

Because of her activities, Anna knew she was somewhat at risk. As a result, she stayed away from her parents and Mickey and Bernie. The last thing she wanted was to carry some deadly germs home to her older loved ones. And she couldn't spend time with Katy, Jim, and Lucy either. Consequently, she felt lonely.

To make up for her solitude, she would take afternoon walks on the beach, breathing in the clean ocean air in the hopes that if she'd been accidentally exposed to anything, perhaps the fresh sea air would cleanse the germs from her. She doubted there was any actual medical rationale to her thinking, but it made her feel better. Plus it was a good place to clear her head . . . and pray that those suffering from influenza would be comforted and healed.

Anna had tried to make the Thanksgiving edition of the newspaper cheerful, including an article celebrating the news that Lawrence Bouchard was alive. He'd been injured by artillery fire but was now recovering in an army hospital on the East Coast. But right beneath that happy article, she once again reminded the readers that until all cases and outbreaks of Spanish Flu were down to zero in their community, any group gatherings to celebrate the holiday should be avoided. Still, she suspected that some citizens, particularly the ones who were starting to complain about the severity of quarantine, would throw caution to the wind in exchange for turkey and dressing.

When Anna picked up groceries for the house, she learned that Marjorie was cooking turkey for

JD. Although she was not inviting her son and Clara, or Ellen and the baby, to join them. But according to Marjorie there were other families who were being less cautious. "Some people act as if they are immune to this disease," she told Anna. "I tried to warn them, and I know JD will be vexed to hear it, but some people just don't listen."

So it came as no surprise that shortly after Thanksgiving, the number of influenza patients doubled at the hospital. And the death toll had now reached ten—and six of them were children. By now Oregon was experiencing a shortage of child-sized coffins. Coos Bay alone needed hundreds. As sad as it was to print that bad news in the paper, Anna felt the readers needed a reminder—this epidemic was not over. Citizens needed to continue to practice restraint.

In early December, with the epidemic still pummeling the state and much of the nation—not to mention the entire world—Anna wondered why they hadn't heard from Daniel. She'd even sent him a second telegram, describing the dire conditions at the hospital and how worn out his father was becoming. She was just finishing her daily afternoon walk, mulling over the possibility that Daniel could've fallen victim to this horrific disease, when she saw someone walking toward her.

She'd been so cautious to avoid all unnecessary

contact that her first instinct was to change direction, but then she noticed a familiarity—and then an extended hand, waving with enthusiasm. "Daniel?" she whispered. "Could it be?"

He waved again, heading directly toward her, and she felt certain it was him. She hastened her pace and as she got closer, she could see him smiling. "Daniel!" she cried, eagerly running to him—and then stopping. "I've been so careful," she said. "Because of the influenza. Are you . . . ?"

"I'm certain that I'm safe," he told her. "Although I've been traveling, I went straight home. I bathed and changed my clothes. And throughout this whole mess, I've never shown any symptoms. So I feel sure that you're okay with me."

"Well, you're the doctor." She smiled, suddenly feeling shy. But when he held his arms open, she threw caution to the wind and ran straight into them.

"I can't believe it." She was trying not to cry. "It's really you."

"I left France as soon as I could. But then I got stuck in England. The hospital was so busy. Servicemen passing through, needing care and discharge and transfers. I was working day and night. And thinking I'd soon be home, I didn't worry about trying to write to you. Then there was the voyage, rough seas and extra time. After that, I got waylaid in the US Army hospitals. Too much to be done, and not enough doctors."

"Speaking of that . . . have you seen your father? Does he know you're home?"

"Not yet. I asked his housekeeper how he's doing, and I can tell she's concerned."

"I'm worried too, Daniel. He's working too hard. I speak to him about every other day and each time, he sounds even more tired."

"Well, I'm on my way there now, but I wanted to come see you first." He leaned down to kiss her. "To thank you for waiting for me. And to apologize for not communicating better."

"It's all right. I know you were busy. I'm just glad you're home. We need you."

"And I need you." With his arm around her they walked toward the stairs, and he inquired about the welfare of her family. She assured him that so far, none had gotten sick.

"But we've taken all the precautions you wrote to me about."

"That's good." He told her about his most recent journey on the train. "It was so crowded with soldiers returning home. And so many stops in every little town. I wanted to get off and send a telegram, but I was afraid I'd lose my seat. I began to feel like Odysseus in the *Odyssey*. I thought I'd never get here."

She laughed. "Hopefully you didn't run across any sirens."

"The only sirens I had contact with were warnings for aerial attacks. Fortunately, that's behind me now." He stopped at the top of the beach stairs, just looking down at her with so much warmth in his eyes, she felt a happy tingle rush through her.

"I'm so glad you made it safely home, Daniel."

"And I'm so glad you're all right, Anna. I had moments when I worried you could've gotten sick too." He kissed her again. "But you look perfectly healthy to me."

"Thanks." She smiled.

"As much as I'd love to stay here with you, I need to go to the hospital and surprise my father—and then I'll send him home to get some rest."

"Yes, I'm afraid he needs it." She stared up at him in disbelief. Was this really happening? Was this really her Daniel? His face looked a bit older and thinner, and his hair had more gray in it, but his eyes were the same.

As they walked toward her house, he asked about the epidemic, how many were affected, how many had died. She sadly told him.

"Well, it could've been a lot worse," he said. "And hopefully, it's on the decline by now."

"We've done our best to keep it under control, but it just doesn't seem to go away."

"Yes, the rest of the country has the same problem. It was like I predicted. But the disease will run its course . . . in time. And if it's handled professionally, it will eventually be completely gone. Some places are already free of it. Of course, they're still picking up the pieces. It seems to touch everyone. The mortality rate is staggering. Already it's predicted to take more American lives than the war did."

She shook her head. "Unbelievable."

In front of her house, they kissed again and said goodbye. Then Daniel went on his way to the hospital. And Anna, feeling suddenly light and hopeful—despite the hard news of the nationwide epidemic—went inside to tell the others the good news—from a safe distance.

CHAPTER 30

Christmastime was somewhat bleak for Sunset Cove households since quarantines were still in effect, but according to Daniel, the tide was changing on their epidemic. JD had invited Marjorie to join him on Christmas Day, and since Daniel and Anna had been stealing time together, she planned to join them.

"Are you sure that's safe?" Lucille called up as Anna stood on the second-floor landing.

"Daniel and JD are both doctors," Anna reminded her. "They think it's safe enough." She hadn't told her parents that she'd already been in Daniel's company almost every day.

"Well, if it's safe for you to be with them, why isn't it safe for you to be with us?" Mac yelled up the stairs.

"I'm just obeying doctor's orders," she said as she fastened her necklace.

"But I spoke to JD on the phone this week," Lucille called out, "and he gave us permission to spend Christmas with Jim, Katy, and the baby."

"Yes, why is that all right, but we can't be with you?" Mac demanded.

"It's because all of you have obeyed the restrictions and taken care not to be exposed to anyone outside of your homes. But you know how I'm out and about all the time—at the newspaper, getting groceries, and so on. Daniel still advises me to keep a distance from my family."

"Yes, I suppose that makes sense." Lucille sounded disappointed.

"Next year," Anna promised them. "And now if you'll both excuse me, I need to get over there."

"Have fun," Mac called out.

"Send our best wishes," Lucille said.

"And give my love to Katy and Jim and that adorable baby that is growing up without me being able to see it!"

They exchanged Christmas greetings and Anna finished getting dressed. Then, using the Runabout, she drove over to the Hollister home where Marjorie answered the door.

"Merry Christmas," she exclaimed, ushering Anna inside. "The doctors are still at the hospital, making their final rounds for the day." She led Anna to the kitchen. "Sally went home to be with her family."

"I thought she wasn't allowed to leave." Anna removed her coat.

"JD was fit to be tied when she told him she was going—and he told her not to come back."

Marjorie chuckled. "But I think it's all for the best. She's not a very enthusiastic housekeeper."

"And JD is always complaining about her cooking skills."

"Well, he's a bit spoiled." Marjorie smiled. "And I suppose I've contributed to the spoiling."

"So I hear." Anna looked at the stove. "Everything smells delicious. May I help?"

"How do you feel about peeling potatoes?"

"I'm great at it." Anna grinned as she reached for an apron.

"This is a pretty good kitchen," Marjorie said as she checked a pot. "But I like mine better."

"I've never been very gifted in the kitchen," Anna admitted. "So I honestly wouldn't know a good kitchen from a mediocre one."

"Well, since I've been over here cooking for JD from time to time, I've wondered which kitchen I prefer. And I'd pick mine."

Anna felt curious. "Does that mean you feel you'll have to choose between kitchens?"

Marjorie laughed. "I suppose I've entertained the idea."

"Interesting."

"I can't speak for JD, although he's hinted."

"It's possible that he's a little gun shy. Remember what happened with Lucille."

Marjorie nodded. "I've had that exact same thought."

"Perhaps it would help to drop a hint."

"Oh, would you?" Marjorie beamed at Anna. "It would sound so much more natural coming from you."

"I—uh—I guess I could do that." Although it wasn't what Anna had intended, she had no compunction about giving the old doctor a gentle nudge. After all, hadn't she been the one who'd encouraged him to dance with Marjorie last summer? "Tell you what, Marjorie. You make an excuse to get Daniel in here with you, and I'll go out and have a private word with JD. I think that would be better."

"Perfect."

So it was, when the doctors came home, Marjorie asked Daniel to help her remove the heavy turkey from the oven. Meanwhile, Anna hurried out to have a word with JD.

"Marjorie is such a good cook," she began. "Everything in there looks absolutely scrumptious. This will be the best meal I've had in weeks. Since the influenza epidemic."

"I've been fortunate to have a number of good meals." His brow creased with suspicion. "Some that were cooked by Bernie and delivered by you. Don't you eat her food too?"

"Well, yes. But to have something straight from the oven. That's different." Anna sat down. "JD, can I have an honest talk with you?"

He blinked. "Of course, I thought we always did that."

She smiled. "Well, here's the deal. Marjorie is very interested in you, but I think she's unsure about your intentions."

"My intentions?" He frowned. "I can assure you they are honorable."

Anna laughed. "Yes, I've no doubt about that. But are you only interested in her friendship? Or could you have a future?"

His eyes twinkled with mischief. "Well, I hope I have a future."

"I mean your future with Marjorie."

"Oh . . ." His thin lips curled into a smile. "I suppose I've had thoughts along those lines."

"Well, I just wanted to let you know that if you feel like taking a swim, the water is fine."

After an enjoyable meal, Daniel and Anna cleaned up while JD took Marjorie aside. Anna suspected he might be asking her to become his wife but decided not to say anything to Daniel. But when the older couple returned, they happily announced their betrothal. Hearty congratulations were shared, and while Marjorie served dessert, JD sheepishly produced a small bottle of California wine. "A grateful patient gave me this last year," he confessed, "and I've been saving it for a special occasion."

"I hope Chief Rollins isn't peeking in the window." Marjorie laughed nervously.

"I expect the chief might overlook this since it was a gift," Daniel assured her as they all lifted a glass in a congratulatory toast. "But just the same, we won't tell anyone."

By the end of the evening, JD and Marjorie's plans were finalized. They would get married at City Hall when it was convenient for both of them. "And JD will come to live with me above the store," Marjorie told them. "That way I won't have to move all my things and I can still keep an eye on my store."

"And Marjorie has a very comfortable home," JD said. "Cozy and warm."

"That means you two can live here when you get married." Marjorie grinned. "And I don't know what you're waiting for."

"Maybe we're waiting for you to set a good example and lead the way," Daniel teased.

JD looked at Marjorie. "I'm ready when you are."

She laughed nervously. "You say the date, JD, and I'll be there with bells on."

"Really? How about this week?" His gray brows arched.

And so it was agreed. They would get married at City Hall on Friday afternoon. As Daniel walked Anna out to her car, he assured her that their wedding day wouldn't be too far off. "I just want to get past this epidemic first," he told her.

"Yes, of course. I'm actually surprised at the haste JD and Marjorie are making."

"Well, they're older." He chuckled. "Naturally, they're in more of a hurry."

She smiled. "I think JD will be more comfortable at Marjorie's house. He never really seemed quite at home here."

"Will you be at home here?" Daniel asked.

"We will make it a home," she assured him. "Together."

He kissed her. "Yes. Together."

On Friday afternoon, shortly before five o'clock and with no fanfare, JD and Marjorie quietly exchanged vows before the judge with only Daniel and Anna as witnesses. Not even Randall and Clara were aware of the wedding. Not because they wanted to exclude them, but because quarantines were still in effect.

Afterwards the four of them went to Marjorie's to share a lovely homemade meal that she'd created for their celebration. And the newlyweds seemed completely at home and content. So much so that Daniel and Anna excused themselves before dessert.

"I'll walk you home," Daniel said as they stepped outside into the foggy evening.

"Thank you. And tell me, how has it been at the hospital this week?" Anna asked as he took her hand in his. "Any new cases after Christmas?"

"We were prepared for it, but so far so good.

Not only that, but most of our current patients appear to be out of the woods."

"So hopefully, no more deaths?" she asked.

"We're hoping to cap the death toll at the current fourteen." He glumly shook his head. "I wish it had been less."

"But it could've been more, Daniel."

"That's true." He slipped his arm around her as they stopped in front of her house. "When the epidemic is completely over, will you be ready to marry me, Anna?"

"You know I will." She smiled up at him.

"Do you still want to get married at City Hall, like Dad and Marjorie did today?"

"I honestly don't care how or where we get married," she confessed. "I just hope it will be soon."

"Are you opposed to getting married in the church?"

"You *want* to get married in the church?" She was surprised since he hadn't before.

"I missed so many weddings while I was gone. First Katy and Jim's. Then Mac and Lucille's. And Clara and Randall. Each time you wrote to me about one of these weddings, I felt envious."

"You did?" She blinked.

"I want to be the groom, waiting for my beautiful bride walking down the aisle."

"You do?" She could hardly believe it.

"I really do. Do you think I'm silly?"

"Not in the least."

He leaned down to kiss her again.

"And I know someone who will be over the moon to hear this."

"Who's that?" He continued to hold her close.

"Katy. She's dreamed of preparing a beautiful wedding for us. But I kept discouraging her because I thought you didn't want it."

"Nothing would make me happier. But not until the epidemic is well behind us."

"Well that will give Katy plenty of time to put together her plan."

"Then let the planning begin." He kissed her again.

Katy was thrilled beyond words to plan an early spring wedding for Anna and Daniel. As soon as the epidemic was nothing more than a memory, Kathleen's Dress Shop reopened, and with the help of Clara and Lucille and Ellen, they went to work on what everyone was saying would be the wedding of the year. Whether Anna liked it or not, she would have three attendants. Her mother, her daughter, and her best friend Clara. Attending Daniel would be his father, Jim, and Randall. The church would be adorned with all the spring flowers that the community could offer, and everyone in town would be invited to attend. A big reception at the Grange would follow, celebrating with food and music and dancing.

The church was packed full when Anna came down the aisle wearing a beautiful tea-length white lace dress, silk stockings, and white satin shoes. She carried white lilies and cherry blossoms. But it was the look on the groom's face that everyone remembered most from that day. His eyes glistening with tears, his face wreathed in the biggest smile anyone had ever witnessed on him, it was obvious he couldn't have been happier. The same was true with Anna. It was a new era for both them—as well as for all of Sunset Cove!

Center Point Large Print
600 Brooks Road / PO Box 1
Thorndike, ME 04986-0001 USA

(207) 568-3717

US & Canada:
1 800 929-9108
www.centerpointlargeprint.com